Praise for CHOSEN FOR DEATH
and for KATE FLORA

"*Chosen for Death* has not only a cunning mystery but an insightful, thrilling, layer-by-layer revelation of human character... With her first novel, Kate Flora hits the ground running as a new writer to watch."

Molly Cochran and Warren Murphy

"An easy, reflexive pace, complex heroine, simple plot, and natural prose should draw an audience to this first novel."

Library Journal

"Flora's characterization is assured and her plotting is tight and credible."

Publishers Weekly

"A fast-paced New England mystery, laced with a wry humor and full of insights into fragile human relationships."

J.S. Borthwick

"Thea Kozak is appealingly tough-minded... *Chosen for Death* is a first novel that sticks in your mind."

Washington Post Book World

"Kate Flora does what all great writers do; she takes you inside unfamiliar territory and makes you feel right at home."

Michael Connelly

"Thea is a great character; she has a thoroughly real set of strengths and weaknesses; she is hell-bent on discovering the truth, even while she knows—just as well as the reader—that truth often comes at considerable personal cost."

Mystery News

Thea Kozak mysteries by Kate Flora:

Chosen for Death
Death in a Funhouse Mirror
Death at the Wheel
An Educated Death
Death in Paradise
Liberty or Death

Also by Kate Flora, written as Katharine Clark:

Steal Away

Kate Flora

Kate Flora was raised on a chicken farm in Maine. She left the rural life behind for college and law school, returned to Maine to practice law, and eventually ended up a lawyer in Concord, Massachusetts. She has since abandoned the law to write full-time but has never given up her curiosity about what motivates bad behavior. When she isn't writing, she's teaching writing or trying to coax reluctant perennials to behave. She is the current international president of Sisters in Crime. She and her husband, Ken Cohen, have two sons. They now divide their time between Concord and Bailey Island, Maine.

Chosen for Death

Kate Flora

CRUM CREEK PRESS
The Mystery Company
Carmel, Indiana

This book is for my husband, Kenneth Cohen
and my mother, A. Carman Clark,
who believed in me.

CHOSEN FOR DEATH

Copyright © 1994 by Kate Clark Flora

ISBN: 1-932325-00-X

Cover art by Robin Agnew (Aunt Agatha's, Ann Arbor, MI)
Cover design by Andy Roberts, www.tangentnet.com

PUBLISHING HISTORY
Forge hardcover edition: December 1994
The Mystery Company paperback edition: February 2003

Crum Creek Press / The Mystery Company
484 East Carmel Drive #378
Carmel, IN 46032

www.droodreview.com

Acknowledgments

Special thanks to the many people who have helped me along the way. First to Grace Livermore and Hannah Bond, who gave me time to write.

To all my readers, who provided an audience and so much helpful criticism: Christy Bond, Christy Hawes, Jim Dillion, Esq., Prof. Frances Miller, Dr. Jacqueline Olds, Diane Englund, Jack Nevison, Nancy McJennett and that wonderful artist, Peter W. Rogers. To Karin Knudsen Rector, for geographical assistance. To writer Jane Langton, whose support meant more than she could know.

To Maine State Trooper Kate Leonard and especially to former Concord Police Chief Carl Johnson for the many times he corrected my grammar, fixed my cops and made my prose more politically correct.

And last but by no means least, to my agent, Carol McCleary, who had confidence enough for both of us, my editor, Claire Eddy, who so gently corrected me, and to Margaret Milne Moulton, who gave Thea her job.

To those who might be offended by my geography or my police procedure, I remind them that this is a work of fiction, and that people and land may have been molded to fit the crime.

CHAPTER 1

NEW ENGLAND WEATHER can be very unpredictable in September. Mornings that start off crisp and cold can be steaming hot by noon. That was how I found myself sitting in the sweltering church slowly baking in a jacket that I couldn't take off. I couldn't take it off because the matching dress was sleeveless and I'd been raised by a mother who knew to the depths of her soul that you couldn't wear a sleeveless dress in church. Everyone else in the Boston area was spending that glorious Saturday outside. Not that I would have been. With the private-school year just getting started, the consulting business I worked for had work stacked up like planes at Logan Airport at five P.M. But I wasn't at the beach or at work.

I was at my sister Carrie's funeral.

It was ironic and unfair. Carrie had always loved flowers. Now she had more flowers surrounding her than she ever could have imagined, heaped everywhere around her small white coffin. But neither the flowers nor the carefully chosen container meant anything to her now. Inside, no less dead for all the pink satin frills and tucks that embraced her, lay my sister Carrie. My little sister Carrie, who was always a lost soul. Carrie, who had never quite accepted our love, who had never believed she belonged. And now there was no way we could ever persuade her. They talk about people with an amazing capacity for alcohol as having a hollow leg; well, Carrie had a hollow leg for love.

No matter what we did or said to convince her she was loved, it was never enough. It must have been hard for her, growing up. Our family was anything but peaceful. Every meal was filled with cheerful, noisy bickering, impassioned political arguments, loud jokes, and everyone's simultaneous reports about their day. No matter what we did to include her, Carrie was never quite a part of it. She drifted on the fringes like a waif,

6

watching and waiting for her chance to speak. We learned to build in pauses, making spaces in our conversations so she could talk. Still, it must have been overwhelming being a small golden presence among the dark, noisy giants.

Reverend Miller paused in his eulogy and looked down at us with sad eyes. The pulpit was very high. I would have felt too vulnerable and exposed up there, but I suppose he was used to it. He looked down at Carrie, lying there in her small white cradle, banked by a million flowers. "I baptized Carolyn McKusick," he said, "the week after Tom and Linda brought her home. She was beautiful. Even as a baby, she had that direct, questioning stare that let no one off the hook, a look that seemed to ask, 'Who are you? Who am I, and what are we doing here?'"

He was right. Carrie's questioning, demanding gaze had followed all of us, seeking answers. Attention. Love. No matter what we gave her, it was never enough. She could never be satisfied.

He looked like he might cry. "Now she is with God," he said. "For all her questions, Carrie believed in God and in His goodness. So, while for all of us who loved Carrie, our sorrow is great that she is no longer with us, we can take comfort from the knowledge that she has now found peace and perfect happiness. Let us pray." Under the trained ministerial cadence, I could hear his sadness.

Dutifully I bowed my head, but I didn't follow Reverend Miller's prayer, and I didn't pray the sort of prayer he and God would have approved of. I prayed, as I sat there bent over my clenched hands, that today or tomorrow, or someday very soon, the police would call and tell us they had found Carrie's killer. I prayed that he would be tried and convicted of first-degree murder. I hoped he fried. I didn't know if Maine had a death penalty, but I hoped so. By the time the prayer was over, my stomach was in knots and sweat was trickling down inside my black dress.

Reverend Miller announced that there would be a brief

graveside service at the cemetery and everyone was invited back to our house for refreshments. He did his best to make it seem solemn. It still sounded like an invitation to a party. We waited while the pallbearers stepped forward to take Carrie's coffin out of the church. Dad, looking ten years older; my brother Michael, almost unrecognizable without his ever-present smirk; our neighbor, Mr. Foster, who had loved Carrie like a daughter; Uncle Henry, who never wore a suit, looking lost and uncomfortable in navy blue pinstripes; Todd, Carrie's high school boyfriend, so pale I was afraid he might faint; and Charlie Hodgson, her high school guidance counselor. Six strong, good men whose love hadn't saved her.

I'd had trouble all morning focusing on the funeral. My mind kept slipping away to other things, other times in Carrie's life. Not because I wasn't sad, because I was. It's just that I'm not the type for public grief. I would do my grieving alone, over a long time. I've heard that funerals are good for people, that they give people a chance to acknowledge their sadness, and I suppose that's right. It just doesn't work for me. Maybe it was working for Mom and Dad, or some of the other people there who'd loved her. I hoped so. The process leading up to today had been so dreadful for all of us, like when Dad and I had gone to choose Carrie's coffin.

The funeral director had tried to persuade us that a white coffin was inappropriate. "We usually use them for children," he'd said.

"Yes, well, she was my child," my father had said. "We'll have the white one. She would have liked it." Buying a coffin is sort of like buying a car. There are lots of options, and getting the right interior package is important. The white one had a soft pink velvet lining, elaborately pleated and tucked, with a deeper pink satin pillow for Carrie's head. It was the only one in the room that didn't look like an executive office suite — and the funeral director obviously didn't want to sell it for the body of a twenty-one-year-old girl who had been murdered during a sexual assault.

Poor Dad had just wanted to buy it and get out, but the funeral director kept trying to steer him to different models. He had an odd, pale face, flat in profile, with a nose the sculptor hadn't finished raising out of the center. His voice was so carefully modulated it had lost all character. He sounded as dead as his clients. When his suggestion that the one we wanted was only suitable for a child didn't work, he tried another tack. "Unless your daughter was very small, sir, it probably won't be large enough." He'd most likely taken a calculated risk with that argument, since my dad is a big man, and I'm tall for a woman at five eleven. He had no way of knowing that Carrie was adopted.

"I'm sure it will do fine," Dad had said. "Carrie was just under five feet tall, and tiny." His voice had broken at that point, and I'd taken over, my grief displaced by fury at this man's attitude. He wasn't selling used cars here. He must have temporarily forgotten the lessons of Bereavement 101, unless there was another course on appropriate choices which stressed that young women who were careless enough to get themselves assaulted and murdered weren't entitled to white coffins.

I could see that Dad was about to lose control. If he did, the undertaker was in serious danger of becoming his own client. Dad was a loud, affable man, a lawyer who rarely showed the arrogance or false indignation so common to his profession. He loved to argue, but rarely lost his temper. When he did, he did it with style. I put a hand under his elbow and urged him toward the door. "I'll take care of this asshole. You can wait for me in the car." Normally, no one takes over from my dad, but Carrie's death had left him bewildered and helpless. He'd gone out willingly, relieved to let me deal with things.

The funeral director was hovering hopefully by a nice black and pewter model. As soon as I was within hearing range, he started extolling its virtues. I shook my head. "Read my lips," I said. "We want the white one. Nothing else. No other model.

9

No discussion. No argument."

He sniffed loudly. "I don't believe you understand, madam," he said. "It wouldn't be appropriate, under the circumstances..."

"Stop right there," I said, holding up a warning hand. "Let's be clear about this. The circumstances are that a lovely young girl who was the victim of a terrible crime needs a coffin. Don't you dare even think about passing judgment on my sister. The white one. Understood? Now, what else do we need to deal with?"

He shrugged his shoulders, an elaborate gesture which would have said volumes about difficult families and women who don't understand the proprieties, but there was no one around to appreciate it except me and I didn't. After that came reams of paperwork, and a dozen additional choices, which I made numbly. I'd had no idea there were so many details and even less idea what the proper choices were. Mom should have been doing this, she was the one who cared about propriety, but she was even more devastated than my dad. So I waded through questions like how many copies of the death certificate we needed, and how many limos for the funeral, and when was I going to bring the outfit she was to be buried in, with the funeral director being deliberately unhelpful to punish me for my impertinence.

The little bit of energy my rage had given me quickly subsided. By the time I'd dragged myself out to the car, I was exhausted. Dad had taken one look at my set face, driven straight to the nearest bar, and ordered us both double bourbons.

My reverie was interrupted by a warm hand on my arm. "Thea, dear, it's time to go," my mother said. I looked around. Carrie was gone, and everyone was waiting politely for the family to follow. I hoped I hadn't been tuned out too long. Probably not. My mother wasn't one to ignore proprieties. It wasn't so much a concern about what people might think as it was consideration for their feelings. No one likes to be kept waiting. I let her steer me out of the pew and down the aisle. I could hear the shuffling of feet and the murmur of voices behind me, but I didn't look back. Numbly, I let my mother lead me out of the church. Carrie couldn't be dead. I still needed my little sister. I'd always need her.

I stood at the top of the steps, watching them slide the gleaming white coffin into the hearse. I still couldn't believe it. How could someone have done this? It takes a long time to accept death. I knew that. It didn't make me feel less sad, or less angry. *They're not going to get away with this, Carrie*, I thought. *Whoever did this to you will be punished. I'll see to that. Thea will take care of it.* I fought off another flood of reminiscence, all the other times I'd made that promise to Carrie. I'd never let her down. My mother tugged on my arm, and I followed her down the steps and into the waiting limo.

CHAPTER 2

I WOKE THE next morning to the smell of strong coffee somewhere very close to my nose. When I tried to sit up, my nose hit
the saucer, rattled the cup, and a few drops of scalding coffee
dripped onto my chest. I fell back against the pillow and opened
my eyes. My brother Michael was bending over me. "Morning,
Sunshine," he said. "As Ann Landers always says, 'Wake up
and smell the coffee.'"

"As if I could do anything else," I said. "You practically
poured it on me." I didn't say it nicely. I hate getting up in the
morning.

Michael ignored me. "You are invited to breakfast with the
assembled multitude, or morning of the living dead, if you can
stir yourself anytime soon." Michael has a sick sense of humor
and no tact. I couldn't figure out what he was doing in my
apartment.

I struggled up against the headboard and reached for the
coffee. "What are you doing here, anyhow?" I asked. Sunlight
streamed in the windows, illuminating old rock posters, a shelf
of dolls, the huge jar of pennies on the desk. I was in my room
at home. At my parents' house. Because Carrie was dead. And
that was why Michael was here, too. "Who's downstairs?" I
asked. The coffee was hitting my empty stomach in a harsh acid
wave. I hadn't been able to eat anything yesterday, after the
funeral.

"Mom and Dad. Uncle Henry and Aunt Rita. Todd and
Charlie and Mrs. Hodgson. Mr. and Mrs. Foster. And my
beloved Sonia, who is in a snit and agitating to leave."

"Why don't they go away and leave us alone?"

Michael shrugged. Introspection isn't his strong suit, and he
doesn't try to figure out other people's reasons, either. "Maybe
they think they're needed. Or maybe they don't want to be alone
themselves. Especially Todd. He's in real bad shape. You'd

better come down and talk to him, Thea." He slouched toward the door, my lanky, handsome, and utterly useless brother. "Everyone around here is waiting for you to take charge. So come down and do it. But put on something decent first, OK?" He disappeared, closing the door behind him.

I inspected myself. Nothing so risqué, really. A Calvin Klein tank top and bikini briefs in a nice utilitarian shade of gray. My usual sleeping costume in spring, summer, and fall. Not something I'd even dream of wearing out of this room. Michael had only mentioned it to make me feel uncomfortable. Such a sweet guy. Even with the family brought together for such a sad occasion, he couldn't resist getting his needles in. I pulled on a faded purple sweatshirt, jeans, and socks, and staggered into the bathroom. The mirror on the wall didn't agree that I was the fairest of them all, but it did say I wasn't bad for a lady who was pushing thirty. I still looked good in the morning.

I dragged a brush across my teeth, splashed cold water on my face, and pulled my half-acre of wild dark hair back into the confines of a barrette. My eyes were very green today, which meant I'd get into trouble before the day was over. My eyes change color. From green to blue-green to blue. Sometimes even hazel. The really green days always mean trouble. I don't need an astrologer; I have eyes. Today my eyes looked like Christmas. Red and green. I'd done a lot of crying last night when I was finally alone.

The banister was smooth under my hand, polished by all those years of little bottoms sliding down it. I turned through the arch and went into the dining room. It was empty, the only evidence of use a few dishes on the table. I was surprised Mom hadn't whisked them off to the kitchen already. She has more energy than anyone I've ever met, and she uses much of it keeping the world in order. I shouldn't be critical, though. She never expected me to be like that, and she was wise enough to let us all make the messes that kids will without fretting about her perfect house. Mostly she'd been a pretty good mom.

Carrie's search for her birth parents had been a notable exception.

There was an elaborate buffet breakfast laid out on the old carved sideboard. I set my coffee cup down on the table, picked up a plate, and began piling up food. I still had no appetite, but my body needed food, and eating was an activity which could delay the moment when I had to confront the assembled multitude.

All the leaves were in the dining table my mother had bought for the large family she hoped to have. It could have seated an army. But then, according to Michael, an army lurked somewhere in the house. I could hear the murmur of voices from the living room.

When she and Dad married, they'd planned to have six children, but it hadn't worked out that way. Before me there had been a series of miscarriages. There were two more between me and Michael, and when Michael was born she'd hemorrhaged so badly they'd had to do a hysterectomy. They'd started immediately trying to adopt more children, but the agencies hadn't been very sympathetic to a couple who already had two healthy children of their own. It had taken six years to get Carrie, and after that they'd given up.

I was eight when they brought her home, a tiny, picture-perfect baby. I loved taking care of her. She was better than any doll. My friends were wildly jealous, vying for the privilege of coming to my house so they could play with baby Carrie. I suppose Michael liked her well enough, but he was busy with his little-boy pursuits, and a baby can be very disruptive when you've just gotten your trucks and cars lined up for a big race, or if you have to keep all the little pieces of a building set on the table so the baby won't eat them.

It always seemed to me that there was something furtive in the way she arrived, in the way the grown-ups always lowered their voices when we came into the room if they were talking about Carrie. Mom says that's just my imagination. Maybe it is.

They were always very open about the fact that Carrie was adopted. They didn't have any choice, really. Carrie was a tiny pink and gold pixie in the midst of a bunch of Neanderthal giants. She couldn't help noticing she didn't look like the rest of us.

Mom and Dad are both tall, big-boned people. Dad is loud-voiced, flamboyant, and opinionated. Scotch-Irish in background, though his family has been here for a long time. He loves to argue. Mom is quieter and more controlling, but she also has strong opinions. Her family is eastern European, more recent immigrants, but they've embraced American middle-class values with a fervor that would make you think they've been here forever. Mom reads etiquette books the way some people read novels. Dad's hair is dark and wavy; Mom's is impossibly thick, black, and curly. I've inherited it. Like our parents, Michael and I are tall, dark, and handsome. Michael has Dad's hair. He's thin and moves like he's connected with piano wire, but he's actually quite a good athlete. Anyway, when we go out together, people stare. When we used to go out with Carrie, they stared even more.

It wasn't like me to sit around like this, lingering dreamily over food. I'm not the lingering type. I'm an active person, like Mom, but today I couldn't keep my mind on the present. Maybe it was being in this house. It was too filled with memories. If I'd been home, in my condo, I could have found a million things to do. Open the week's mail. Do the dishes. When all else fails, I just go to work. I like to go in to work on a Sunday. You can get a lot done when no one else is around.

The idea of immersing myself in work was very appealing. Maybe I could leave soon. If I left by noon, I could still manage a few hours in the office. Which meant I'd better get into the other room and fix whatever it was they were all expecting me to fix. I poured a second cup of coffee and carried it into the living room.

It was a beautiful room. It ran the whole width of the house,

15

front to back, with tall windows and elaborate moldings where the walls met the ceiling. The walls were painted a strange shade of green called Banshee, which looked perfect with the flowered chintz curtains and overstuffed chintz sofas. There was a huge Oriental rug on the floor. Plenty of comfortable chairs. And today, all the seats seemed to be taken. It looked like the set for a high school play. A dozen pairs of eyes rose to watch my entrance. I almost wished I'd worn a dress. I set down my coffee, hugged my parents, and took the seat reserved for me between Todd and Uncle Henry.

Michael hadn't been exaggerating. Todd looked dreadful. His unshaven face was white, and the circles under his eyes could have been painted on by a kindergartner. I put my hand over his, and he seized it as if it were a lifeline. "Thea," he said, "what do I do now?" The others were watching me, covertly, waiting to see what I'd do. I knew they were waiting for me to "fix it," whatever that meant.

"You need to talk, Todd," I said. "Let's go out on the sun porch." He nodded, got unsteadily to his feet, and headed toward the French doors.

I sat on the porch swing. I've always sat on the porch swing, ever since I was tall enough to crawl into it. Todd sat facing me in a green wicker chair. "I would have protected her, Thea," he said. "Why wouldn't she let me? Why did she have to go off and live in Maine by herself like that, working in that lousy restaurant? It was probably someone she met there who killed her." His voice had a forced, rasping quality. He was the picture of dejection, sitting there. "I shouldn't have let her go."

I suppressed my urge to tell him that he was grabbing blame he had no right to. He'd beaten himself up enough already. Right now, what he needed was reassurance that he wasn't responsible. "Todd," I said, "this is not your fault. Carrie loved you. But you know how Carrie was. She didn't go away because of you. You know that, don't you?" He nodded, but it was perfunctory. He wasn't really listening. He was remembering.

16

I slid off the swing, went over to him, and put my hands on his shoulders, forcing him to look at me. "Listen to me, Todd. This is important. She didn't go to Maine because of you. She went for herself. There was something she needed to deal with on her own, without any of us, that took her to Maine. Even when she was very little, Carrie had a lost quality. No matter what we did — you, me, Mom and Dad, any of us — to make her feel loved and secure, she never felt like she belonged. It isn't something any of us did, or failed to do." I shook him gently. "Are you listening, Todd?"

His head was bent so I couldn't see his face, but he nodded. "I'm listening."

"There was never a person more loved than Carrie. But you can't make someone believe something. I've read that it's quite common for adopted children to feel this uncertainty about who they are and a sense of not belonging. Going to Maine was part of Carrie's attempt to find herself. Her true self. She told me she couldn't settle down and commit herself to anyone until she was clear about who she was."

"I know, Thea, I know," he said. "But I just keep thinking I ought to have done something more. Or that if I'd just done things right, she'd still be here."

I pointed toward the doors. "Everyone in there is thinking the same thing, Todd. Carrie's vulnerability captured all of us. We all felt responsible. We each should have saved her. But it's very arrogant of us to think like that, Todd. Carrie was a grown woman. She had her own agenda and she was acting on it. Sure, we could have tried to keep her here and protect her, but it wouldn't have worked. She would have gotten angry and frustrated and hated all of us."

"But at least she'd still be alive," Todd insisted.

"Yes," I said, "and still fighting with you, and with Mom, and everyone else, and doing who knows what sort of self-destructive things. Look, Todd, you can flagellate yourself endlessly with the might-have-beens, and it won't do you or

Carrie any good at all. I know this will sound selfish, but you've got to pull yourself together and get on with life. Start thinking about the positive, about how much joy we all got out of knowing her. Let her memory be a source of good..." But Todd wasn't listening again. He was preparing his rebuttal, and it came bursting out before I could finish.

"Right," he said angrily. "It's easy for you to say that; she was only your sister. We were lovers. My loss was different! You don't understand how it is for me."

I knew I'd been sounding a bit too much like Pollyanna, but when Todd said that, my self-control flew right out the window. "I don't understand how it is for you, Todd? Because you were her lover? Have you forgotten about David?"

Todd's mouth snapped shut and he fell back in his chair like he'd been slugged. He made a few futile attempts before he finally got some words out. "Oh, God, I'm sorry, Thea. I forgot." He got up and walked shakily toward the outside door. "I'm just going to drag my miserable body out of here before I make things worse. Tell your folks thanks for breakfast."

I took his hand and pulled him back, pushing him firmly onto the porch swing. "Not so fast, Todd," I said. "We aren't finished." I sat beside him and put my arms around him. He buried his face in my chest, shoulders heaving.

"Oh, Thea," he said, "what am I going to do now, without her?"

"It won't be easy," I said, "but you go on, somehow. When David died I was furious, at first, that I hadn't died, too, instead of being left behind to face every day without him, surrounded by his things. Everything I touched, everywhere I went was a reminder of what I'd lost. I was too numb to do anything. I just sat home and cried. For a long time I was sad, then I got really mad at him for leaving me. Eventually I learned to do what I just told you to do, to be glad we had the time we did, and to find pleasure in that, instead of feeling angry and cheated because of what we might have had. It's been almost two years now, and

I still miss him. I'll always miss him."

I looked down at his dark head, laid so trustingly on my chest. He was so young, poor thing. Everything seems so monumental when you're young. Kids like Todd could make me feel a million years old. "I didn't mean to dismiss your pain, Todd," I said. "I know it hurts. All I'm saying is that it gets easier, and you go on."

I never talk about David. My family doesn't mention him anymore, and neither do my friends. I used to dissolve in tears whenever they did, so they learned to be careful. Except for my boss, Suzanne, the people at work don't know about David. David was my husband. I met him on the rebound from a guy I'd loved passionately who didn't love me. I'd finally broken the hold of that unrequited love. To celebrate, I'd gone to a movie with two friends. It was an intense, somewhat inscrutable foreign film. Afterward we'd gone to a bar for a drink to talk about the movie. David pulled up a chair and invited himself to our table. His opening line, a model of stupidity, was, "I knew three such attractive women didn't come here just to talk to each other."

In my most charming way, I'd urged him to get lost, but he wouldn't.

"I can't," he said. "I know that was a dumb line, and I apologize. The truth is that I'm mesmerized by your fabulous green eyes, and I've come to claim my right to spend eternity in their orbit." My two friends laughed derisively and I, who earlier in the evening had resolved to maintain a heart of stone ever after, fell hopelessly and irrevocably in love. My friends went home, and I stayed with David. That night, and every night after that until the night he didn't come home because the friend who was giving him a ride wanted to show off his new Camaro and wrapped David around a tree.

The friend escaped with a few bruises and a broken wrist. When he came around after the funeral to say how sorry he was, I gave him two black eyes and a broken nose. So I knew how

Todd felt.

I just sat and hugged him for a while, letting him cry. He left quietly through the outside door, saying he was going home to sleep. I thought he'd be OK. I went back into the living room to join the family. "Todd's gone home," I said. "He says thanks for breakfast."

Mom nodded. "He just needed someone to talk to. We knew you'd understand." She began collecting coffee cups. Mom can't stand clutter, and she can't sit still. "A policeman who is working on Carrie's case just called," she said. "He wanted to know if he could come over and talk with us. I said he might as well, since everyone is here right now. Except Todd. But I suppose he can go to Todd's house, can't he? I know you're anxious to get going, Thea, but you can wait a little longer, can't you? It would be nice to have you here."

My mother knows me so well. I hadn't said a word to her, but she knew I would want to get away as soon as possible. I need a lot of time by myself, or I get crazy. "No, Mom. That's fine. I suppose we might as well get it over with."

Sonia, Michael's perennial fiancée, got up and stretched. Sonia is white-blonde, ivory-skinned, and rail thin. She likes loose, fluffy clothes in unmatched colors, and when she's sitting down, she looks like a pile of unfolded laundry. She doesn't like anyone in the family except Michael, though she's polite to Dad, and she hates family gatherings. She's a rich, spoiled workout queen, and I don't like her. She checked her watch, a wide swath of magenta on her skeletal wrist. "Michael, if I don't swim today I'll feel wretched all week. There's no reason for me to stay around and wait for the cops, is there?" It was a simple enough question, but with the whine in her voice and the elaborate body language that accompanied it, she made it sound like Michael had inconvenienced her enormously by having the audacity to have his sister get murdered. Michael shook his head. He was probably glad to see her go. Their relationship is based on a contest to see who can make the other more miserable.

"No, Sonia, you don't need to stay around," said my mother. She turned away from Sonia, who was wasting no time on good-byes, and frowned at my sweatshirt and jeans. "You might want to put on something a little different, Thea," she said. By which she meant she didn't think it was right for a respectable widow my age to meet a policeman in my present unkempt state. I'd used up my energy on Todd. I didn't have any left to argue with her, so I excused myself and went upstairs to change.

CHAPTER 3

EVERYONE PRETENDED THEY didn't mind, but I could tell by the rise in volume, by all the projects that suddenly needed to be done, that the family was nervous about talking to a policeman. Not because we had any secrets, but because we'd be forced to deal with the reality of Carrie's death in front of a stranger. Until now, we'd faced it together, sharing the burden, there to comfort each other. We all had a common bond, so much remained unspoken. It would be different with an outsider. We didn't know whether we'd have to talk with him alone or all together. It didn't matter. We knew we had to help the police; it was just that none of us wanted to talk about her. There was something else, too. No one had asked exactly how she died. We didn't want to know and we were all afraid he might tell us.

The Fosters and the Hodgsons excused themselves and left. Mom let them go reluctantly, clinging to them at the door. Having the distraction of people to feed and wait on kept her from thinking about what had happened. Uncle Henry and Aunt Rita stayed.

I helped Mom clear the buffet and put food away. Rita and Henry did the dishes. As soon as everything was put away, Mom, who couldn't stand being idle, began getting things ready for lunch. Dad laid a fire in the fireplace, an elaborate process which involved sweeping up ashes, carrying in armloads of wood, arranging newspaper and kindling, and getting the damper set just right. Only Michael seemed unconcerned. He sprawled on a sofa, reading the Sunday paper. He didn't even look up when Sonia yelled good-bye as she went out the door.

At twelve, precisely the time he'd said he would arrive, Detective Andre Lemieux of the Maine State Police rang the doorbell. Aunt Rita dropped the plate she was drying. Dad lit the fire. Uncle Henry gave Mom a quick hug and bent to help Rita pick up the pieces. Michael stayed on his sofa, inert. Which left me to answer the door.

I don't know what I was expecting. Something bad. The devil, maybe. We were all dreading this interview so much. The man standing there seemed perfectly normal, no horns or tail. He wasn't even wearing a uniform, just a simple tweed jacket, blue shirt, and corduroy slacks. As he stepped past me into the hall, I realized we were almost the same height. He seemed surprised at that. Maybe he'd expected we'd all be small and fair, like Carrie.

I held out my hand. "I'm Theadora Kozak."

His handshake was firm and dry. "Detective Andre Lemieux, Maine State Police." He smiled. "I guess that's obvious, isn't it?"

I hadn't expected a policeman with a sense of humor. It might make things easier. He seemed puzzled about who I was. "I'm Carrie's sister. Was, I mean," I explained. "My parents, Mr. and Mrs. McKusick, are here, and my aunt and uncle, Henry and Rita McKusick, and my brother, Michael. They're waiting in the living room. But one thing, before you go in. Please be gentle with my parents. They're taking this very hard..."

He didn't say anything, but he gave me an odd look. I couldn't tell whether it was amusement at my presumption or displeasure at being told what to do. Otherwise, his face was unreadable. An attractive, square-jawed blank beneath a bristle of dark hair. He looked like an ex-marine. Or a classic, tight-assed cop. I just hoped he was good at his job. I turned and walked into the living room. Maybe I'd just imagined that look. It didn't matter. It's my experience that cops can't resist power-tripping. I had neither the energy nor the inclination for mind games today.

Maybe I just had a chip on my shoulder. A boulder, actually. When David died, the police were awful to me. First with a phone call asking to speak to his next of kin, but refusing to talk to me because the card in his wallet listed his mother rather than

23

his wife. Who thinks of things like that? No one expects to die young. Then, when they reluctantly told me which hospital he was in, another officer refused to let me in to see him because they wanted to talk to him if he regained consciousness, so he died asking for me and getting a policeman instead. They did let me see him then, while he was still warm, but after the life had gone out of those wonderful brown eyes. So I didn't like cops, and this one, despite his good manners and firm handshake, was no exception.

I took a seat on the far side of the room, near Michael. Lemieux introduced himself to everyone, sat down, and pulled out a notebook. My parents sat together on one sofa, holding hands. Uncle Henry and Aunt Rita were also holding hands. The four of them, the giants of my youth, suddenly looked old and diminished. This detective had better behave, or I'd throw him out on his ear. But I didn't get the chance. He behaved. He sat quietly, not picking his nose, asking questions in a gentle voice, and writing down their answers, also taping the conversation. He accepted the coffee Mom offered, and declined lunch.

He asked all the predictable things. Why had Carrie moved to Maine? When had she moved there? Did we know who her friends were? Had she spoken to us about any serious boyfriends? Told us about any trouble she was having with anyone? He asked us what Carrie was like. We took turns answering, or supplementing each other's answers. He made it easy to talk about Carrie, and it seemed like we talked for a long time, but nothing we were telling him looked like it would help him catch Carrie's killer. No one wanted to say anything bad, or even too personal, about Carrie, in front of everyone else.

Not that we knew much about her life in Camden. Even though Mom and Dad and I had all been up to visit her, Carrie had been pretty distant since her move to Maine. He seemed disappointed that we didn't know more about her life up there, but it wasn't surprising, really. Carrie was a very private, secretive person. Being adopted had made her insecure about her identity. She guarded information about herself closely, as though someone might find it out and take it away from her. I was closest to her, and there was a lot she didn't even tell me.

The most revealing stuff was what Mom told him, reluctantly, in response to his question about why Carrie had gone to Maine. About a fight they'd had. Carrie had wanted Mom to help her search for her birth parents. Mom has always been a wise, understanding parent, but on this subject she was adamant. She wouldn't discuss it. Maybe it was because she had had to work so hard and wait so long to get Carrie, or because she'd tried so hard to be a perfect mother to her. Whatever the reason — and since she wouldn't talk to me about it I didn't know, either — she was so threatened by Carrie's curiosity that she refused to even consider her request.

"The last day, before she left," Mom said, "Carrie tried again to persuade me that she was right. She said she didn't look anything like us. That she'd always felt odd and out of place and not like one of us. Disconnected. Not chosen, like we'd always told her, but abandoned. Unwanted. She wanted to know who had discarded her, and why they'd given her away. Why they didn't love her enough to keep her. She said she needed to find them and ask them why. She said she might have real brothers and sisters, as if Thea and Michael were fake." She started crying.

Dad gave her his handkerchief and put his arm around her, pulling her tight. "You don't need to talk about this anymore, Linda, if you don't want to."

The detective sat impassively, letting her decide. After a minute, she drew her head away from Dad's chest. "It's OK, Tom," she said. "Carrie said she couldn't understand why, if I loved her, I wouldn't help. She wasn't interested in how I felt. Of course, her head had been filled with nonsense by that search group she was involved with. It was as though we — her family — meant nothing to her. Not our love, or our lifetime together.

What mattered were some people she'd never known, who didn't even want her."

Mom shook her head. "She had no idea what she was getting into, and she wouldn't let me tell her. Carrie believed her birth parents would provide all the answers, fix everything that was wrong with her life. Once she found them, she would know who she was and where she came from, and she would finally be satisfied. Nothing I said, about us being her family, or the risks of such a search and the dangers of disappointment, made any difference." Her voice was getting weaker, as though talking about this exhausted her.

"Linda," Dad began again, "you don't have to talk about this." She put a finger over his lips. "Thea," he said, "will you get your mother a glass of water?"

She took a few sips and set the glass heavily on the coffee table. "Carrie was always searching for something. I guess I shouldn't have been so surprised. Or reacted so strongly. But I did. She told me that she had a friend who was going to spend the summer in Maine, working in a restaurant. The friend could get her a job, and she was going up there to put some space between us and think about things for a while. She packed up that very day, and she left."

"When was that?" Lemieux asked.

"Early June."

"And was that the last time you saw her?"

Mom smiled. "Of course not. Tom and I drove up to see her twice. Carrie might have been mad at me about that one thing, but she was still a loving daughter." She said it defiantly, as though the detective might not believe her. "Thea visited her once, too, didn't you, dear?" I nodded obediently.

Lemieux asked a few questions about the visits, but it was clear that none of us had seen or heard anything, or met anyone who appeared to dislike Carrie or had any reason to hurt her.

The whole interview made me impatient. Impatient with his questions, with the time it was taking which was keeping me there, instead of at home, getting on with my work. I had to fight my own urge to take over and ask different questions — questions which would have made everyone furious with me. When he was finished, I felt like I do after a bad restaurant meal — dissatisfied and still hungry. He hadn't followed up on things he should have, like why searching for her birth parents was so important to Carrie, or even why it was that we knew so little about her. No one had even uttered the words private or secretive or lost, and they were important words in describing her. He didn't have enough information to understand Carrie yet, and if he didn't understand her, how could he find her killer?

I stifled the impulse to tell him so. I was too tired to bother. I'd been following the interview like a coach at a tense basketball game, watching the conversational ball as it flew up and down the court, silently urging everyone to open up, do more, say more, until I felt as though I'd asked and answered every question myself. I knew that memories of Carrie, and the sense that we'd failed her, rested heavily on everyone in the room.

Yesterday I'd made her a promise that her killer would be found. Today that didn't look so easy. This detective wouldn't be here talking to us if the police had an obvious suspect or anything better to go on. And we weren't giving him much. There had been a couple of calls from Carrie on my answering machine in the last month. Calls I hadn't gotten around to returning yet, because I'd been so busy. If I'd answered them, I might know something that would be useful to the police. Or they might have been calls for help.

"Do you have any idea who killed Carolyn?" my mother asked.

"I'm afraid we don't, Mrs. McKusick," he said. "Not at this point in time." He seemed genuinely sorry, but then, catching criminals was his job, so maybe he was just sorry because it meant more work to do. Maybe he'd hoped one of us would confess. I didn't know why I was letting this detective bother me so much. He hadn't said one harsh word to anyone. Maybe it was because it was so important that he find Carrie's killer and he admitted he didn't have a clue. Maybe I was just worn out from the scene with Todd. And remembering David.

I got up to see him out and found my legs were so shaky I barely made it to the door. I had to lean against the wall to keep from falling over. He didn't miss it, either. He hesitated in the doorway. "Mrs. Kozak," he said, "are you all right?"

"Fine," I said, too loudly. "I'm just tired."

"Mr. Kozak isn't with you?" he asked.

"Mr. Kozak," I said, "is dead." I shut the door in his face.

CHAPTER 4

AFTER DETECTIVE LEMIEUX left, my mother served lunch. It was a generous spread, her usual, and everything looked delicious, but no one had much appetite. The only one who did it justice was Uncle Henry. Dad and Henry used to have eating contests when they were kids. Their mother, my grandma, used to tell us about it when we were little. Once Dad and Henry ate almost an entire turkey between them. The only trouble was that Grandma had cooked it to make turkey salad for a church supper and she wasn't pleased.

I was thinking about what Mom had said and wondering if she blamed herself for Carrie's death because of the fight. It wasn't something I could come right out and ask her, but it was something to watch for. Mom wasn't the type to let others know she was worried. She believed in putting up a good front and keeping her troubles to herself. We were a strange bunch, really. Right up front about opinions, politics, and current events, and very private about feelings.

As soon as I decently could, I said good-bye to everyone, threw my things into a suitcase, and left. Michael was right behind me, though why anyone would be in a hurry to get back to Sonia was a mystery to me. The weather was gloomy, which suited my mood just fine. It was a real nothing sort of day — too warm to be cold and too cold to be warm. Too cloudy to be sunny and too bright to be cloudy. Mid-September isn't a big time for Sunday drivers, those mindless cruisers who can drive you to distraction and folly when you're trying to make time, so the traffic was light. My Saab carried me smoothly along, lulled by its husky throb, at only slightly more than the speed limit, and it was a quick trip up Route 128 from south of the city, where my parents lived, to my condo. Route 128 is the major road that loops around the city. In boom times, back before Massachusetts lost so many jobs, it was aptly called America's

Technology Highway. The impressive buildings are still there, crowning the hills along the road, but now a lot of them sport big banners proclaiming space for rent.

I pulled into the lot and past the wide swath of brown bark mulch and blooming chrysanthemums outside my door. I guess it looks neater but I'm no fan of covering the world with bark mulch. I think of it as the browning of America. Still, it was stylistically consistent with the condo complex. My condo is serviceable and impersonal — a civilized form of living out of a suitcase, and it's just minutes off the highway and only a few more minutes from the office. The office is my true home.

The condo smelled stale and musty. I had left in a hurry, and last week's mail and dishes were still piled up on the counter, while several pairs of shoes I'd kicked off lay in front of my favorite chair. A trio of glasses representing my nightly shot of bourbon were stuck to the glass coffee table. My cleaner only came every other week, and this had not been her week. It hadn't been anybody's week. At least, now that I was home, I could lose myself in work. Work was all that kept me sane.

I got a diet soda, sank into the chair, and pressed the message button on my answering machine, kicking off my shoes beside all the others. There were a few condolences from friends, the usual collection of gasps and clicks from people too shy to talk to a machine, a dinner invitation from a guy who wouldn't take no for an answer, a bad joke from David's friend Larry, who worried about my morale — "What do you get when you pour boiling water down a rabbit hole? Hot cross bunnies," — followed by a long message from my boss, Suzanne, explaining that she'd made a mistake about the date our report was due for Acton Academy.

Suzanne is small and dynamic. A workaholic, like me, but unlike me, she tries to lead a normal, satisfying life. We do consulting for colleges and private schools, focused primarily on identifying and attracting new pools of applicants. I met Suzanne a few years after college. I was wandering blindly about, trying to figure out what to do with degrees in sociology and journalism. I'd tried working for a small-town weekly, getting paid in peanuts, and discovered that it wasn't for me. I couldn't get used to being pushy and intrusive just to report some minor story, even though I liked to write.

Then I'd tried the sociology angle, working for the Department of Social Services, but that didn't suit me either. It took me less than a year to burn out, sick of processing desperate, unhappy people, never getting enough done, and worrying constantly about some serious case falling through the cracks. Salvation came in the form of an ad in the paper for a self-starter who liked people and liked to write.

I answered the ad, liked Suzanne, and quit my job the next day. That was five years ago. Our work styles are very compatible. We're both independent, overachieving workaholics, but we can work well together. And the business is quite successful. There was some friction after I met David. He objected to my working all the time. David liked to play, and I discovered I liked to play with him, so for the two years we were together, I practiced being efficient about work at work and leaving it behind when I went home. David and Suzanne liked each other, and were good-natured about their attempts to get a larger share of my time. When David died, it was a lifesaver for me to have a job I could throw myself into. I've been throwing myself into it ever since.

Suzanne's message, once I got over my shock at having only one week instead of the three I'd expected, offered just the opportunity I needed. I'd planned a leisurely week, starting to work on the report and writing a couple of proposals. A fifty-page report due on Friday meant an eighty-hour work week, and that was if things went well. I wouldn't have time to think about Carrie. My cleaner could worry about the shoes, dishes, and dust, and by Friday I was bound to find another distraction to take me through the weekend.

The messages subsided with a final beep. I picked up the

phone and called Suzanne. "Hello?" She sounded sleepy, and it was only seven-thirty.

"It's Thea. I got your message. I'll get started on that report right away. Have we got everything we need?"

Suzanne sighed. "Thea, honey, it's Sunday night. You know, the weekend. Can't you wait 'til morning?" I was about to tease her about losing her competitive edge, but I heard deep male tones in the background, and immediately understood what was going on. Suzanne works too hard for the same reason I do, as a distraction. But she readily admits she'd like to get married and have a family and lead a normal life. Most of the men we meet in our business are married, but she'd found one somewhere.

"Of course," I said. "See you in the morning?"

Before I could hang up, Suzanne said, "Wait. How did things go at home? Are you OK?"

"It was bearable," I said. "Just. Tell you about it tomorrow." I cradled the phone. I changed into some decent pants and a sweater, stuffed a yogurt and diet soda into my briefcase, and grabbed my keys. The phone rang before I got to the door.

"Thea? It's Mom. You got home all right?"

"Sure. Easy driving today. I was just on my way to the office."

Mom sighed. It worries her that I work so hard. "There's something I forgot to ask you, dear, while you were here. I got distracted, with so many people around, and that policeman."

"I know what you mean," I said. "I didn't like him much, I don't know why. There was just something about him."

"Well, Thea, he was just doing his job. He seemed polite enough to me, although of course I would have preferred not to discuss it. It's about Carrie. The thing I wanted to ask you, I mean. I hope you don't mind. Someone has to go up there and clean out her apartment. The rent's paid until the end of the month, but her landlady says it makes her nervous having a dead person's things around." Mom's tones conveyed her disgust with someone so irrational. "If it bothers her so much, I don't know why she won't just pack them up herself and ship them, but she says she won't touch them. So would you mind too much, dear, going up there next weekend and getting her stuff? You could treat it kind of like a minivacation, couldn't you? Camden is very pretty."

I didn't bother to ask her why she didn't do it herself. She wouldn't have called me if she could do it. She wasn't superstitious, like Carrie's landlady, but she had her own reasons for not wanting to touch Carrie's things. Memories. Even if she went, it would take her forever to do it. She'd be inundated with memories every time she touched something.

I should have expected this call. The family persists in believing that I can do anything, that I am the model of calm capability. "Thea will fix it," could be the family motto. It's partly my fault because I don't just say no. I'm flattered that they think I'm capable, but it can be a real nuisance sometimes, since they also don't think my work is important enough to merit any consideration. This was one of those times. I'd wanted a distraction that would get me away from thinking about Carrie, not one that would immerse me in memories.

The last time I'd been called in to fix things was when they wanted me to persuade Carrie to abandon her notion of searching for her birth parents. I'm ashamed to admit that I tried, too, but that was one that even Thea couldn't fix. Carrie was calm, cool, and resolute. She explained her reasons, dismissed our parents' concerns, and gave me the number of someone I could talk to in the search group she had joined. When I reported my failure, my parents weren't surprised. What I didn't report was Carrie's disappointment in me for failing to understand. That was personal, and it opened a chasm between us that we never bridged. Shortly after that, Carrie moved to Maine. I visited her once, uncomfortable about the distance between us. She didn't mention the search, and neither did I, so I assumed she'd given it up.

I'd done it again. Drifted off into my own thoughts. Mom was talking and I hadn't paid any attention. "I'm sorry," I said. "I missed what you just said."

"It's not like you to be inattentive," she said. "You were the same way at the funeral. Are you feeling all right these days?" She didn't wait for a reply. "I expect you're just working too hard, dear. A long weekend in Maine will do you good. Anyway, what I said was that the landlady expects you on Friday, so she can let you in. She must be planning to go away for the weekend or something. You know that we don't have Carrie's keys. Her purse disappeared when she was attacked..."

She rattled on, oblivious to the fact that she'd just added an impossible complication to my life. "Mom, I've got an extremely busy week. I can't go up on Friday. I have to work."

"Oh, just tell Suzanne that you have to have the day off. She'll understand. She works you too hard anyway." Mom is very good at compartmentalizing things. Although on the one hand she persists in assuming I can do anything, she doesn't entirely accept the idea of professional women who manage their own work schedules and meet their responsibilities any way they can. She is like this despite running an impeccable household very competently while also coordinating all the volunteers at the local hospital and working part-time in Dad's office. Besides, it was convenient for her to think Suzanne controlled my schedule. I've given up trying to change her.

"Why don't I go up next week instead?"

"Well, you know, dear, I suggested just that to the landlady, but she was very insistent. Maybe you'll have better luck with her than I did. You're very persuasive. I've got her number right here. Do you have a pencil?" I dug one out of my briefcase and wrote the number on the edge of a magazine.

"Dad and I really appreciate your doing this. You're such a good daughter," Mom said, and hung up before I could argue. Such a patsy was what she really meant. I was halfway down the stairs before I realized I should have suggested she get Michael to do it. Michael, my incredibly talented and lazy brother, lived off his rich girlfriend, dabbled at his art, and had plenty of time on his hands. I'd call him from the office.

CHAPTER 5

MY CALL TO Mrs. Bolduc, Carrie's landlady, was unsuccessful. I felt like I was conversing with a pet-store parrot. No matter what I said, she repeated her standard line, "Come on Friday or I get my husband to throw the things out." She answered none of my questions, including why her husband could throw things out but not pack and ship them, and she managed to imply that Carrie was an immoral slut who deserved what had happened to her.

By the time I hung up, my hatred for Mrs. Bolduc was so intense that it was a good thing I had four days to cool off before I met her. Otherwise there would have been another homicide.

My efforts to pass the job along to Michael were equally unsuccessful. On Sunday his line was busy, and when I finally got through on Monday, his girlfriend Sonia's nasal voice on the answering machine informed me that they were in Bermuda for a few days and would be glad to return my call as soon as they got back. Good old Michael. He sure knew how to deal with grief. I gave up and threw myself into writing the report.

Acton Academy was a staid old all-girls prep school with a dwindling enrollment. Our interviews with Acton alumnae, current students, prospective students, parents, and faculty showed that the school was perceived by applicants as old-fashioned and dull, although it actually provided an excellent education, especially in math and science, in an environment where girls felt it was safe to excel. Acton had asked us to advise them whether it would be necessary, or successful, to accept boys.

Our research had included focus groups with various sections of the school population, telephone surveys, hours of interviews, class visits, and a review of the promotional literature. It showed that including boys wasn't the solution. What the school needed to do was update their curriculum slightly, adding some "sexy" courses in areas like video production, photography, and computer science, and find ways to give a truer picture of their strengths and promote their overall strong academic program, especially the math and science curriculums.

Our clients had started out pessimistic, but the progress reports that we had given them had lifted their spirits dramatically. We expected the final report to sustain that optimism. Our telemarketing surveys with high school students who were potential candidates and their parents indicated that Acton could increase its enrollment by targeting anxious parents in medium-sized cities and large towns where an eroding tax base was beginning to affect the quality of the schools.

My job was to write all of this down, in a lucid and persuasive way, in a report of not less than fifty pages. Some of those pages I could fill with charts and graphs, some with recaps of answers from questionnaires, but it was always a challenge to make about fifteen pages of succinct prose become fifty pages of rhetoric. Our contract was to produce a fifty-page report, and fifty pages was what the client would get. Our clients, whether they acted on our recommendations or not, usually liked our reports.

Suzanne was aware of my deadline dilemma, and she had offered to do the final edit and check on Friday. I raced the clock all week, feeling like a soldier crawling through a mine field. Every time I sat down to concentrate on the report, my secretary, Sarah, interrupted me with a client who thought he had an emergency or a question that just couldn't wait. I finally, after a couple of almost-all-nighters, staggered into the office on Friday morning, tossed the revised draft and twelve new pages on Sarah's desk, and collapsed into my chair. "Make the changes, type those last few pages, and get it to Suzanne as soon as you can," I said.

"Of course, Thea." She handed me a pink memo slip. "Your mother wants you to call her before you leave."

Maybe it was a reprieve. I grabbed the phone eagerly and dialed her number. "Mom, it's Thea."

"Have you heard anything from the police about your sister's killer?" she asked, not wasting any breath on a greeting.

I felt a tingle of excitement. "No. Have they found him?" I hoped that they had. My attitude hadn't altered a bit since the funeral. I'd tried to avoid thinking about Carrie, but her face had come floating into my head nightly as I pored over the documents I was consolidating into my report. Her direct blue eyes seemed to be asking me why I wasn't doing something about her death. I suppose that was just me, feeling guilty. Even Carrie had always believed Thea could fix it.

"No. They haven't. A whole week and a half gone by, and nothing. No news." My mother sounded outraged. "Well, there was something, dear. A call from that policeman, asking more questions. I told him I didn't have any more time to waste talking to him, I had to get on with my life, but that you were coming up today. He's working at the Thomaston barracks and he wants you to stop in and see him on your way through. He said to ask for him at the desk."

How nice of her, I thought, to have my life all arranged. "Be prepared for a rude awakening, dear," she went on. "He may have seemed nice the other day, but he isn't a nice man at all. The questions he's asking are quite terrible. I should refuse to answer them if I were you. About her sex life! Can you imagine? I don't know why he thinks I might know something like that." She sputtered on into silence and hung up, having dropped her latest bomb into my lap.

I sat staring at the phone, stunned into immobility. I was running on less than eight hours' sleep in the last two days. I had a four-hour drive ahead of me and now, before I even reached Mrs. Bolduc — and I needed all my energy to keep from harming her — I was supposed to have a chat with Detective Andre Lemieux about my dead sister's sex life. Wasn't life grand?

"Here. Drink this," Suzanne commanded, setting a large glass of bright pink liquid on the desk. She took the phone out of my hand and replaced the receiver.

"What's in it?" I asked suspiciously. Suzanne has been known to embrace some pretty weird diets.

"Strawberry instant breakfast. Protein powder. Wheat germ, fresh strawberries, milk, and an egg. I promise it won't hurt you. Drink it. You need the energy." Reluctantly I raised the glass to my lips and took a tentative sip. Not bad. And I hadn't done much eating lately. I'd been too busy. Suzanne beamed like a mother watching her child use a cup for the first time. "Have you looked at yourself in the mirror, Thea?"

I shook my head. I hadn't had time yet. I hadn't even combed my hair today. "Well, don't," she said. "You'll fall into terminal depression. Are you going to be able to drive to Maine without falling asleep?" She fumbled around in the gigantic leather bag she euphemistically calls a purse. Pony express riders used them to carry a whole town's mail. "Here," she said, fishing out a small brown prescription container, "you'd better take one of these." She opened it and shook out an orange pill shaped like a rounded triangle.

"What is that?"

"Dexedrine." She chuckled in disbelief. "I can't believe you've never tried it. I'd never get my work done without it." She ignored my skeptical look. "These are really mild. Take a half or a whole, whatever works for you, and you're energized for hours. They're great for killing your appetite, too, not that you, with the world's fastest metabolism, need to worry about that. If I ate like you do, I'd weigh two hundred pounds."

"Are these legal?" I asked. "I thought doctors weren't allowed to prescribe them anymore."

"They're for my narcolepsy," she said with a perfectly straight face.

"Right," I said, "and I'm the Queen of Sudbury. How do I know this won't make me crazy?"

"You don't," she said, "but chances are it won't. I've been using them for years, and I'm not crazy, am I?"

"I'm taking the fifth," I said.

She looked worried for a moment, but my smile reassured her. "Just take it with you, Thea, in case you need it. I don't want to lose my valuable partner in a car accident because she fell asleep." She dropped it into my hand as she passed, and sailed on out the door.

I put it in my jacket pocket, drank the rest of her concoction, and headed for the exit. As I passed Suzanne's office, her last remark finally hit home. She had said "partner." But I was just an employee. Highly paid and well regarded, but not owning a piece of the action. I stuck my head around her door. "Did you mean that?" I asked.

She grinned. "A bit slow on the uptake today, aren't you, Thea? Of course I meant it. It's about time, don't you think?" Yes, I did think it was time. I'd been psyching myself up to introduce the subject for some time, and I was about ready to do so. Now Suzanne had saved me the trouble, and paid me a major compliment. I felt a little less weary as I started my car and swung out onto the highway. The psychological lift, and maybe even Suzanne's weird concoction, made the drive seem easier.

I stopped at the mile 24 service area on the Maine turnpike and had a large coffee and a salad. I lingered in the rest room long enough to brush my hair and put on some lip gloss. That was enough prepping for my interview with Detective Lemieux. He'd better not take too long. I couldn't afford to be late with Mrs. Bolduc, or I'd find the door locked.

The drive was easy as far as Bath, where the four-lane road ran out. Good old Route 1 had been awful when I'd come up in the summer. It had taken me more than twenty minutes to cross the bridge, and the drawbridge wasn't even up. Today things were easier. There was one imbecile driver who pulled out in front of me at the last minute, making me jam on my brakes and say bad words, and who then proceeded to creep along at twenty-five. It took a while to get by him. And there was the weaving pickup truck with the occasional beer can flying out the windows, one of which bounced off my windshield. If I'd only brought my bazooka along I could have blown him off the face of the earth, but I'd forgotten to pack it. Otherwise, the traffic wasn't bad, which was a good thing, because despite the coffee I was running low on energy and my mind was on cruise control.

Coming down the big hill in Waldoboro, I was struck by the ugliness of the landscape below. In the valley between the hills were clustered masses of gas stations, car dealers, and other businesses. It looked as if a giant, playing with toy buildings, had set them carelessly on the hillsides and they had all rolled down. At the bottom of the hill, almost obscured by the ugliness, there was a pretty little river flowing through the valley.

Route 1 wound its way along toward the coast, past tree farms and animal farms, past gift shops lurking behind huge wooden lobsters and gift shops lurking behind Viking ships, a tribute perhaps to Leif Eriksson, that early explorer. Everyone who wasn't having a yard sale seemed to be selling wooden sheep with fleece, birchwood reindeer, or the silhouettes of bent-over ladies to decorate your yard, or pretty wooden butter-flies to perch on the side of your house. My condo association would have a fit if I mounted a few of those butterflies on the front of the building and installed a few sheep in the yard.

I crossed the St. George River and headed uphill toward Thomaston, the "Town that Went to Sea." According to Lemieux, via my mother, the state police barracks was at the top of the hill. I pulled up in front of the building and got out. I wasn't dressed for an interview. My mother hadn't called me before I left home and reminded me to wear a dress. Instead, I was wearing an indigo T-backed tank top under an oversized blue and white shirt, baggy tan pants, and an indigo washed-silk bomber jacket. The kind of clothes I love, but not what my mom would consider suitable. And not what I would have chosen if I'd known I'd be doing this. It was a fine outfit to wear to a discussion of someone's sex life.

Lemieux was waiting for me. Today he had the height advantage, because I was wearing jogging shoes, not heels, but I was still better looking. Not everyone would think so. A lot of people probably found his clean-cut, paramilitary look and sturdy build attractive. And some misguided people think my hair is too wild and my mouth is too big. We shook hands and he asked me to follow him back to his office.

It wasn't much of an office. Utilitarian, crowded, and too small. There wasn't much around to give a clue about the occupant, either. No pictures on the wall, except a calendar, and that was from an insurance company. A man with a blank face and blank walls. Maybe he saved his passion for his work.

He noticed my scrutiny. "My office is in Augusta," he said. "I just borrowed this one." I sat down in the chair facing the desk. There was an ashtray between us, filled with little putty-colored balls of chewed gum. He pulled a file out of the drawer, flipped it open, and pulled out a yellow lined sheet.

"Mrs. Kozak, I'm afraid that the questions I'm going to ask you may be unpleasant. Murder is an unpleasant business." He had a deep, resonant voice, the kind that would be nice reading Dickens aloud. "I'd appreciate it if you would concentrate on answering my questions instead of getting upset about the fact that I'm asking them." He was trying to be helpful, but he made me feel like a naughty child being lectured by a grown-up. "You're an intelligent, capable woman, and I'm sure you'll understand why I'm asking these questions when we're through. If you don't know the answer, just say so, and we'll move on. If you find you're getting upset — "

"You can skip the lecture," I said. "I'm in a hurry. Just get to the questions." I was being rude, but I didn't much care. I wasn't there for tea. He wasn't the soul of tact either, according to my mother.

"Certainly," he said. His eyes were amused, but his face stayed blank. I think he wanted to push me around a little, but his priority was asking questions, at least for now. "Were you and your sister close?" he asked.

"Yes," I said. "Maybe not so close recently." The truth was that since David's death I'd been withdrawn, burying myself in work, and I hadn't always been there for Carrie. After nineteen years of being a second mom to her, I'd let us drift apart. Which was one reason I felt so guilty about her death.

"Was your sister promiscuous?" he asked.

He didn't beat around the bush, did he? "No," I said.

"Was she sexually active?"

"She was an attractive, red-blooded American girl," I said. "Free, white, and twenty-one. Of course she was sexually active." I'd better start exercising some serious self-control or I was going to get into a fight with this guy. His chairside manner left something to be desired.

He nodded. "Sexually active, but not promiscuous. Did she have steady boyfriends, or did she play the field?"

"Both. She dated several boys in high school, then settled down with one, Todd, although she and Todd had their ups and downs. During the downs she sometimes saw other guys." I didn't add that she sometimes slept with those other guys for the sole purpose of driving Todd crazy. Nor did I tell him that it had had the desired effect — Todd was driven crazy. Carrie had been pretty young then. Young and acting out.

"Did she sleep with Todd?"

"I think she did."

"She never told you?" His tone implied disbelief.

"Well, yes, she did tell me that she was sleeping with Todd, but it wasn't a routine subject of our conversation. I don't like to know too much about people's intimate affairs." He made me snappish no matter how hard I tried to stay cool.

"Did she sleep with any of the other guys?" I tried to avoid an answer with a vague shrug, meaning to suggest I didn't really know. I wasn't used to dealing with people who make their living getting people who don't want to talk to tell what they know. "Is that a no, or an I don't know?" Lemieux asked.

"Sometimes," I said.

"Sometimes what? Sometimes you know, or sometimes she slept with guys other than Todd?"

"Sometimes she slept with other guys," I said, knowing I sounded like a sulky child. "But she wasn't promiscuous." He lifted one dark eyebrow, a subtle insinuation of skepticism. I could tell he was dying to get into a debate about our different definitions of promiscuous, so I said, "Was there anything else you wanted to know?" I glanced at my watch. I had to get out of here soon.

"Was your sister a tease? Did she like to turn men on and then say no?"

"Not that I ever knew."

"Was your sister into kinky sex?"

My hand flew to my chest in a perfect imitation of an offended dowager. "I'm afraid I don't know what you mean."

He laughed in my face. "Did she like to be tied up? Spanked? Rubbed all over with salad oil? Penetrated with vegetables? Fucked in the ass? Do it with two guys at a time? That's what I mean by kinky. Did she like any of that stuff?"

I couldn't believe the things he was saying. How could he talk about my sister like that? It made me sick just listening to it. I stood up. "I'm leaving," I said. "I am not staying around to listen to any more of this. And if you can get your mind back above your belt, maybe you should devote your energy to finding out who killed my sister." I headed for the door, but he beat me to it, blocking my exit.

He glared down at me. "Go sit down."

"I won't," I said, glaring back. "I'm leaving. Please let me by." He didn't budge. "I'm not under arrest, am I?" I asked. He shook his head. "Good. Then let me go. You have no right to make me sit here and listen to you say filthy things about my sister. You shouldn't violate her privacy like that."

He stayed there, filling the doorway. There was no way I could get around him. He sighed as though he'd heard that line too many times. "Look, Mrs. Kozak," he said, "I'm sorry I upset you. I tried to tell you..." Amazingly enough, he really did look sorry. "I thought you understood. Before you storm out of here in a fine state of moral outrage, please sit down for a minute and listen." I was so astonished at the change in him that I did what he asked.

Once I was back in my chair, he stopped guarding the door and sat down, too. "I'm going to speak very frankly," he said, "so that you can understand. Murder isn't nice. It isn't polite, and murderers are not respectful of people's feelings. The unfortunate but necessary result is that murder investigations aren't nice, either."

He leaned back in his chair, arms folded, staring at the calendar. "Murder victims don't have a right to privacy. The killer takes their privacy when he takes their life. When we don't have much to go on — and we don't in this case — we need to know as much as possible about the victim to help us know where to look. That's why you're here, to help me learn about your sister so we can find her killer. I'm not asking these questions because I enjoy it."

"OK," I said, "so you want to learn about my sister Carrie. I can understand that. I can tell you what she liked to read, the kinds of places she liked to go, her favorite music, what she drank, how she dressed, how she liked to spend her spare time. Lots of things. I'd be glad to tell you all those things..." I checked my watch again. I didn't have any more time if I was to get to Camden before Mrs. Bolduc left. "... when I have time. But I don't understand why you want to know about her sex life. Maybe you can explain it to me some other time. I'll be around all weekend. Right now I have to go."

"Where?" he said.

"Where what?"

"Where do you have to go?"

I hesitated about telling him. It was really none of his business, but I had no reason to lie. "I have to go clear out Carrie's apartment. I don't have a key, and her landlady said she'd only wait until five and then she's going away for the weekend or something. She says if I don't get the stuff out she'll throw it away. She is an impossible woman and she won't listen to reason, so I've got to get there on time."

He opened the file and flipped through some papers. "Mrs. Bolduc, right, on Mountain Street?" I nodded. "I'll take care of it," he said. He got up and left the office. He moved quickly and quietly. I stared at my fingernails, which were badly in need of a manicure, wondering what he was up to.

He wasn't gone long. "It's all taken care of," he said. "A trooper is going by now to pick up the key and bring it here. I don't think she'll refuse." The idea of the police leaning on Mrs. Bolduc pleased me.

"Now," he said, "you want to know why I'm asking about your sister's sex life, right? Do you know how your sister died?"

I was beginning to wish I'd walked out while he was gone, even though he was being almost pleasant now. My lack of sleep and the long drive had caught up with me. I was light-headed from fatigue. I felt like leaning back in the chair and going to sleep. And I didn't want to hear what he wanted to tell me. "She was killed by a blow on the head," I said, "by someone who wanted to assault her. We didn't want to know the details."

"I think maybe you should." Lemieux pulled out a thick manila envelope, tipped it up, and dumped out a stack of photographs. He selected one and set it down on the desk, facing me. It showed a wide gravel path going uphill through the woods. Far ahead, something was lying on the path. He waited until he was sure I'd seen it, then dropped another picture on top of it. Now I could see the something was a person. A person with blond hair. I assumed it was Carrie. I'd always known that eventually I'd have to find out how she died. It looked like that time was now. Another picture. A closer shot, showing only the top half of her body. The side of her head toward the camera was OK, but there was a smear of blood across her face. She looked surprised.

He flipped another photograph onto the pile. This one showed her from the other side. Most of that side of her head was bloody. Toward the back, her skull was pushed in. I'd never seen anything like it. Her head was lopsided and awful. My stomach lurched and felt like I was going to be sick. I looked up at Lemieux, struggling for control. Was he trying to shock me into cooperating? "What did he hit her with?" I asked.

"We don't know," he said. "Something big and blunt. A sledgehammer, or a rock. We haven't found anything that matches the wound, and there were no traces of the weapon in the wound itself to give us any clues. And here's the answer to your question." He set another picture in front of me. Carrie's body, looking up from her feet. She was naked below the waist, her legs spread wide. There was a stick between her legs, smeared dark. He dropped another photograph beside it. It was a close-up of her crotch, with the stick disappearing up inside her. The stick and the ground around it were dark with blood.

"Oh my God," I said. I was definitely going to be sick. I hoped I could make it to the ladies' room in time. I pushed myself out of the chair. "Where?" I mumbled through the hand over my mouth. Lemieux was out of his chair in a second. He grabbed my arm, dragged me down the corridor, opened the door marked "Women," and shoved me through it. I made it as far as the sink.

When the heaves finally subsided, I leaned against the wall, panting, until the worst of the shakes were over. Then I washed the pathetic bits of lettuce out of the sink, tied back my straggling hair, and splashed several handfuls of cold water over my face. I studied myself in the mirror. I looked like someone who had just seen a ghost. My eyes were huge and green in a dead-white face. I walked back to Lemieux's office, my legs wobbling, hands shaking, and breath ragged. The only thing that was in working order was my temper.

Lemieux was leaning back in the chair, hands clasped behind his head. The pictures were gone. There was a key sitting on the desk where they had been. I picked up the key, my purse, and my jacket. His eyes were watchful, waiting for my reaction. I don't know what he expected. Maybe that I'd come back babbling. Or that I'd be reduced to tears and putty in his hands. He didn't say, and his face gave nothing away. I said nothing either. My thoughts were unspeakable. He'd probably heard everything included in my opinion of him before. His dark, shiny eyes followed me as I walked out the door.

CHAPTER 6

IT WAS A miracle that I didn't have an accident on my way to Camden. I was in no shape to drive a car. I gripped the wheel tightly to still my trembling hands, shaking from exhaustion, rage, and shock. And all the way there I saw, not the road, but that wide dirt path, and Carrie's body lying sprawled on the ground, violated by a tree branch. I'd read that people don't bleed much from injuries after death, which meant it had been done while she was still alive. My poor baby sister.

I lowered the window and let the cool air blast me. Shook my head furiously from side to side. Dug my nails into my palms, and even tried singing, but nothing I did would drive that picture out of my mind. I even tried to think about David, but I couldn't quite remember his face. Why had Lemieux shown me those pictures? He hadn't seemed like a brutal man. Was it something about me? Would he have done the same thing to my mother? They say a picture is worth a thousand words. Those words would have been so much kinder.

I've come to believe that my Saab has a superior intelligence, and can pilot itself when I'm incapacitated. It always gets me home when I'm tired, or when my mind is on an audit we're conducting or an interview I've just completed, and even on those rare occasions when I've had too much to drink. It didn't let me down today; it brought me to Camden without incident. I hoped Mrs. Bolduc had gone wherever she'd planned to go. I couldn't face an encounter with her right now.

The directions Carrie had sent were in my glove compartment, but I thought I'd remember the way. Downtown Camden has only one main street, and since it's also Route 1, I arrived in the center of town without having to ask directions. The road slid downhill past a row of big old houses, past stores on one side and a pocket park on the other, and then through a tunnel of inviting shops before starting back uphill past another park and the library. The library was my landmark. I turned left onto Mountain Street. Carrie's address was Mountain Street, but her apartment was in the ell of a big house stretching back along a side street.

Her battered little Chevette wasn't in the driveway. No one had mentioned it; I'd have to track it down at some point. Maybe the police had it, but contacting them to ask where her car was would mean I might have to speak with Lemieux, and I never intended to do that again. My dad the capable lawyer could handle it.

I parked, got out my suitcase, and walked up the little brick path to her door. From the corner of my eye, I saw a flicker of movement. Someone was standing in an upstairs window, watching me. Ignoring the invisible figure, I let myself into the apartment, and shut the door behind me.

The apartment still smelled faintly of Chantilly, Carrie's favorite perfume. A bouquet of late roses, their pink faded to pale brown, dripped petals onto the pine dining table. Something was wrong, though. Something that wasn't the same as when I'd visited her. I studied the room, trying to identify it. Someone had been looking through Carrie's things. Books were off the shelves, magazines were scattered around, and many of the drawers were half open. Carrie was neat, like Mother. She would never have left things like that. Probably the police had done it while they were looking for information about her sex life. I wondered what they'd found in her diary. Carrie had always been meticulous about keeping it up to date.

I lugged the suitcase upstairs to the bedroom and set it on a chair. Like the living room, this room showed signs of a search. I went to the linen closet in the bathroom and got some clean sheets. I wasn't going to sleep in the same sheets she had used. I automatically dumped the dirty sheets into the hamper, which was silly. I'd only have to take them out again to pack them.

Whatever Mrs. Bolduc's faults, she hadn't been stingy about furnishing the apartment. The furnishings were pretty as well as useful, and the apartment was bright and inviting. Some of it was Carrie, of course. She'd added pictures, pillows and knick-knacks, books, and the flowers. Carrie always had to have flowers. When she was little, she was always picking other people's flowers and bringing them home. Poor Mom, she couldn't get mad at a little girl handing her a special bouquet, and yet she had to stop Carrie from taking the flowers. She'd solved the problem by helping Carrie plant her own little flower garden in the backyard. In the winter, Dad would take Carrie to the flower shop each week to pick out a bouquet for the family. I wondered if Mrs. Bolduc had let Carrie plant some flowers here.

I felt lousy. The past week had left me bone-weary, and today's interview with Lemieux hadn't helped. I needed a cup of tea to settle my stomach and soothe me with its heat, but I was too tired to go back downstairs. I got a drink of water from the bathroom, kicked off my shoes, and lay down on the bed. I fell asleep thinking about a little blond girl clutching a bouquet of stolen flowers. The picture gradually faded and became a wooded path. Someone was walking toward me, out of the shadows, holding out flowers. As she stepped into a shaft of sunlight, I recognized Carrie. She came closer, and I could see that one side of her head was matted with blood. A bold, almost jaunty streak of blood ran across her face. She was half-naked, walking awkwardly because of the stick between her legs. She held out the flowers. They were faded roses. "You've got to help me, Thea," she said.

I took the roses. Her hands, as they touched mine, were cold as ice. "You're cold, Carrie," I said.

"No, Thea, I'm dead." She giggled. "Cold as death." She spread her hands in a supplicating gesture. "Find the person who did this to me, Thea."

"You've got to help me, Carrie," I said. "Tell me where to start."

"I can't," she said. "I'm dead." She fell backwards on the

ground and lay there like she had in the picture. I put my hand over my mouth and fled backwards, screaming. My screams woke me up.

Drenched with sweat, I staggered into the bathroom, stripped, and stepped under the shower. The icy water woke me up in a hurry. The towel I grabbed smelled like Carrie. I dropped it and went back into the bedroom, still dripping. The sun was gone, but the sky was still light. My growling stomach reminded me I'd subjected it to serious abuse. I pulled on some black sweats and a loose sweater and went downstairs to see what I could find to eat. I put on water for tea and was rummaging through the canned goods when someone knocked. So Mrs. Bolduc hadn't gone away after all.

I pulled the door open, prepared to dismiss her curtly. Detective Lemieux was standing there, holding two brown grocery bags. "Go away," I said, and shut the door. He knocked again. *Go away* probably wasn't in his vocabulary. People who indulge in Gestapo tactics aren't usually amenable to polite dismissal. I tried ignoring the knocking, but he wouldn't give up. Finally I opened the door, prepared to do battle. Behind him, silhouetted against the light in an upstairs window, I could see someone, Mrs. Bolduc, I assumed, watching.

I stood aside and let him in. He carried the bags into the kitchen and set them down. "I brought dinner," he said. "There isn't much here for you to eat." In a soft plaid shirt and pleated cords, he looked more human, but he still looked ready to jump to attention. Maybe he was just naturally stiff. Nothing a little yoga couldn't cure.

"You've got to be kidding," I said. "What am I supposed to do? Forgive you for being deliberately sadistic because you brought some groceries?"

"I was hoping," he said.

I kept the counter between us, watching from a distance as he unpacked the bags and made himself at home, stunned by his bravado. He set out steak, salad stuff, a loaf of crusty bread.

Mushrooms, peppers, and onions. Threw the grocery bags into the trash. And started to cook. Cool as a cucumber while I was trembling with rage. He got out a cutting board and a knife, sliced up the vegetables, and tossed them into a frying pan with some olive oil. He took a bottle of Scotch down from the cupboard above the sink, fixed two drinks, and handed one to me. "Maybe you could set the table," he said.

I hadn't said anything before because I was speechless with fury; now I found my voice. "What on earth do you think you're doing?" I said. I meet all sorts of people, doing the work I do, and I spend a lot of energy working out my approaches so I can get the information we need to write successful reports without being too threatening. I'm good with people. I've spent endless hours on the phone and in meetings with people who are difficult to comprehend, or who don't want to be understood, and I can usually make the situations work, but Lemieux was in a class by himself. Maybe he was from another planet.

"Making you dinner," he said. "You don't look like you take very good care of yourself." He put the steak under the broiler, and the bread in the oven to warm up. Neither of us said another word. I just stood there, stunned, watching him. He acted like he'd been in her kitchen before. But then, he probably had, if he'd searched the apartment.

"I don't want you here," I said. "I don't want your wretched dinner. I don't want anything from you, except for you to leave. I don't think you can have any idea what you did, showing me those pictures." He ignored me, and I didn't know how to make him go. I was still dopey from my unrestful nap, and although I'm not usually at a loss for words, I was confused about what to do. He seemed determined to make me dinner no matter what I said. "Does this mean you won't leave?" I said.

"That's right," he said, handing me two plates. I took them to the table, returning to the kitchen with the vase of fading flowers. I shivered slightly, remembering my dream. It was only a Pullman kitchen. I squeezed by him, determined not to touch him. I put the flowers in the trash, dumped the foul green water down the sink, and rinsed out the vase. Lemieux tapped a drawer. "Silverware's probably in here," he said. Automatically I picked out what we needed when what I wanted to do was throw myself at him and rake his face with my fingernails. I put silverware on the table. We were like a warring married couple who spoke only when necessary. I found two placemats and some napkins in a drawer.

"Shall I put out wineglasses, dear?" I asked sarcastically.

"You could," he said, refusing to be drawn.

I found two pretty cobalt ones, part of a set I'd given Carrie for her birthday, and put them on the table. She liked blue things. The placemats were blue and white Indian cotton. Then, because I didn't know what else to do, my Scotch and I went and sat on the sofa, as far from the kitchen as I could get, and tried to figure out what to do. Since he seemed set on feeding me, maybe I should just eat and then ask him to leave again. But what if he wouldn't leave? What could I do, call the police? I sat on the sofa, fuming, trapped with one of the most detestable men I'd ever met. It was worse than a blind date from hell. Lemieux ignored me, concentrating on his cooking. He was completely comfortable in the kitchen, a quality I'm not accustomed to in men. The whole situation was absurd. But, resentful as I was, I had to admit the food smelled good. Breakfast had been that weird pink stuff, I'd left lunch at the police barracks, and I was starved. But I was afraid to eat with him. Afraid of what he might do.

I was feeling vulnerable and confused, especially here in Carrie's apartment, surrounded by her things and her scent, knowing she was never coming back. Having another person there could have made it easier, but not when it was someone I neither knew nor trusted. I sipped my Scotch, which probably only made things worse, and tried to summon the energy to deal with my feelings about Carrie and my antagonism toward Lemieux. When the phone rang, I almost dropped my drink.

"Hello?" I said.

"Oh, Thea, dear, I'm glad you arrived safely," Mom said. "How was the drive?"

"Fine. And I had no trouble getting into the apartment."

"Good." I could tell she was not in a mood to chat. She was just doing her duty. "Dad says we can store all Carrie's things over the garage until we decide what to do with them. You don't mind dropping them off here, do you, dear? It's almost on your way." "Almost" meant an hour's detour each way.

"I have some space at my place, too. It will depend on what time I get back on Sunday. I'll call you before I leave."

"Well, dear. All right. You do what you must, but I was hoping you'd bring it here. I've sort of promised some of her things to the church fair. That's next week."

I couldn't believe what I was hearing. Carrie dead less than two weeks and Mom was already selling off her things. "I'm not sure we should be so hasty, Mom," I said. "Mike and I may want some of the stuff, and you may want to save things, too. I don't think any of us are ready to make those decisions right now."

"Thea, dear, you know I'm sentimental about people, not things. Things just clutter a place up. I hope I'll see you on Sunday." She hung up, annoyed. She liked people to do what she told them. I drank the rest of my drink and tried not to think bad thoughts about my mother, but I was already in a foul mood and her call hadn't helped. My anger and unhappiness were simmering just beneath the surface, threatening to boil over at any minute.

"Soup's on," Lemieux called from the kitchen. He carried the steak to the table, set it down, and went back for the hot bread and salad. He went back a third time for the wine, then sat down across from me. I looked down at my plate, unwilling to meet his eyes. Afraid that my own words, as hot and steaming as the food, would come spilling out. I'd already lost control in front of him once today. I didn't want to do so again. Dinner looked delicious. The steaks were smothered in a thick layer of sautéed mushrooms, onions, and peppers. He poured wine into my glass, then into his, and lifted his glass. "Cheers," he said.

And I boiled over. "Let's not carry this charade too far," I said. "This is not a social evening we're enjoying together and we're not friends. I don't like you. I don't trust you. And I don't understand why you're here."

"To talk about your sister." His dark eyes stayed on my face, waiting. His own face gave nothing away.

"You can just forget about that, Detective. If that's what you came here for, then prepare to be disappointed. In fact, you can leave right now. I am not telling you one more goddamned word about Carrie, do you understand?" The words were coming now, as unstoppable as a rushing train. I was tired of being polite to this awful man. "I don't know how you can live with yourself doing the things you do. It must take a pretty sick kind of man to show people photographs that awful of someone they loved."

He just sat impassively and stared at me. "Isn't it bad enough," I said, feeling the awful, choking sensation of tears behind my anger, "that the two people I loved best have died so violently? Why did you have to rub my nose in it? Don't you see I'll never get those pictures out of my head?"

"I'm sorry," he said, his voice so quiet I almost didn't hear it.

I wanted to argue with him about that, to tell him I didn't believe he was the least bit sorry, but he seemed so oblivious I didn't think it would do any good. I tried to get back on more neutral ground. I'd spent enough time being out of control in front of this man. My anger, like my sorrow, was a private thing. Not for public view. "Look, I'm grateful for the food. It looks delicious and I'm hungry. But otherwise, I don't have anything to be cheerful about." I cut a bite of steak. It was good. So were the vegetables. So was the wine. I concentrated on eating. Because I was hungry and because I hoped maybe the sooner I ate the sooner he'd leave.

He still hadn't said anything more. He just ate quietly, watching me. Then he smiled. "I was right. You were hungry."

Boy, he was a genius of a detective, wasn't he? What was he doing here, cooking for me and saying nothing? Was this another one of his ploys? He seemed so normal, almost pleasant, sitting across from me, eating his dinner. "What am I supposed to call you?" I said. "Trooper? Officer? Detective?"

"Trooper is OK. Or Detective. Or you could just call me Andre."

"Ok, Trooper," I said. "I don't know what you're up to here, but don't expect that just because you cooked me dinner, I'm going to be good company. I have no reason to trust you, no interest in talking to you. You might as well know that like Macbeth, you have murdered my sleep. Those pictures will keep coming back to me." No need to go into detail. He didn't have to know that I have terrible dreams. It was none of his business.

"I'm sorry." That was all he said.

"Maybe it's just the difference between you, as a policeman, and the rest of us," I said. "For you, seeing Carrie's body is just part of the job, the beginning of your quest. But I loved Carrie. Seeing that... knowing what was done to her... makes me feel sick, angry, bewildered. How can one person do that to another? And why show those pictures to me? What were you trying to accomplish? Why would you want to hurt someone like that? Were you planning to do that to my mother, if she'd come instead?" I was practically yelling, yet the words seemed to bounce off him without effect. His face stayed as blank as if I'd been reciting recipes. The futility of my anger made me angrier.

He refilled my wineglass. "You think I'm made of stone, don't you?" he said. "The cold, cynical policeman, right?"

"I have no reason to think anything else, have I?"

He waved his fork at my plate. "What about this?"

"I don't understand about this," I said. "I admit it. But after the pictures, I assume it's just another trick. Shock didn't work.

57

Perhaps this is the attempt to get me relaxed and in a good mood, and then I'll cooperate with you and tell you all about Carrie and her wild sex life. It's a reasonable assumption, isn't it, now that I know how far you'll go?"

He frowned briefly as he considered and rejected a reply. Then he nodded. "It is. Wrong, but understandable. For some reason, Mrs. Kozak, you have a deep prejudice against police. A lot of people do, often for good reasons. But it makes you hard to deal with."

"But I'm not!" I said. "You're the one who's hard to deal with."

He threw his napkin down on the table. "Yes, you are." His voice was still controlled, but he was angry. "You give out information grudgingly and sparsely. You want to control the information and you want to censor the content. Your whole family is like that. On Sunday I was handed a charming version of your sister. The picture of family solidarity was pleasant, too, but I couldn't get a true feeling for what Carrie was like. The only glimpse was when your mother talked about their quarrel, and once she'd said what she wanted to say, she didn't want to discuss it any further."

"But it was your fault," I burst out. "You didn't try hard enough; you didn't ask the right questions. I was angry with you. I wanted to tell you what you should ask, so that you could get a picture of Carrie, but you gave up and went away." He had a lot of nerve, blaming us for his failure.

"It wouldn't have worked," he said.

"Why not?"

"Can you get your mother to discuss things she doesn't want to talk about?"

I had to tell the truth. "No, I can't."

"And who controls the family dynamics?" he asked.

"I don't know what you mean," I said. "More bread?"

"Two slices, please." I cut two for him and one for myself. It was unreal. In the midst of this long, raucous quarrel, we were

58

both eating like pigs. The steaks had been large, and both our plates were clean. But then, the whole day had an element of unreality. "I mean," he said, "if your father is talking about something your mother doesn't want him to discuss, what happens?"

"She shuts him up. Politely. With a distraction. Or she just starts talking through him, until he gets the message."

"And what about you?" he said. "Does she control you, too?"

I thought about that. I don't usually spend much time analyzing my relationship with Mom. She's a wonderful woman. I've always envied her energy and organization, her generosity. She was always helping people. I didn't like what Lemieux was suggesting, but he was right. None of us discussed things around her if she didn't want them discussed, and challenges were masterfully diffused. Carrie was the only one she hadn't been able to muzzle. He passed me the salad. "I'm here, aren't I?" I said.

"I'm not surprised they sent you," he said. "I knew someone would have to come up, and I had only two candidates. You or your uncle Henry. There seems to be an attitude in your family that you will take care of things. Is that right?"

"Bear with me for a minute," I said, rubbing my temples wearily. I wished he would just go. I was so tired and I needed to save my energy for tomorrow. Packing Carrie's things would not be easy. "I am really confused. Everything you are saying is so insightful. You seem to understand us all very well, which makes sense, in your line of work. So explain this to me. If you read all of us... if you read me so well, why did you do what you did to me today?"

He hit himself in the forehead with the heel of his hand, mocking the classic how-could-I-be-so-stupid gesture. "I'm just a dumb cop, right? I lost my temper."

I recalled his impassive face. His cool voice. The determined, methodical way he had thrust the pictures at me. "You did not," I said. "You were cool as a cucumber."

"Wrong!" He slammed his fist down on the table so hard the wineglasses rocked. "I don't have to do this every time I get mad. I've got self-control, just like you. But sitting there watching you — beautiful, exhausted, so obviously sad about your sister — acting like the president of the Junior League confronting a difficult housewife, refusing in your prim, pig-headed way to tell me anything useful, while you pretended you were being helpful and I was being prurient, made me furious. Mad enough to try and shake you out of that role."

"Oh fudge you, you anthole," I yelled, slamming my own fist on the table.

His angry face was transformed by an astonished grin. "What did you say?"

"I said, fudge you, you anthole. Sounds nasty, doesn't it? It's a remnant from childhood, when swearing wasn't allowed. Michael came up with that one, and it's still one of my favorites. Listen, in your job, you have to exercise self-control even in the face of provocation. Besides, I've never been called prim before, and I resent it. I resent everything about you. I resent this whole blatant attempt to manipulate me when I'm vulnerable. I think it stinks and I wish you'd leave!"

Now he was looking a little more animated. "I don't blame you," he said, ignoring my request that he leave. It didn't surprise me. He was about as malleable as a pit bull. "Prim doesn't suit you, but you were being prim. I don't want to know about your sister's favorite colors, or what she liked to read. This isn't a fanzine interview. I'm investigating a sex crime. I don't want to write her profile, I want to find the person who killed her. To do that, I need to get inside her head. I need to know how she was with men. Was she a tease? Did she confuse them about the nature of her involvement? Was she willing to sleep with more than one man at a time, or was she monoga-mous? Was she practical about birth control? What kind of men did she choose? Was she likely to pick up strangers? I know I offended you, but I don't know of any graceful way to ask about sex practices. No one talks about that stuff easily."

It was quite a speech. And he was right. I hadn't understood why he was asking those questions. Still, it wasn't all my fault. I'd been tired, impatient, and anxious to protect Carrie, but he'd been cold and awkward. "You didn't try very hard, you know," I said. "You could have practiced being human."

He looked genuinely bewildered. "I'm not human?"

"Well, I did wonder if you might be from another planet. What I mean is that you didn't show you cared about any of it. First you were impassive and then you were cold and angry, like I was an adversary or I'd already offended you. You didn't try to help me understand why you needed to know that stuff about Carrie. The pictures were just the final blow. For such a smart man, you've got some big blind spots. And now I wish you'd go..."

"Mea culpa," he said. "I confess to being human. I'm sorry about the pictures, I really am. I was trying to shock you into cooperating."

"I know. I can't imagine that ever works."

"You'd be surprised," he said.

"Please spare me any more of your surprises, OK, Detective? I don't think I could take it."

"Look," he said, sounding somewhere between aggrieved and apologetic, "I said I was sorry."

"Sometimes sorry isn't good enough," I said. "I felt so violated today in your office. Do you mean you do this routinely to people when their loved ones have been killed? Show them graphic pictures of the bodies?"

"No. Of course not. Look, I told you. I was frustrated. I was angry..."

"And that's supposed to make things OK, is that it? Cop loses it, cop brutalizes witness, so what? I thought you guys saved the Gestapo tactics for the bad guys."

"If you're trying to make me feel guilty," he said, "you're succeeding." I almost fell off my chair. "Look, before you throw me out, can I tell you a story to try and explain why I did what I did?"

I hesitated, still angry, still not trusting him, even though he had a boyish, pleading look on his face that seemed genuine. I desperately wanted him to find Carrie's killer but I was afraid of his tricks and his traps and his brutality. I wanted — I needed — some kindness and comfort, and he'd offered that in the form of food. I wanted to trust him. Maybe he was going to give me a reason to. I folded my arms protectively against my chest. "OK," I said, "why did you do it?"

"Two years ago I investigated the apparent suicide of a twelve-year-old girl. Excuse me, but I'm going to be very graphic here. It's not a nice story. Not nice at all. If you want me to stop — anytime — just say so and I will." His dark eyes bored into me, daring me to refuse.

"Go on," I said.

"There wasn't any doubt that she'd killed herself," he said, "and when we got the autopsy results, there wasn't any question why, either. That little girl — and she was little, too, under five feet tall and she weighed about ninety pounds — had been sexually abused, vaginally and anally. She'd been beaten and tortured. Her body was covered with scars and burns. And she was pregnant." He paused, his face tight with anger. "Everything pointed to the stepfather. He was a vicious drunk who beat everyone in the family. But no one — not his wife, the neighbors, the teachers at school — no one was willing to risk his wrath to tell what they knew. The mother claimed her daughter was promiscuous and must have been sneaking out to meet an abusive boyfriend. The neighbors said they'd never noticed a thing. Neither had the teachers. And there was nothing I could do..." He stopped, studying my face. "That's why I did it, you see."

But I didn't see. "I'm sorry," I said. "It's an awful story. But I don't see what that has to do with me. Why the fact that someone brutalized that girl justifies your brutalizing me..."

He rubbed his forehead with long, blunt-tipped fingers. "I'm not doing this very well, am I? OK, here's why. Because that girl had a little sister. Still living in the house with that monster. And now she's almost eleven years old and you know what that means?" He leaned across the table and grabbed my wrist. "It means that any day now he'll start doing the same things to her, until he kills her or she kills herself, and there isn't a damned thing I can do about it because everyone is too scared or too lazy to get involved and protect that child."

He spread his hands in a gesture of resignation. "I'm sorry. I know it's no excuse for what I did to you. For a minute I pictured your sister lying there helpless and violated and I flashed on that other little girl — she had those blond curls like your sister — and I just couldn't bear to let you sit there all complacent and uninvolved when you might actually be able to help me. It was cruel and I was wrong and I'm sorry. I didn't mean to make you sick."

For the first time, I saw him as a human being and not the enemy. I didn't know that many men, cops or otherwise, who'd be willing to tell on themselves like he was doing. I was still angry and wary and I was hurt, but the situation felt different. "That was kind of counterproductive, wasn't it?" I said.

He nodded. "We have a common goal. To help your sister." He pushed back his chair and stood up. "Now I'll leave if you'd like..." He hesitated. "But please consider talking to me, frankly, about your sister. I need to know her better." Then the solemn face vanished, chased away by the trace of a smile. "Or we could call a truce and I could stay and do the dishes. Maybe you'd like some dessert. I brought something good. You'll be surprised..."

"I've had all the surprises I can stand today."

"That's too bad," he said. "It's the ultimate in chocolate decadence..." His story had explained a lot. Not that I exactly forgave him, but it made his behavior more understandable. Now, as a peace offering, there was chocolate, and I was a hopeless chocoholic. He picked up our plates and carried them to the kitchen. I followed with the salad bowl and the bread. There was only an end left. "Truce?" he said.

"Truce," I agreed.

"This is your lucky day," he said. "We have a chocolate mousse cake that will knock your socks off."

I looked down at my bare feet. "Too late," I said. He set the cake on the counter and reached into the cupboard behind me to get some plates while I got out forks. As he did, his hand brushed my shoulder. I felt a tingle, like an electric shock. He was staring at me with astonishment, and I knew he'd felt it, too.

"Excuse me," I said, and fled upstairs to the bathroom. I stared at my face in the mirror. It looked just the same, too pale, with dark smudges under my eyes. My mouth was still too wide, my hair too wild. And my heart was pounding. I washed my face with cold water and went back downstairs, prepared to accept his truce, tell Lemieux what he wanted to know, and get him out of there as quickly as possible. I hadn't felt a shock like that since David, and I wasn't going to take a chance on something like that again. It hurt too much.

CHAPTER 7

WE HAD OUR cake and coffee in silence — a more comfortable silence this time — and adjourned to the living room. I chose the sofa; he sat across from me in a big chair with the coffee table between us. I think we both needed that physical barrier. Neither of us had mentioned it, but that brief touch had created something between us that lurked on the fringes like an unasked question. I was determined that it would remain unasked.

Fatigue lay on me like a layer of heavy fog, clouding my brain. My body felt heavy and useless. Despite the coffee, I knew I couldn't stay awake much longer. I wanted to get this over with, get Lemieux out of here, and sleep the rest of the weekend. "OK," I said, "ask your questions, and I'll try to answer them. I hope you won't be disappointed." Even though I'd decided to be cooperative, I was uneasy. He was right. People do have difficulty talking about sex. It's hard enough with someone you know well; it was going to be much harder with a stranger. It still seemed wrong to discuss personal things about Carrie with an outsider. But if that was the only way to find her killer, I would have to do it. At least fatigue had a numbing quality.

He leaned forward into the light. I'd avoided really looking at him before. I'd been too angry to care how he looked. His skin was pale, almost sallow, and this late at night, the dark shadow of his whiskers showed. His nose was thin and almost pointy, his eyes dark and lost in shadow so I couldn't see their color. His eyebrows were very dark, and rose above his eyes in crescents that gave him a perpetual questioning look. An attractive face, if only he allowed it some expression.

"You've heard some of these questions before," he said, "but I'll try to be more civilized about it this time." He was nervous, too. He wasn't used to wearing his own face, to being vulnerable himself. The impassive facade was a good barrier. But the day, with our clashes and anger, the odd kindness of dinner and his confession, had created a cautious intimacy between us. It would be difficult for him to retreat now. "First, maybe you should tell me about your sister," he said. "What was she like?"

"Lost," I said. "That's the first word that comes to mind when I think of Carrie. And the second is complicated. She had an air of vulnerability, of needing to be rescued. People were always trying to rescue her, to help her — her teachers, our neighbors, her boyfriend, Todd. But she resisted it. Part of it was just the way she looked. Like a perfect little doll. People treated her like a toy and not a person. She had that curly blond hair, and perfect pink and white skin, and an adorable turned-up nose. And she was so small. Of course, beside the rest of our family, she looked even smaller and blonder. So people perceived her as helpless, even though she wasn't particularly helpless. And yet, even though she resisted all attempts at rescue, I think she always hoped she'd be rescued. To prove you truly loved her, you had to rescue her, and she made rescue impossible."

I searched for the right words to explain Carrie. "I don't know much about the psychology of adopted children, but I think the fact that she was adopted played a big part in Carrie's life. The family made no secret of it. Mom always told Carrie that she was extra special because she was 'chosen' to be a part of the family. That with Michael and me, they had had to take whatever they got, but with her they'd been able to choose. Carrie never believed it. She didn't feel chosen. She probably shouldn't have been given to us. She should have been an only child in some nice blond family."

"Why?"

"The physical differences. She couldn't identify with the family. Part of her air of being lost was genuine. She was lost because she didn't feel like she belonged to us, and she didn't have anyone else to belong to, so she had no identity. Our love, caring, and support, and all our efforts to include her and make her feel like a part of the family, couldn't keep her from feeling alien. It was like we were a different species. Am I making any sense?"

He nodded. "How did Carrie get along with your mother?"

"I think you already know," I said. "Not very well." I hated to admit it. "Carrie was always defiant. Difficult. Once she became a teenager, they didn't get along at all. Mom would never admit it, of course, but I think she felt as alienated from Carrie as Carrie did from us. Carrie represented the failure of her dreams of the large, perfect family. My parents wanted lots of children. After Michael, they couldn't have any more. It took them a long time after that to get Carrie. I think they both expected too much from her."

I didn't want to say bad things about my mother so I tried to change the subject. "Detective," I said, "do you really need to know this stuff, about Carrie and my mother?"

"Hard for you, isn't it?" he said. "But it does help me understand her."

"Mom never said this. She'd never admit it, but this is what I saw. She had taken Carrie in, and lavished love and attention on her, and she got rebellion and ungratefulness in return. They just didn't understand each other." I had a clear vision of Mom and Carrie in the kitchen, making cookies. Mom trying to teach Carrie; Carrie determined to do it by herself. Ending up with burned cookies and hurt feelings. "Of course Mom got rebellion from me, and from Michael, but Carrie's was different. And Mom didn't handle it as well. She was older when Carrie was a teenager; maybe that was part of it. The worst thing was Carrie's desire to search for her birth parents."

"Your mother mentioned that on Sunday," he said. "Was that something that went on for a long time?"

"On and off. Carrie always wanted to know who her 'real' family was, but she rarely mentioned it, because Mom always seemed so threatened by it. More recently, she got involved with a search group — a group of adopted children all interested in finding their birth parents — and with the group's support she

67

got more demanding. She felt that Mom should help her, since the records are sealed and available only to the adoptive parents. And Mom refused. I thought — we all thought — that when Carrie came up here she was taking a break from her search."

"Carrie didn't pursue her search while she was here?"

"Not as far as I know. But the fact that she didn't mention it doesn't mean she wasn't doing it. Carrie was much more secretive than the rest of us." Now that I understood his reasons, I wanted to cooperate, but talking about Carrie, especially here in this apartment, made her seem so close. It was hard to talk around the big lump in my throat. "I know what you said, about the dead having no privacy. I still feel like I'm violating her memory somehow, talking to you about her private life," I said. "All this stuff makes her sound so bad. But if you'd only known her."

He handed me his handkerchief. "This is the only way I can know her," he said. "Your feelings are normal, but by protecting that privacy, you protect the killer. I meant what I said about murder victims having no privacy. It used to bother me like it bothers you, prying into the lives of the dead, getting their family and friends to share the intimate details of their lives. I look at it differently now. I see myself working with the murder victim. I need to know Carrie, to understand her. The closer I come to knowing her, the better my chances are of finding her killer."

He seemed uncomfortable with what he'd just said. I sensed it was something he didn't usually tell people. And he didn't want to say any more. Instead he picked up his coffee cup and got to his feet. "You want more coffee?"

"It wouldn't help. I'm beyond reviving. But I'd like some water, please."

I heard him go into the kitchen, and then heard his footsteps on the stairs. When he came back, he had a blanket over his arm. He set down his refill and my water, and handed me the blanket. "You looked cold," he said.

"Thanks," I said. I wrapped myself up, thinking what an odd combination he was. So gruff and so kind.

"Was Carrie sexually active in high school?"

"Yes. She asked me about birth control when she was fifteen, because she didn't want to talk to Mom. She was usually monogamous, but sometimes she slept around. Her problem was that she chose lousy guys. She loved them and they were using her. It was the adoption thing again. She'd been discarded once, so she didn't think she had any value. We were all relieved when she got involved with Todd."

"Why?"

"Because he was a nice guy. Is a nice guy. The only decent guy she ever picked. He's heartbroken about what happened. Not that it was a smooth romance. Carrie loved Todd, but she couldn't stand his protectiveness. She had to lash out at anyone who treated her well, because she felt she didn't deserve it. She would periodically break up with Todd and take up with some lowlife. Todd always waited patiently, and was there when things went wrong. A real sucker, but he couldn't help himself. He loved her. That's how we all were about Carrie. I'd left home by then, but I was always like a second mother to Carrie, so it was me she called for advice. She used to confide in me a lot."

"Used to?" he said.

"Since David died, I've been less accessible. Most of the time, I work. I haven't been a very good sister to Carrie."

He had the grace to let it go. "Suppose Carrie went too far, flaunting other guys in his face, could Todd have snapped and killed her?"

"Have you met Todd?" I asked. He nodded. "Well, then you must see that he couldn't possibly be a killer. He's devastated by Carrie's death."

"Killers often are," he said. "Passion killings are very common."

I thought of the photograph. "I know your experience is different from mine. I know that the killer is sometimes a most unlikely person, but I know Todd. I can't believe he could commit this crime. Maybe, if he were extremely provoked, he might have hit Carrie. That other thing, though, with the stick. He couldn't do that. Whoever did that hated women, or hated Carrie, or was just terribly sick. Todd's not sick."

"Tell me more about the lowlifes, as you call them. What sort of people were they?"

I couldn't help it. I laughed. "You don't know what lowlifes are?"

He tried to look wide-eyed and innocent, but it didn't work. He just looked foolish. "I see so many different kinds, in my business," he said. "Tell me about the ones Carrie was attracted to."

"She liked the drink-too-much, use-and/or-sell-drugs, don't-read, indifferent, all-girls-are-pieces-of-ass types. Guys who cared more for their cars than for their girlfriends, who bragged about the girls they'd slept with, mooched their girlfriend's baby-sitting money for beer and gas, who didn't go to school, except as a diversion, and who believed that using condoms was an affront to their divine manhood. You get the picture?"

I thought of the countless hours I'd wasted trying to talk Carrie out of seeing some of them. Of the times she'd called me in tears because she'd been used, mistreated, or abandoned. You can't transfuse self-esteem, and Carrie had badly needed some.

"Any of them ever hit her?"

"Now and then."

"Did she talk to you about that?"

"I talked to her. There was this one guy, Chuck, she dated her last year of high school. She was so crazy about him that she couldn't think straight. He used to pinch her until her arms were all black and blue, and once he gave her a black eye. She insisted he was just teasing, with the pinching, even though she admitted it hurt. She said she deserved the black eye, because she'd kept Chuck waiting, and he hated to be kept waiting."

Carrie had called so much that year that David had briefly taken to answering the phone "Mother Thea's Counseling Service." Not that anything I said to Carrie made much difference. But she always said it made her feel better to talk to me.

"You're drifting away," Lemieux said.

"Sorry. I was remembering. I tried to tell her that guys who care don't hurt you for fun, but she just couldn't hear it. Chuck used to break up with her, take her back, and break up with her again, just to jerk her around. He was a real pretty thing — handsome, smooth as a snake, smart, and charming, but a real bastard." I drank the rest of my water. I was beginning to lose my voice, and my eyes kept closing. It was cozy under the blanket and I was ready to curl up and sleep.

"I'm losing you," he said. "Bear with me just a few more minutes and I promise I'll go away and let you sleep." I tried to shake myself awake.

"What happened to Chuck?" he asked.

"Went to jail for car theft. And Carrie went back to good old Todd. Oh, I forgot. Chuck liked kinky sex. He used to tie her up, and sometimes he wouldn't untie her for hours. He was older and had his own apartment. Carrie said she hated it — the tying, not the apartment — but it made him happy. Making him happy was all-important to her. We were so glad when he was sent away that we celebrated. Mom made Carrie's favorite dinner, and the whole family came home. Carrie spent the whole evening crying on David's shoulder, while Todd watched helplessly. Later David said we'd have to give Todd iron pills if he was going to have the energy to handle Carrie. What he really meant was he thought Todd was a wimp."

"Who is David?"

"David was my husband," I said. Lemieux leaned forward as though he was eager for more information about David. "I don't talk about David. He's dead."

"Why don't you talk about him?"

"It hurts too much," I said. That's all I was going to say. My feelings about David were private, for me alone. They had nothing to do with this and were none of Lemieux's business. "Is there anything else... about Carrie? It's been a hard week and I'm awfully tired."

"I know you are," he said. "I'm almost done. What about Carrie's other boyfriends, after Chuck?"

"I don't know much about them. There was Todd, of course. He and Carrie were both in the Amherst area. She was at U. Mass. and he was at Amherst. I was busy, so I didn't see much of her. She called me a lot. Then David was killed, and I sort of withdrew from the family; well, from everything, except work, for a long time, and so I rarely saw her. She didn't call me with any crises, so I figured she'd settled down. I'm afraid I sort of abandoned her. So I don't know what she was up to. But everything will be there in the diary, so you can read about it. She used her diaries like an imaginary friend, confiding everything to them. You *do* have her diary, don't you?"

Lemieux looked surprised. When he was surprised, his eyebrows flew up and gave his face an appealing, elfin quality. He'd probably have hated it if he knew. "No, we don't. Why did you think we had it?"

"The apartment looked like someone had searched it. Carrie was very precise and neat. She'd never leave books lying all over, or drawers half open. I assumed you'd looked through her things and taken whatever might be helpful. Are you telling me you didn't search?"

"Of course we did." He sounded discouraged. Fatigue had replaced his stiffness. He no longer looked like he was about to jump to attention. He slumped in his chair, staring blankly at his empty cup. The light shining down on him deepened the lines in his face, making him look older and weary. "We didn't find anything personal," he said. "No diary, no notes, no letters."

But Carrie didn't throw personal things away. Since she had no past, her present was doubly important. She guarded it carefully. "What about in her purse?"

He shook his head. "We haven't found her purse. And there were no papers in the car, except a little slip of paper from a library, the kind you write down the call numbers of books on, stuck down between the seats. Some sort of list." He tried to recall it. "First there was a letter. Just 'C.' Then 'certificate, papers, park trail,' and the word 'mother.' 'Mother' was underlined."

"What does it mean?" I said. He just shrugged. "But, Andre, Carrie kept everything. All her cards and letters, and she always kept a diary. They must be somewhere." And suddenly I wasn't sleepy at all, realizing what must have happened to Carrie's papers. Whoever killed her had taken the papers. "He must have come here. Did you check for fingerprints?" My mind, so sluggish all evening, was racing. "What about Mrs. Bolduc? Did she see anything? I know she keeps an eye on the place. An eye — ha! Two eyes and a nose. I've seen her looking out the window. If she does it to me, she must have done it to Carrie. She must have seen something. On the phone, she implied that Carrie was a slut..." I couldn't stop. A whole host of suggestions and ideas came tumbling out.

Lemieux's mouth twitched. I watched him struggle to keep his face blank. He lost the fight. The twitch became an amused grin. "Did you call me Andre?" he asked.

"I guess I did. I won't do it again," I said.

"You can call me Andre if you want. I'd like that. Andre, not Andy. No one who knows me calls me Andy."

He seemed pleased that I'd called him Andre. Too pleased. And I didn't know why I'd done it. It could only lead to trouble, and I was allergic to trouble. Besides, I had enough trouble already. I was noticing too much about him — how tired he was, his five o'clock shadow. Elfin eyebrows. Bristly military hair. Broad shoulders. The richness of his voice. And an electric shock that made me tremble. The trouble with getting all stirred up is how easily one intense feeling, like anger, can transform into another, like passion, especially when you're sitting around late at night with an attractive man and you've had a few drinks. But I'd sworn off passion. It was time I put a safe distance between us. Distance and a locked door. Just as soon as he reassured me that some murderer wouldn't be coming in. We could talk again tomorrow, in daylight. In a public place. "But if someone has her keys, couldn't they come back? Is it safe for me to stay here?"

"I think whoever it was took everything they wanted the first time. And anyway, Mrs. Bolduc had the lock changed as soon as she found out your sister's keys were missing."

I stood up, glad the coffee table was still between us. "I'm sorry," I said. "I've got to get some sleep. I'm just too tired."

"I'd love to join you," he said. There was a husky catch in his voice, almost a growl, that roused something deep in my numb, weary body. For a fleeting second I wanted to say yes. But only for a second. We'd reached an understanding and I'd agreed to cooperate but that didn't mean he hadn't hurt me. I crossed my arms defensively.

"I prefer to sleep alone," I said, knowing I was sounding prim again.

"That," he said, "is a tragedy." But he dropped the subject. "May I call you tomorrow if I have more questions?"

"I'll be here."

"I could come back and do the dishes," he suggested.

"You did the cooking. I believe in a fair division of labor."

He threw up his hands in a gesture of surrender. "I give up. This girl is strictly business, right?"

"Right."

I walked him to the door so I could lock it after him. He hesitated on the threshold, then held out his hand. "Thanks for a nice evening, Thea," he said. I took it gingerly. The electricity almost made my hair stand up. I shut the door quickly and fastened the dead bolt. The rush of energy I'd had subsided as rapidly as it came. I put the dishes in to soak and went up the stairs. They seemed very steep.

I fell across the bed, not bothering to undress, and was asleep in an instant, but an hour later I was awakened by some noises outside. Maybe the lock had been changed, but I still didn't feel safe. I went downstairs, wedged chairs under the front and back doors, and went back to bed.

CHAPTER 8

No ONE TRIED to break in during the night. But, except for that first hour when I'd slept like a log, I slept badly. In the morning, feeling like something the cat dragged in, I crawled downstairs, reheated a cup of last night's coffee, and drank it while I did the dishes. Then I went out to the car and brought in boxes so I could pack Carrie's things. It was sunny, and the sky above Mount Battie was a brilliant blue. Just up the street was a trail leading to the top. I planned to climb it later, if the weather held, and make at least a bit of the weekend a vacation.

I started in the bedroom, putting a couple of boxes together. I set them on the bed and began taking the things out of her closet. Her clothes were ridiculously small. The dresses would have been obscene minis on me. I couldn't have gotten her jeans to my knees. All the clothes smelled like Carrie. Despite my resolution to be cool and matter-of-fact, I went through ten tissues emptying the closet. The apartment was suffused with memories. Carrie's presence was everywhere.

When I wasn't dissolved in tears, either from the scent of her ever-present Chantilly or from remembering her in a particular garment, my mind was racing. Yesterday's encounter with Detective Lemieux had had a strange effect on me. Before coming up here, I'd been content to let the police search for Carrie's killer. Now I wanted a more active role in that search. It was my nightmarish dream which triggered things. The vision of poor battered Carrie, standing there asking for my help.

What was driving me was guilt, my feeling that I'd neglected Carrie. Wrapped up in my own sorrow, I'd abandoned her when she needed me, when she'd needed an ally in the family who understood her drive to find out who she was. Instead I'd tried to talk her out of it. No wonder she hadn't stayed in touch. From the time she was tiny, I'd been like a second mother to Carrie.

76

It was me, Teea, as she'd called me, she'd come to for Band-Aids, hugs, and help. Her little face would be pressed against the glass beside the front door, watching for me to come home from school. I taught her to ride a bike, told her the facts of life, went with her to buy her first bra and high heels. Mom never showed it, but she must have resented her determined little daughter's rejection every time Carrie seized my arm and insisted, "I want Thea to help me." Perhaps not. Maybe she was grateful to have confrontation averted.

During her funeral, and again yesterday in my dream, I had felt Carrie asking me for help. I wasn't some wacko who believed in the occult or in visitors from beyond the grave. It wasn't some ghost calling to me, it was what remained now that she was gone. My connection to Carrie. My understanding, my love. My obligation to see that things were set right. I had no basis for it other than the note that Lemieux had mentioned, but my intuition told me that despite the nature of the attack, her death was somehow connected to the search for her birth parents. The missing papers could cut either way, of course — boyfriend or relative who didn't want to be found. Lemieux could track down boyfriends and perverts; tracking down Carrie's birth parents was a way that I could be involved.

Andre Lemieux had had another effect on me as well. I wanted to sleep with him. Something nice girls never admit, but I admitted. I wanted to make love with that inscrutable, fiercely controlled trooper who hid a secret human being inside, and I was scared stiff by my feelings. I'd only been involved with one man since David, and it had been a complete disaster. We'd met through a mutual friend who thought we'd be perfect for each other. Once I got to know him, I wondered how she must perceive me, to think I'd get along with such an asshole, but at first I'd thought she was right.

Steve was a banker. He made bright, witty conversation, played a mean game of tennis, and had impeccable manners. He pursued me with flowers and small romantic presents. He was no David. His touch didn't make me tremble, and I didn't feel like he'd ever be my best friend, but we had some fun together. The only problem was that he couldn't wait to get me into bed, and I wanted to take things slowly. He reminded me of a high school boy trying to score so he'd have something to tell his friends. While our dates weren't wrestling matches, they were battles of will, and it got harder and harder to handle his advances.

One night we shared a bottle of vintage champagne to celebrate my birthday, and when he began making his moves, I didn't say no. Partly, I admit, I slept with him because I needed sex. Sexually I'm conservative and careful, but I like sex, and I'd missed it. Steve was not the answer to a maiden's prayers. He was a classic wham-bam-thank-you-ma'am lover. He attended to his own needs, rolled off, and fell asleep, leaving me lying there in the dark feeling cheated. And because I'm Thea of "Thea will fix it" fame, I decided I had to teach Steve something about loving a woman. I started by waking him up, and I gently told him about my own unmet needs. He turned out to be a grouch when awakened. Accused me of being some sort of nympho and went back to sleep.

I must have been a slow learner, because I didn't give up. Three more times I slept with Steve. The total foreplay for all four times couldn't have been more than ten minutes. I never got close to orgasm, and I didn't get much closer to a conversation about the situation. Steve didn't believe he had a problem, but he sure thought I did.

I decided I'd be better off without Steve and his problem. I started being too busy working to see him, and eventually he moved on to another woman less demanding than I. He married her, and now they're expecting a baby. I see them sometimes through the mutual friend. He still hasn't learned anything about pleasing a woman. I can tell by the way his wife squirms on her chair.

The last thing out of the closet was Carrie's shiny black

raincoat. I slipped it off the hanger and folded it in half. When I did, something rustled. I unfolded it and checked the pockets. In one I found a white envelope stuffed with papers. The return address was the Town Clerk's Office, Hallowell, Maine. It had been sent to Carrie at this address. I pulled out the papers and spread them on the bed. They were notes of some kind, in Carrie's handwriting, but they didn't make any sense to me. The only thing that did make sense was her heading. At the top of the page she had printed: BIRTH MOTHER SEARCH. So she hadn't stopped searching when she came up here.

I stuck the papers in my pocket and started on the bureau. Whatever her killer had been looking for here in the apartment, it hadn't been money. Her jewelry, some traveler's checks, and the two hundred-dollar bills Dad always insisted she keep were still in her drawer under the sweaters. Looking at her jewelry turned on the faucet again. My family likes to give jewelry for significant occasions, especially antique jewelry. In her jewelry case she had the pair of enameled gold bracelets she'd gotten for graduation, Aunt Sylvia's gold earrings, the Art Nouveau locket I'd given her for her eighteenth birthday, her sweet-sixteen pearls. I shut the box with a snap and set it on the bureau. I couldn't bear to look at those things.

I managed to clean out the linen closet without any tears. I don't get sentimental about sheets and towels. Not usually. After David died, I didn't wash the sheets for two months, because they still smelled like him, and I kept all his dirty clothes for the same reason. Suzanne finally washed them when she came to nurse me through a bout of flu. I cried and carried on like an infant. But I was sick, and sad, and she didn't hold it against me. I still have one of his shirts, unwashed, that I sleep in sometimes. After two years, it still smells faintly of him.

I moved to the bathroom, sweeping everything from the medicine cabinet into a big plastic bag. I rolled up the bag, stuck it in one of the boxes, and lugged the boxes downstairs.

By noon I was starving. There wasn't anything in the house

I wanted to eat, and it was time for a break anyway. A walk downtown to get myself some lunch might clear my head. I laced up my spiffy new cross trainers. I often joke that my idea of cross training is walking briskly to the table and rhythmically raising and lowering a fork. It's not quite true. I march off to aerobics at the end of the day like all the nine-to-fivers and pound off the extra flesh.

I was still wearing the sweater and pants I'd put on last night, but only I knew that. I stuck the apartment keys in my purse, slung it over my shoulder, and went out. Mrs. Bolduc might be away, but her curtain was still twitching. I waved at the window and the twitching stopped. Carrie must have hated being spied on. She probably gave Mrs. Bolduc the finger, and that's why Mrs. B. gave Carrie such bad press.

The big trees along Mountain Street were beginning to show a hint of fall. A few yellow leaves blew along the sidewalk. The air was cool, with a gentle wind that lifted my hair. I turned right onto Main Street and walked down past the shops. The windows were full of attractive clothes in rich fall colors. A sage-green fisherman's sweater that was meant to go with my eyes beckoned, and I vowed to stop and try it on on the way back.

I hadn't thought about where to go, but my feet were leading me to the bar and restaurant where Carrie had worked. Leadbetter's was in the basement of a four-story brick building. It had once been an auto repair shop, but now it was just a large room stripped back to bare brick walls, broken into sections by the occasional waist-high partition or raised platform. Seating in the bar was on old sofas and chairs from Grandma's attic. In the restaurant section, beyond, there were regular tables, and some booths along the wall. On the right, just inside the door, a small stage was cluttered with musical paraphernalia.

The bar looked more inviting. I never eat on the sofa at home, because I might spill something. Then I'd have to get it cleaned, and that would be a big hassle. So I eat in my big leather chair, when I bother to eat at all. Then I can wipe the spills right off.

The idea of lunch on someone else's sofa appealed to me. I chose a big faded chintz one off in a corner, plopped down, and waited for someone to notice me. The place wasn't busy, and I didn't wait long. My waitress was heavy, with curly brown hair corralled on top of her head with a bright elastic band. She planted her hands on her hips and looked at me placidly. "You eatin' or just drinkin'?"

"Both."

"Good," she said. "I need some business." She handed me a menu. "Get you somethin' from the bar?"

Drinking in the middle of the day is always a disaster for me, but I could always go back and take a nap, and the place invited drinking. Dark and comforting, with soft rock, the kind you hum along with, in the background. "Do you have Sam Adams?"

"Does a bear..." she began, and stopped herself. "Yeah. Be right back." She turned and walked away. The waitress's uniform was pretty informal. I'd packed a couple of them this morning. She had a white polo shirt with "Leadbetter's" over her large left breast, and a black miniskirt that rustled when she walked. Her legs were thick, but well-shaped, and her moon face had pretty features. She was back in a flash, and slid my Sam Adams, in its tall brown bottle, onto the table. She set a frosty mug down beside it. "The guy who makes this must be getting rich," she said. "Everybody orders it."

I ordered a reuben and fries and a green salad. She bustled off to put in my order. I poured beer into the mug and watched the frosty glaze disappear. The first icy sip tasted so good. I wondered idly if Suzanne had been pleased with the report. Would it be harder or easier being her partner? Sometimes a small change in title can have a big effect on a relationship. But she would have thought of that before she made the offer. Suzanne is not impulsive about business. Now that I wasn't strung out and unable to focus, it made me feel really good to be valued.

The walk had made me thirsty. I finished the beer before the food came. The place was gradually filling up around me, the muted hum of conversation drowning out the music.

My waitress came with the food, set it down in front of me, pulled some silverware and a napkin out of her pocket, and grabbed the empty bottle. "You want another?" She didn't hesitate. She was a good waitress. "Of course you do. Be right back." And she was gone before I could say no. A drink when I'm hungry always makes me ravenous. I attacked the sandwich, oblivious of the sauerkraut seeping between my fingers. It was not disappointing. The meat was lean, the kraut tangy, and there was plenty of dressing to ooze out of the holes in the bread. I licked my fingers delicately.

She came back with the beer and another frosty mug. "Good, isn't it?" she said.

"Great," I said. "May I have another napkin?"

She pulled a stack out of her pocket. "Sure," she said. "I should of thought of that. Don't spill on that couch, now."

"I won't," I said. "Did you know a waitress named Carrie McKusick, who used to work here?"

Her expression stopped being friendly, and became defensive. "She's dead. She got murdered," she said. "Why're you askin'?"

"I was just wondering. She was my sister."

Her whole body projected disbelief. "Yeah, right," she said, "and Twiggy is my sister."

I wasn't offended. I was used to it. She might not be polished, but this girl was refreshingly real. "Carrie was adopted," I said, "so we don't look alike. I came up to clean out the apartment."

Her face turned a deep shade of pink. "I'm sorry," she said, "but you know, people are so curious when someone is murdered. It's real sick. I've waited on a bunch of people who came in here just to ask questions about Carrie. I figured you were one of 'em. Know what I mean?"

I did know. There are always vultures around who can't wait to get the details. There had even been some people like that when David died — casual friends who asked the most outrageous questions while pretending to comfort me. "I know what you mean," I said. "People can be such jerks. Packing up her things depressed me. I felt like talking to someone who knew her." It wasn't quite the truth. What I felt like was talking to someone who might be able to tell me what she'd been up to these last few months. But a little white lie didn't seem like a bad idea.

"It ain't... it's not me you want to talk to, anyway," she said. "I only been workin' here a month. I hardly knew her. She was real sweet to me and all, but we wasn't friends. But she and Lorna" — she pointed toward a tall woman on the other side of the room — "they hung around together. I'll see if she'll talk to you, but don't be too surprised if she don't. People've been bothering her a lot about Carrie. The cops, too." She left to serve someone else, and I finished my lunch. Every bit of it, including the garlic pickle. There's nothing like a brisk walk and a bit of alcohol to stimulate the appetite. And require a trip to the ladies' room.

Years ago, I was in a restaurant in Vermont that had a chalkboard on the wall for people who can't resist writing when they're in the john. I thought it was a brilliant idea. Someone had written, "You don't buy beer in this place, you just rent it." Which was true. I returned the rented Sam Adams to the establishment and went back to my sofa.

The tall waitress, Lorna, was waiting with my check. "Meg says that you're Carrie's sister." Her gray eyes were angry. "Can you prove it?"

I was used to dealing with defensive people. Suzanne and I often had to interview admissions directors and other staff people who were afraid or resentful because the administration had brought in outside consultants. There I knew why they were angry. I didn't have a clue what was going on with Lorna, but I didn't mind humoring her. Maybe it was just what my waitress had suggested — too many people asking questions. I fished around in my bag, pulled out my wallet, and handed her the battered family picture taken when David and I were married. She snatched it out of my hand and studied it. "That's you," she said, "and that's Carrie."

I stood and peered over her shoulder. "And that's our parents. And our brother, Michael. And my husband, David."

She shot a look at my left hand. "You aren't wearing a wedding ring."

"No, I'm not," I said. "I'm a widow."

"Widows are old," she said, coldly. "You're young."

I took back the picture, and the check, which she was still holding. I put the photo back in my wallet, and gave Lorna the check and twenty dollars. I'd done my best. If she still didn't believe me, that was her problem. "I don't know what you're so angry about," I said, "and I'm not waiting around for you to tell me. But I'll tell you what I'm angry about — the job the police are doing finding Carrie's killer. I'd hate to see whoever it was get away with something like this, wouldn't you? I thought maybe her friends might know something that might help. Something I might understand was a clue, even if the police don't, since I knew her so well. But if you're any example, I guess that was a crazy idea. Give the change to Meg." I shut my purse with a snap and headed for the door.

"Carrie said you were tough," Lorna said, coming after me. "I see what she meant. You staying at her place?" I nodded. "I get off at eight. I'll come by then."

CHAPTER 9

I WALKED BACK to Carrie's apartment and went to bed. This time there were no dreams. No one, living or dead, came and asked me to do anything. I slept like a log until someone pounded on the door. I stumbled sleepily downstairs to let Lorna in, excused myself, and went back upstairs to wash my face. When I came down, she was in the kitchen making coffee. She was about my height, and about as thin. There the similarities ended. I like to work hard, and I enjoy being alone, but I also like people and have a generally upbeat attitude. Lorna must have been born angry. Her face was tight and fierce, and she moved things around in the kitchen like even the pans and dishes were her enemies.

"There's no milk," I said.

"I like it black," she said. "There's maybe some of that coffee lightener in the freezer."

"Black is fine," I said, which was a lie. I drink coffee because I'm addicted to the caffeine, but I like it tan and sweet. Right now, though, I didn't want to dwell on coffee; I wanted to get down to business. Lorna wasn't going to be a fun person to spend time with. We carried our cups to the table and sat down, eyeing each other warily. "So, why did you come?" I asked.

"I thought you wanted to talk to me," she said. "That's what Meg told me."

"She told me that you were Carrie's friend," I said. "Were you?"

She shot me an angry look. For a moment, I thought she might walk out, but she controlled herself. "What do you think?"

"You're here," I said. "That tells me something. Otherwise, I have no basis for thinking anything, except that Meg said the two of you hung around together."

"Yeah," she said, "we were friends." She pulled a pack of

cigarettes out of her bag. "Mind?" I shook my head. Lorna went to the kitchen and got an ashtray, which told me that she'd been there enough to be familiar with the place. She lit up, drew deeply, and blew the smoke out through her nose. "That's good," she said. "I can't smoke at work. Customers don't like to get their food from a waitress who smells like smoke. That's what Mr. Hoggins says. He's the boss. A real jerk. Carrie tell you about him?"

"She mentioned him. She said work was fun, except when the boss was around, and then it was a drag. I suppose she meant him."

Lorna nodded vigorously. "She did. He didn't like Carrie too much after he tried to hit on her and she shot him down, but he couldn't fire her because his wife liked Carrie a lot. She didn't hold it against Carrie, that Mr. Hoggins went after her, I mean. She's good people. Lily, I mean. Awful name, though, Lily Hoggins, isn't it?" Despite her initial hostility, Lorna seemed to be in the mood to talk. When people want to talk, the best thing to do is shut up and let them.

"Carrie was popular with the customers, too," she said. "She had a real knack for getting them to order all sorts of extra things. Made for some nice, fat tips. She was so little and all, I guess they felt they had to help her out. She'd joke about it in the kitchen. Come in, throw down a big order, and say, 'Gotta take good care of these people, they've just adopted me.' And then she'd say, 'People are always adopting me. They've been doing it ever since I was born.'" Lorna stubbed out the cigarette and lit another one. "I didn't know what she meant, at first. It was a big deal with her, being adopted. But you know that."

Lorna had a funny way of talking. Her words came in spurts, and she spat them out fast, like they tasted bad in her mouth. "Were you her only friend at work?" I asked.

She thought about that. "Probably. After that college girl left. The one who was her roommate. Everyone liked Carrie, but she was kinda secretive. Private. She didn't talk about herself much, except for being funny about the adoption thing. But that was how she spent her time. On her 'search,' as she called it. Searching for her parents. It was so sad. Were your folks mean to her, or what, that she had to go find some other ones?"

"They weren't mean," I said. "They were good parents, and they loved her very much. The need to search doesn't happen because the adoptive family is bad. A lot of adopted kids just have a powerful need to find their roots, to see what their biological heritage is. Maybe it was harder for Carrie because she was so different from the rest of us."

"You can say that again," said Lorna, lighting her third cigarette.

"Did Carrie talk to you about her search?"

"Sometimes. A few weeks ago, she said she thought she was getting very close. She'd gone down to Massachusetts, a few weekends. I think she found something there that got her real excited. She never told me what it was."

"Did she find her birth parents?"

Lorna shrugged. She was getting bored with this conversation. "She didn't tell me." She got up and began prowling restlessly around the room, aimlessly picking things up.

"What about her boyfriends? Did you meet them?"

"I don't know about her boyfriends," she said quickly. But I could tell that she did.

"Did the police talk to you about Carrie?"

"A couple different ones. I only remember this one. Big guy with bristly hair and a poker up his ass. Like some hot-shot ex-marine. Mr. Detective Trooper. I don't remember his name." That was OK. I knew whom she was describing. "He wanted to know who she hung out with and if they were kinky. I told him I didn't know."

"But you do know, don't you?" I said.

"Look," Lorna said, making a show of checking her watch, "I've gotta go now. OK? Nice talkin' to ya. I'm real sorry about your sister. She was a good kid." She grabbed her bag and headed for the door, but I beat her to it. She glared at me. "Come on. Move it, will ya? I said I've got to go."

"I heard you," I said. "Answer my question and you'll be out of here in a flash. Maybe we can talk about whatever it is that's making you hesitate, but you've got to understand something — there is no way Carrie's killer will ever be caught unless people are willing to tell what they know. He isn't going to walk in and surrender." I guess I wasn't being very persuasive. She was still glaring, and she didn't seem to be about to tell me what I wanted to know. I tried again. "Carrie is dead now. You don't need to protect her. It won't do her any good. There's something you're holding back, something you know that you don't want to tell me, and I need to know what it is. It's about some guy, right?"

Her reaction told me I was right. "So what?" she said. "How will catching the guy do her any good?"

"It will get him off the street. He won't be able to do it to someone else. And he won't get away with it. No one should be allowed to do what was done to Carrie and walk away from it. Do you know what he did to her?"

She refused to meet my eyes. "Hit her on the head with a rock," she muttered.

"The detective didn't tell you the rest?"

"What rest?" she asked, suspiciously.

"That he raped her with a tree branch while she was alive, and left her lying there in the dirt with that thing sticking out of her. Did he tell you that?" It made me sick to say it, but I had to find a way to shock her out of her reticence.

Lorna backed away from me like I was crazy. "No," she said, shaking her head slowly from side to side. "He didn't tell me that. Oh, God! That is so sick!" Clutching her stomach, she dropped onto the sofa. "How do you know that's what happened? It wasn't in the papers." She pulled out a cigarette and lit it with trembling hands. "Is there anything around here to drink? I need something real bad."

I got out Carrie's cheap Scotch and poured one for each of us. Scotch is not my drink. I prefer bourbon, but Scotch is what we had, and I didn't want Lorna to feel like she was drinking alone. She downed hers in one gulp. I took the glass back and fixed another. She set it on the table and stared at me with troubled eyes. "How do you know?" she repeated.

"I saw pictures of her body," I said. "They made me sick. I couldn't believe someone did that to Carrie. To my baby sister. I loved her, Lorna. I fed her and changed her when she was tiny. Read to her. Stuck Band-Aids on her cuts. Taught her to ride a bike. I can't let the person who did this to her get away with it — smash her head and violate her like that and then just walk away. If you know anything that might help find the person — the monster — who did that to her, you'd better tell me."

She considered what I'd said, obviously shocked but still reluctant to share what she knew. "It might not be a good idea," she said, hesitating. "Carrie was mixed up with a guy... she was seeing two guys, maybe more, but two was all I heard about. This cute guy, I never heard his name, blond, like her, sorta looked like he could have been her brother — I don't know anything about him — but there was this other guy who was kind of a bad dude. You've probably got much worse, down in Massachusetts, where he came from. Handsome guy, but sort of mean, and some of the guys he hangs around with are real bad news. He does some dealing, you know what I mean? I don't know if he'd like me telling you about him. He might come after me, if he knew it was me that told you about him."

"Not if he's arrested and taken off the street. If he's a dealer, it shouldn't be hard to get him arrested."

"There's parole, honey," she said. "Everybody gets parole, and besides, he's got friends."

"Did you tell this to the police?"

Lorna laughed. A short, bitter bark. "Sure, and have them go right to him and tell him that I'd sent them? Do I look that dumb? The guy likes his privacy." She swallowed half her drink.

"Look, honey, you aren't from around here. To you this probably looks like a peaceful hick town with some friendly locals and the nice rich folks who moved here from away — flatlanders they call 'em now, but that's not a Maine term — and all the happy tourists. But that ain't all that's here. There's lots of people so poor they don't mind what they do to make a buck, and others so far gone on booze or drugs they don't know what they're doing. And then there's the smart ones, who just like to make money, running the other two groups. This guy is one of the smart ones."

Now it was my turn to gulp some Scotch. "Are you telling me Carrie was mixed up with drugs?"

She smiled faintly. The worn smile of a burned-out teacher whose feeble pupil finally gets the point. "I'm telling you that Carrie was involved with a guy named Charlie. And that anything that has to do with drugs around here has Charlie's name on it. And that's all I know. The cops know all about Charlie, but they can't lay a finger on him. He's one smart dude. I doubt if the cops know Carrie and Charlie were an item, but I'm not going to be the one to tell 'em." She tilted her glass and drained it. "You got any more of this stuff?"

I poured out the last inch, added an ice cube, and gave it to her. "What's Charlie's last name?"

"Who knows? Just Charlie the gorgeous hunk." Her words were beginning to blur.

"What does he look like?"

She smiled. "The devil. A handsome devil. Big, with wide shoulders and hips like a snake. Strong as an ox. Black curly hair like a rock star. A thin, mean mouth." She got a dreamy expression on her face as she described him. It sounded to me like the reason she hadn't told the police about him was that she had hopes in that department herself and didn't want to screw things up.

"All I want to do is talk to the guy," I said, "and see if he has any ideas about what happened to Carrie. Do you know where he lives?"

"I do," she said coyly. "Yeah, I've been there. With Carrie. He's got a nice place. But don't get any ideas. I'm not going with you. You wanna go, you go on your own. You unnerstand? But he's mean. I think he hit Carrie sometimes. I wouldn't let no man do that to me."

"Just give me directions," I said. "I'll find my own way."

She leaned forward, exhaling a long cigarette and booze sigh, and put a hand on my arm. "Don't waste your time," she said, digging in her long fingers. "Stay away from him. Why would he want to talk to you about a dead girl? He likes 'em lively." She laughed. A foolish, alcoholic snort. "And he likes to be left alone."

"Do you think he killed her?" I asked.

She shook her head. "Naw. If I did, I never would have mentioned him to you, or I'd of told the police about him."

I didn't believe her last remark, but I let it pass. I pulled a notebook and pen out of my purse, and shoved them toward her. I had an idea about this Charlie from Massachusetts. He sounded a whole lot like a nasty brat named Chuck that Carrie used to hang around with. "Directions," I said. "How do I get there?"

She got a little unsteadily to her feet. "Oh, hell, you'd never find it on your own," she said. "I'll show you the road. It's just a dirt track leading down to the lake. But I'm not driving down it. You can do that part alone. I wouldn't want Charlie to know I sent you. You promise you won't tell, OK?" I promised, and that seemed to satisfy her.

If she hadn't had three drinks, I was sure she would have refused to help me. From what I'd seen of Lorna's nature, refusing to help just to be perverse would have been more in character. But she was helping, which was all I could ask, and if I was lucky, she'd stay awake and on the road long enough to lead me to this guy Charlie. I locked the door and followed her uncertain steps out into the night, wondering what kind of a friend she could have been if she was so hot for Carrie's guy. Not, if it was Chuck, as I suspected, that that would have been any loss.

CHAPTER 10

LIKE A DOG of uncertain parentage, Lorna's car, which had once been an olive green Fury, sported the characteristics of its mongrel lineage. One fender was blue, the other yellow, each bravely defending the pale green hood. One headlight had been bent skyward, the front bumper had been replaced by a battered two-by-four, and only one tail-light worked, except when she hit a bump. Then the other came on momentarily, flickered, and went out again. It made her easy to follow even though the combination of flickering lights and three quick drinks made her progress somewhat erratic. Eventually, after I'd followed her down what seemed like every narrow country road in the state, she pulled over. I parked behind her and walked up to her open window.

"It's that dirt road there on the right," she said. Her face was grim. In her mind, I knew, she thought she was making a mistake, leading me to Charlie. "The cottage is about a mile down the road, first one you come to, right on the pond. He's got a red Bronco, so if that's there, he's probably home. You be careful, especially if he's got people there. Some of the guys he hangs with are real scum. And no matter what, don't you tell him it was me that sent you. You're wasting your time, you know." She gunned the engine and took off in a shower of gravel and oil fumes.

I got back in the Saab and started down the road. I could see why Charlie owned a Bronco. It wasn't much of a road. The bottom of the car kept bumping on the hump between the tracks, and the tracks themselves were pitted and studded with rocks. My headlights leapt drunkenly through the darkness as I rolled over the washboard. Halfway down, if Lorna was right about the mile, a smaller track forked off to the left, into a clearing where someone was building a house. I drove on down the road, watching for Charlie's cabin.

The night was clear, with a gibbous moon, and the road stretched out white in front of me, making the visibility good. I hardly needed my lights. The window was open and loud insect sounds filled the night. The wind was light, and I was almost warm enough with the window down, but I wished I'd brought a jacket for later. It showed that I wasn't thinking too clearly. If I'd been thinking clearly, I might not have been doing this at all. But my instincts told me that the guy I was going to see was Carrie's old boyfriend, Chuck, and even though Lorna had tried to portray him as a bad, maybe even dangerous drug dealer, I knew Chuck, and he was nothing more than a punk, and a bully. An overgrown brat, and I wasn't afraid of brats and bullies. Besides, I just wanted to talk to this guy, Charlie, and that couldn't be too bad.

The faint lights ahead became windows as I got closer. Windows in a small white two-story cottage with decorative black shutters. A shiny red Bronco was parked in the driveway. I pulled the Saab in behind it, shut off the engine, and got out. Loud rock music poured out through the open windows, jarring in the tranquil night. I could have been the Russian army approaching, and no one would have heard. In the pause between tracks, I heard the lunatic call of loons out on the water. Little waves slapped the shore. The night smelled green and good, more like spring than fall. I walked over to the nearest window and looked in. The windows were small and high. I could just see in if I stood on tiptoe. Four men sat around a table playing cards, surrounded by empty beer bottles. There were more bottles on the floor. I couldn't see any of their faces.

I inched my way along to the next window, hoping for a better view. When I raised myself back onto my toes, the muscles in the arch of my foot cramped, refusing to support my weight. My leg buckled, slamming my knee loudly into the side of the building. Four faces turned toward the window, three I didn't recognize and one I knew too well. Chuck, or Charlie as he was now known, got up and headed for the door. I lowered myself to the ground and went to meet him.

Suddenly, I had a brief, absurd vision of myself as the heroine in some gothic novel, all alone miles from the nearest house with the villain coming toward me. I wondered if I really knew what I was doing. If I'd been foolish to come here alone like this. I knew Chuck, so I hadn't been worried, and I was determined not to let Carrie's killer go unpunished, even if it meant taking a few chances. I'd never learn anything if I sat at my desk in Massachusetts and worried about the admissions statistics of independent schools. My mother would have been shocked at what I was doing, insisting that we let the police handle it. But even if the other police were as competent as Andre seemed to be, nearly two weeks had passed and they didn't have a suspect. If I was going to get involved I had to ask questions, and Chuck was a good place to start.

I raised my hand to knock, but before I could, a bright light came on overhead, half blinding me. The door opened and a rough hand grabbed my arm and pulled me inside. "Whooee, lookit this," my captor yelled. "It's a girl." There was a scuffle of feet as the others came over, and more hands pulling at me. They backed me up against the wall and surrounded me. I knew how a deer must feel, trapped by hunters.

Another voice, deep and authoritative, said, "Back off, you cretins, and let's see what we've got." I knew that voice. Charlie, the bad-guy dope dealer, and Carrie's old flame, Chuck the car thief. I had suspected as much when Lorna described him, which is why I wasn't as scared as she seemed to think I should be. I still thought of him as a punk kid, but people change and not always for the better.

Charlie pulled me away from the wall, where the light was dim, and shoved me out into the room. He followed, pushing me along with a series of little shoves, until I was directly under the light. He stared at me, not saying anything, then gave me a powerful shove that propelled me across the room. I landed in a heap on the floor, scrambled quickly to my feet, and turned to face them. This was no time to be in a humble position. I waited to see what Charlie would do. He brushed the hair roughly back from my face, grabbed my chin, and pushed my head up until our eyes locked. "Well, well," he said, "if it isn't the lovely Theadora."

The other three hung back a bit, staring at me, waiting to take their cues from him. Only one of them, a slight, tidy blond kid who looked too young to be hanging around with the others, looked like a civilized human being. The other two were the products of too many generations of inbreeding. Spotty chinless wonders with scanty facial hair and rabbity eyes. They had to be brothers. Looking at them, I felt like I'd driven down a peaceful Maine road and ended up in a moonshiner's hut in Tennessee. They all three reeked of alcohol.

"There's no need for this, Chuck," I said, trying to sound calm and controlled, not easy when someone has a hand on your throat, pressing your head back. "I'm sorry I came unannounced, but I needed to talk to you. About Carrie."

"Still trying to look out for your little sister, I suppose," Charlie said. "But she's all grown up now. She doesn't need your help. She doesn't want it either, Theadora. She came up here to get away from all of you." He took his hand away. I resisted the urge to massage away the ache, knowing it would please him to have hurt me. I concentrated on staying calm. "It was just by luck," he said, "that we met again. If you'd had your way, that never would have happened. You and your fine family. You didn't think I was good enough for your little sister, did you?" His handsome face was twisted with hate. "When I went to prison, you all had a party to celebrate, didn't you? Maybe tonight I can return the favor. We can have a little party of our own. A little pay-back party."

I'd been watching his face instead of his hands, so I didn't see the blow coming until it was too late. His open palm smashed against my cheek, knocking me backwards. The sting radiated from my cheekbone, surprisingly painful. I glared up into his grinning face. He was enjoying this. "That's right, Chuck," I said, "you weren't good enough for her then, and I can see you haven't gotten any better, except at hurting people. There you're a real prize."

I realized, now, that he hated me. That I should be afraid of him. That I shouldn't have come out so blithely on this mission. For Chuck the Brat, prison had been the finishing school that turned him into a lethal character, and I'd delivered myself neatly into his hands. I was a "people" person. It was something I should have anticipated, if I hadn't been so single-minded in my determination to do something to help find Carrie's killer. It was a little late for second thoughts now. I had no idea how I was going to get out of here. All I knew for sure was that if I begged or pleaded or cringed it would please him. I had to stand up to him, whatever he did. If I could. Part of the fun of hurting people is humiliating them. I'd come here thinking of him as a source of information, not a potential killer. Now I wasn't so sure. "What else are you good at, Chuck," I asked, "murdering people?"

He checked to be sure his buddies were watching. "If necessary," he said. "I wouldn't mind killing you. In fact, it would give me great pleasure." He sounded matter-of-fact, as if killing was something he did every day. It might have been, for all I knew. I'd come expecting a mean punk kid. Prison had hardened him into something more dangerous. "Stop calling me Chuck," he said. "No one calls me that. It's Charlie now."

My face stung where I could feel the print of his fingers. A warm, salty trickle of blood from my split lip ran down into my mouth. The others were watching us like Charlie and I were stars in a show being staged for their benefit. I decided to stay on the offensive. I had nothing to lose. It looked like he was going to hurt me, and he wouldn't hurt me any less because I begged him not to. "Charlie," I said, "did it please you to kill my sister?"

The mocking smile faltered and fell away, replaced by

confusion. Grabbing my arms, he pulled me toward him until our faces were only inches apart, suffocating me with his beery breath. "What the fuck did you say?"

"You like to hurt people, Chuck. So I want to know did you enjoy killing Carrie?" I yelled back, emphasizing the "Chuck," mad at him for the way he was treating me, for making me scared, for all the times he'd hurt my sister. "Was it you who left her lying there on the ground with her head crushed?" I wrenched one arm free and slapped his face. "Did that please you? Did it, Chuck? Was it fun to watch her die? Did she beg you not to, Chuck? Did you make her beg?" He had always brought out the best in me. Time hadn't changed that.

"Shut up. You're not making any sense," he said, hitting me again. Harder this time. A hard right to the jaw that knocked me off my feet and slammed me against a chair. He followed me, grabbed me by the shoulder, and slammed his fist into my stomach. A sensible person would have been scared witless by now. Normally I'm sensible, but all this was doing was bringing my simmering rage to a boil. The more he hurt me, the more tenacious I got. He brought out the pit-bull side of my personality. This must have been how he'd treated my sister, too.

I didn't scramble up as quickly this time; I spent a minute on the floor curled protectively around my stomach, pressing my hands against the pain and trying to catch my breath, discovering that people really can see stars, or something resembling stars, and that unlike studying the skies on a clear evening, it was not a pleasant experience. Beyond the stars, Charlie dropped heavily onto a chair and pointed to the one I was leaning against. "Sit," he said. "Lenny? Bruce? You want to help the lady?" The chinless wonders picked me up and set me on the chair. I huddled there, still bent protectively around my stomach. If I could have pulled my head in, turtlelike, I would have done so. He was probably destroying my brain cells at a dangerous rate. That accounted for why I sat there dumbly and let him hit me.

So far, all the blond kid had done was stare. Us tough guys

were out of his league. Charlie looked dazed, like he was the one who'd been slugged a few times. "I don't know what the fuck you're talking about," he said.

"About Carrie," I said, "and murder." I turned to the kid. "Could you get me some water, please." My mouth was dry, but I couldn't have drunk from a glass either of the others had handled without boiling it first. He looked at Charlie, waiting for permission like good lapdog.

Charlie nodded. "Bring me a beer," he said. The boy trotted off obediently to fetch. While we waited, I looked around, noting possible escape routes. The cottage had a big living room running all along the front, where we were sitting. In one corner was the door I'd come in. Another door led to a big porch facing the lake. Behind it was a dining room, where they'd been playing cards; beyond that, I assumed, was the kitchen. That was where the kid had gone. In the corner, a pine staircase led to the second floor.

Fear, or confusion, was distorting my sense of reality, making the room seem too bright and too loud. The chair I was in felt soft and yielding. I rested my head against the back, smelling the leather. The chinless wonders lit cigarettes and the sound of lighters filled the room. I flinched at the sound. I felt light-headed, felt like relaxing into the rich, buttery leather and letting life flow around me, but this was no time to lose control.

Charlie and I sat staring at each other until the kid came back. He gave Charlie a beer and then handed me my water. The glass felt like it had been rolled in grease. I shut my eyes and drank. At least his hands were clean. "Thanks," I said. The kid shrugged and retreated.

Charlie's face was unreadable. He wore a mustache now, which covered much of it. I'd forgotten how handsome he was. Handsome and cocky. He'd always drawn stares, wherever he went. Carrie had been proud of that. It ought to be hard to be a successful crook when you stand out like that, but he seemed to be succeeding. The furniture was real leather, and the focal point of the room was a big-screen TV. Real marks of prosperity, especially in rural Maine. There was probably a satellite dish out in the yard to improve reception. Charlie looked good even though he was unshaven, his hair needed washing, and his clothes were dirty, like some rugged, outdoorsy guy just back from a camping trip. "What makes you think Carrie is dead?" he said.

I couldn't tell if his ignorance was feigned or genuine. He'd always lied as automatically as most of us brush our teeth. "There's no think about it, Charlie," I said. "Carrie is dead and buried. I chose her casket. I took her favorite dress to the funeral home. I kissed her good-bye before they put on the lid. Don't tell me you didn't know."

"This is just another one of your family's tricks to keep me from seeing her," he sneered. "Send her away somewhere and pretend she's dead, right? Where'd you send her this time? Europe?"

"Hey, Charlie," I said, "where have you been, on the moon? Don't you read the papers? Carrie's been dead for two weeks. Murdered. Right here in the picturesque town of Camden. I figured you were just the guy for a crime like that. A guy who likes to hurt people. Carrie was hurt real bad." I watched his face as I spoke, hoping he'd give something away, but I couldn't read anything.

He turned to the gallery. "Any of you guys know what she's talking about?" The chinless brothers just shrugged. They probably couldn't read.

The kid murmured a quiet "Yeah," but he didn't volunteer anything further. He seemed intimidated by Charlie, but otherwise unconcerned about what was going on. I couldn't figure out what he was doing there.

"Yeah?" Charlie said loudly. "Yeah? What the fuck does that mean?" The volume hurt my head.

The kid studied his feet. "I don't know much," he said. "I've been away, like you, Charlie. At that dumb school my parents sent me to. But there was a murder in Camden, couple weeks ago. Young girl found on one of the Mount Battie trails by some hikers. But I didn't know it was Carrie." His speech was disjointed, as though retrieving words and putting them into sentences was hard work. When he finished he smiled. A goofy, inappropriate smile, and I knew why he hung around with Charlie. Drugs. The kid was high on something.

"Thanks, Kev," Charlie said. "You're a real asshole, you know that?" He didn't seem upset. It was just more news. There's a sixty percent chance of rain today, the blueberry crop looks good this year, Carrie McKusick is dead, the Sea Goddess will be crowned on Friday. I was on a futile errand. When he was just a punk kid, Charlie lied for fun and had no scruples, but underneath you could still see the kid, trying to act tough. That reality, the kid, was gone now. Score one for the correctional system. They'd taken a kid who might have been rehabilitated and turned him into a man who was beyond redemption. I'd never know from watching him whether Charlie had killed Carrie and was just toying with me or he was truly surprised. So far I'd seen anger and a touch of confusion, but it looked like sorrow and remorse were no longer in his emotional repertoire.

"I'm leaving, Charlie," I said, getting up carefully. The floor didn't wave and the walls stayed straight, so I guessed my head was OK. His chair was between me and the door. I started walking. He reached out casually as I passed and jerked me back. "Not so fast, beautiful," he said. "We're not done talking, you and I." I was standing beside his chair, looking down at him. "Tell me how she died, Thea."

"She was hit on the head with something heavy and it crushed her skull. I don't want to talk about it, though. It makes me sick to think about it. I'm tired, Charlie. Can I please go now?"

He was on his feet now, too. "No, you can't go. I want to talk about this some more." Kevin wandered off into the other room. The chinless wonders giggled. "Shut up, you nitwits, you're distracting me," Charlie said.

"Sorry, man," one of them muttered. He was missing several teeth and the remaining ones were rotten.

Charlie turned his attention back to me. "You aren't kidding, are you? This isn't some trick your family thought up. She's really dead?" I nodded. "Was she raped?"

"Why do you want to know?" I asked, unwilling to answer, knowing it would annoy him. I hoped he wouldn't hit me again, but it was a faint hope. "It doesn't matter anymore if there's been another man, Charlie. She's dead."

He grabbed me by the hair and pulled my head back so that I had to look up at him. His face was twisted with anger. "It matters to me," he said. "Was she?" He waved his fist. "You've only got two choices, Thea. Answer my questions, or I'll knock your teeth out. You know it won't bother me to hurt you. For years I've wanted to knock that smug look off your mother's face, but I'll settle for you."

Two could play at this macho game. I didn't answer. It didn't matter. Whatever I did now, or said, Charlie was going to hurt me. It had been naive of me not to realize how much he hated me, hated all of us. I'd forgotten how badly we treated him. While he was in prison, he wrote to Carrie. Mom destroyed all the letters she could intercept, and discouraged Carrie from answering the others. By the time Charlie was out, she was back with Todd and had gone off to college.

I managed to duck my head so that the fist missed my mouth, but not my nose. Charlie released me and let me fall. Stunned by the intensity of the pain, I sat on the floor, futilely trying to contain the gush of blood. It ran between my fingers. Across my mouth. In a disgusting stream that rushed down my throat, gagging me. Dizzily, I tried to get up and face him again, blinded by my watering eyes. All I saw was a blur as he kicked me. His foot connected with my ribs and knocked me onto my back, driving the air out of my lungs. My side felt like it had exploded. I tried to locate Charlie to see if he was going to hit

102

me again. My eyes refused to focus. My body refused to move. I gave up the struggle and lay where I was, letting my faculties regroup.

He knelt and brought his face down close to mine. "There," he said. "Now we both hurt." His feet scrunched away across the floor. "Kev," he called, "come here." There was a conversation my disabled brain couldn't follow, and the door opened and shut with a bang. I stayed on the floor, defiance abandoned, fighting nausea, feeling the blood pool under my cheek. More footsteps. I could see feet near my nose. Two pairs of worn, dirty boots. Fuzzy voices, heavy with the down-east drawl. "Can't we fuck 'er before she goes, Charlie? It won't hurt her none."

And Charlie's voice, amused. "I can't believe you're interested. She's a bloody mess."

"Just her face. Wasn't her face we was thinkin' of," one of them said.

I waited tensely for his response. "I don't think so," was all he said. I heard the door open and shut again, and Kevin's voice. "Bring her outside," Charlie said. Two sets of hands picked me up, taking indecent liberties with my body. I couldn't do anything to stop them. One of them bumped my side and it felt like I'd been kicked all over again. It hurt too much. I gave up fighting for consciousness and control and took refuge in oblivion.

CHAPTER 11

No ONE SHOULD ever paint walls pale blue. It's a cold, unfriendly, depressing color. I'm sure industrial psychologists advise against it, recommending instead something like fresh mint, lemon mist, honey almond, or even peach. I opened my eyes to pale blue and it screamed institution so loudly I didn't have to look further to know where I was. I didn't want to look around anyway. What woke me up was a persistent pounding in my head made by Lilliputians with jackhammers. When I moved to find a more comfortable place for my aching head, a vicious mule kicked me in the ribs. I was a hurting cowgirl.

I rested quietly until the worst of the pain subsided, moving my hand inch by careful inch toward the edge of the pillow, where, if I really was in a hospital, the call button ought to be. I didn't know where I was, what time it was, or how I'd gotten there, but the ugly blue paint said hospital, and my body felt like that was where I belonged. I could have crossed the Mojave Desert in the time it took me to reach the button and call for help.

Help arrived in the form of a sturdy, freckled redhead with a practical bedside manner. The red hair helped. My eyes were practically swollen shut and it gave me something to focus on. I was viewing the world through narrow slits. She strode in, surveyed me calmly, and announced, "Well, you look like hell. How do you feel?"

"Guess," I croaked. She poured me a glass of water and helped me drink it. "My head hurts," I said.

She consulted my chart, found that painkillers were authorized, and dispensed relief most efficiently. Quick relief, delivered by injection. No waiting for pills to take effect. Soon I was floating somewhere just beyond the pain, aware of it but not quite feeling it. It was a better place to be and I wanted to stay there as long as possible. Eventually I fell asleep. I woke up because I hurt again, but this time it wasn't unbearable, only terrible. Andre Lemieux was sitting beside my bed.

"Please go away," I said. "I can't talk to anyone now." That one sentence took all my energy, and he showed no signs of departing. I knew how stubborn he could be. The Lilliputians, made bold by my failure, were cranking up for another go at my head. Ignoring them and their friend the mule, I rang for the nurse. A different person this time. This one was so starched and prim she rustled when she walked. "Nurse, can you make this man go away, please," I asked.

"I'm sorry, Mrs. Kozak," she said. "The police have been waiting very patiently to ask you about the accident. I'm sure he won't be long. I'll just go and get your medication." Her tone implied that it was very rude of me to have taken refuge in sleep when very important people wished me to be awake. She reminded me of my mother, ever mindful of the proprieties. She rustled out, leaving me alone with Andre.

"What accident?" I said.

"You don't remember what happened?" he asked.

I thought about that. My head hurt too much to think very clearly, but I tried. The last thing I remembered was lying on the floor of Charlie's camp, with the chinless wonders begging for a chance to assault me and Charlie saying no. Or saying something. I remembered the unpleasant sensation of lying in my own blood, unable to move.

"Up to a point," I said. My jaw hurt when I talked. So did my head. And my swollen nose felt like a huge turnip stuck onto my face. Everything hurt, and moving made it hurt more. And talking meant moving my face. All of which made me reluctant to talk, but I knew how persistent he could be. The sooner I got this over with, the sooner he would go away and let me suffer in peace. "I went to see Charlie, this guy Carrie was seeing, who turned out to be the same Chuck she used to date in high school. I told you about him."

"We know Charlie," he said.

"He denied that he knew Carrie was dead. I don't know how

105

I got here, but this was no accident," I said. "Charlie knocked me around a little and kicked me a few times to establish male superiority. I told you he liked to hurt people. Where is here, anyway? The last thing I remember is lying on Charlie's floor."

"Bay View Hospital," he said, looking at me like I'd lost my mind. "You were brought here by ambulance after your car ran off the road and hit a tree. The EMT found empty beer bottles in your car and said you smelled strongly of beer."

"I'll bet," I said. "Maybe you should fingerprint the bottles. You won't find my prints. The only beer I've had in the last three weeks was yesterday noon at Leadbetter's, in the company of about thirty strangers. Did they do a blood-alcohol test on me?" I shifted carefully on the pillow, trying to find a position that didn't hurt so much. If that nurse didn't hurry up, the construction crew working on my head would succeed in blasting right through my brain.

"I'll ask," he said.

My mouth was dry. "Could you give me some water, please?" I asked. He poured a glass and helped me drink it. It felt good in my mouth, but the cold hit my stomach like a fist. I closed my eyes, breathing slowly until the nausea passed. I didn't have to work very hard to close them; they were practically swollen shut. My nose was swollen shut, too. I must have looked like hell, and I ached all over. "I suppose you think I got drunk and ran off the road," I said, "but it's not true. If I was behind the wheel of my car, someone put me there. When Charlie and I finished talking — or rather, when he stopped hitting me or I stopped taking it — I couldn't stand up, let alone drive. I couldn't even have crawled that far. Ask Charlie. Or Kevin. Or Lorna." Foolish to suggest it. He'd get nowhere with Charlie, and I didn't even know Kevin's last name. And Lorna didn't know anything about what happened. She'd just hate me forever if I sent the police back to bother her.

Andre's face was a study in confusion and disbelief. He believed I'd gotten drunk and run into a tree, and didn't know what to make of my story. He didn't seem to know what to ask next, so he just patted my hand. A good choice. It was about the only point on my body it was OK to touch. I wrapped my hand around his and held on, torn between wanting him to go away and needing someone there to reassure me that I was OK. "Your car's been towed to the Saab dealer," he said. "Your dad called the insurance company. They're coming up tomorrow. Your parents, I mean. Who are Kevin and Lorna?"

The nurse must have been out in a swamp picking medicinal herbs or something. How could Andre be so businesslike? Didn't he understand how awful I felt? I wanted to scream at him to leave me alone, but it would have hurt me a lot more than it hurt him. If the nurse didn't come soon, I was going to crawl over and throw myself out the window. I'm not stoic when it comes to pain. I can go without food or sleep or work sixteen-hour days without complaint, but I don't handle pain well at all. I watched the door through my sore, slitty eyes, waiting for relief.

"Who is Kevin?" he said again.

Ignoring him wouldn't help. Like a mosquito in the bedroom at night, he'd just keep on buzzing until he got what he wanted. "Kevin is a druggie kid who hangs around with Charlie. Lorna is a waitress at Leadbetter's. Carrie's friend."

The door opened and my friend the freckled nurse came in. She didn't waste any time on chitchat but got right down to the business of pain suspension. Pills this time. No instant relief. Still, I was so grateful I could have hugged and kissed her. I hunkered down and waited passively to be transported to a state of dreamy lassitude, too inert to do anything. Making conversation, with my swollen face and pounding head, had moved me to a place somewhere beyond exhaustion. She checked my vital signs, establishing for the record that I did have a pulse and a temperature, and then asked Andre to leave while I used the bedpan. Except she didn't mention the bedpan, she just told him to leave, and he did. Reluctantly, because he clearly had more questions.

"Was I raped?" I asked.

She didn't bat an eye. A good nurse. She looked quickly through the information on my chart. "No signs of recent sexual activity."

"Thank you," I said.

She straightened my covers very gently, like Mom used to tuck me in when I was little. "Would you like something to drink?" she asked.

"Do you have ginger ale? I always like ginger ale when I'm sick."

"I'm sure I can find some," she said. "Shall I send the detective back, or do you want him to stay away?"

A good nurse and a mind reader. "He can come back," I said. "I don't care. I'm going to sleep soon anyway."

"You sure are," she said. She went out so quietly I didn't hear her leave. Andre came back a few minutes later with my ginger ale.

"My turn to ask some questions," I said. There were things I needed to know before I left for sleepyland.

"Go ahead," he said reluctantly, obviously wanting to ask his own questions first.

"My car. Is it OK?"

"It looks better than you do. It'll need some body work, but it still runs."

"What about me?" I asked. "Am I OK? Do I still run?"

He took my hand again, very gently. "You'll be fine," he said. "They didn't give you a rundown on damages?"

"No. Tell me." The list had better be short. I was already half-asleep.

"You have a mild concussion, a broken nose, black eyes, some cracked ribs, and assorted facial and body bruises. I've had the whole list myself, so I know how rotten you feel." I liked having him hold my hand. "I'm going to see if I can find Charlie, and ask about last night," he said. "And see if they did a blood-alcohol level on you. Your doctor says he'll probably let you go tomorrow."

"Andre," I said, gripping his hand, "persuade my parents not to come. I don't want them to see me like this. They've had too much trouble already. Call them. Say I'm fine, or something. Anything. Say you will." The last came out as a whisper. I was too tired even to speak. Rotten as I felt, and though I desperately wanted to be taken care of, Mom's kind of care, complete with sighs and lectures, was something I couldn't handle. Dad alone was a different story. Dad's great when you're sick. But not Mom. Her hand is gentle and her soup is ambrosia, but she's a fretful presence. Not conducive to good health.

"I'll try, Thea," he said. He raised the bed and stuck the straw between my lips. The ginger ale went down better than the water, and I was asleep before the straw left my lips.

CHAPTER 12

IT'S NOT THE first day after an injury that's bad, it's the second. That's the day you first feel well enough to notice how awful you feel. At least, that's how it was for me.

I woke up on Monday hungry and crabby and totally miserable. My nose had bled during the night, leaving the pillow and my cheek stiff and nasty. My side ached and my head hurt. I could now see a little better with both eyes, which I suppose was a sign of progress. I woke determined to get to the bathroom on my own. No more sessions with that revolting bedpan. The effort it took to get to my feet almost changed my mind, and the floor rocked alarmingly, but I shuffled across the room to the sanctuary of that ceramic cubicle without further mishap.

I couldn't resist a peek in the mirror. I was surprised it didn't crack. I had honestly never looked worse. It took all the good humor in my nature not to lose it completely. I hoped Andre had been able to persuade my mother not to come. She'd have a hard time, seeing me like this. I drank some water and tried to clean up my face, but the effort was exhausting and only partially successful. I gave up and shuffled back to my bed. I found a nurse staring anxiously at my pillow.

"Oh, there you are," she said.

"Right," I said, collapsing back onto the mattress. "I was just out jogging." She looked at me suspiciously for a minute before she decided I was joking. If she believed that, even for a second, I wasn't sure I was in safe hands, but she got me cleaned up and the bed changed very efficiently, and recorded my vital signs. All the evidence suggested I was still alive. "Do you feel like something to eat this morning?" she asked cheerfully.

"Three cheeseburgers, a large salad, some fries, and a chocolate milkshake," I said. My voice lacked its usual animation. It still hurt to move my face.

"Well, we'll just see what the dietitian has ordered for you today, dear, shall we?" She left, leaving me hungry and uncomfortable, waiting for the dietary mysteries to be revealed. It was some time before revelation. I passed the time recalling my evening with Charlie, wondering whether I'd learned anything from it. My head felt awful, but at least today it worked. I could remember what had happened. I even had a vague memory of being carried to a car. The conversation I didn't understand must have been Charlie sending Kevin to find my car.

I knew he couldn't be trusted, but Charlie's ignorance about Carrie's death seemed genuine. I hated to think he hadn't done it; it would have given me great pleasure to see him put away for life. The man was a walking time bomb. If he hadn't killed this time, sooner or later he would. If he hadn't killed her, I was back at square one. As soon as I was more mobile I'd have to find Lorna again, and ask her about other guys in Carrie's life. She'd mentioned others, hadn't she? She hadn't been forthcoming about Charlie, so probably there was more she'd decided not to tell me. If she'd even speak to me. By now Andre might have paid her another visit. If so, she probably wouldn't talk to me at all.

Then there were those notes they'd found in Carrie's car. What did *C* mean, if not Charlie? Had she gone to the park to meet someone else whose name began with C? How did that connect to *certificates* and *mother*? Were they birth certificates or marriage certificates or some other kind of certificate? Was I just trying to make logical connections among a bunch of unrelated things on a list? It seemed to me that there were three possible sources for her killer — a boyfriend, which was what the police assumed, someone she'd found through her search who didn't want to be found, or a random stranger.

What if she had gone to meet someone connected with her search? Someone perhaps pretending to be a source? How could we ever find that person? Maybe the notes I'd found in her raincoat pocket would help me. If she was still searching for her birth parents, the answer to what had happened to her could be connected to that search. Why else was she supposed to bring her notes and birth certificate? What else could *mother* mean? Andre hadn't seemed terribly interested in the things I'd told him about Carrie and her obsession with finding her real parents, but then, he never knew Carrie.

Breakfast finally arrived, delivered by a twinkling gray-haired lady whose volunteer name tag identified her as Ida Weeks. Mrs. Weeks set the tray on a mobile table, raised the bed, and lifted the covers on the dishes. I was the lucky recipient of a bowl of wallpaper paste, a cold poached egg on sodden toast, and pale yellow orange juice. No coffee. Too stimulating. I made a face. "How far to the nearest McDonald's?"

She pretended not to hear. "Can you manage by yourself, or would you like some help?"

"I don't know," I said, which was the truth. I was a little worried about cutting the toast, soggy as it was. That twisting motion threatened my ribs. Mrs. Weeks didn't dawdle. She picked up my knife and fork, cut the egg, and spread my napkin over my chest. "I know it doesn't look great, dear," she said, "but you'd better eat it. It will help you get well." She departed to deliver culinary delights to the other captives.

I was a good girl and ate my egg and all the wallpaper paste. I was hungry enough to have eaten four breakfasts, but the effort of transporting food to my mouth exhausted me. By the time I set down the juice glass, I was ready for a nap. I didn't know which was more tiring, my lousy physical condition or all the energy I was using up fretting about it.

Hospitals, however, are not designed for the well-being of patients. They are run to fit the schedules of the staff. I had just pushed the tray away and wiggled down under the covers, looking forward to sleep, when the door opened and a man wearing a white coat and stethoscope came in, accompanied by the slightly dim nurse. Reluctantly, I abandoned sleep and gave him my best smile. At least my teeth weren't broken. "Ah," I said, "I see by your outfit that you are a cowboy."

He didn't crack a smile, and I filed him under slightly dim, too. "Well, Theadora, how are you today?" he asked. "I'm Dr. Tabor." Dr. Tabor had wispy blond hair, a wispy mustache to match, and aviator glasses.

"Mrs. Kozak," I said.

"Excuse me," he said, looking puzzled.

"Mrs. Kozak," I repeated. "If you are Dr. Tabor, I am Mrs. Kozak, not Theadora."

"Oh, yes. All right, Mrs. Kozak," he said, twitching with irritation. "I'm glad to see you're feeling better." The nurse handed him my chart, which he scrutinized briefly. Then he did some eye tests with a little flashlight, peered into my nostrils and my ears, and generally poked and prodded me in a wonderfully impersonal manner. I felt like a roast meeting the USDA meat inspector until his probing fingers hit a particularly tender spot and the roast revealed her humanity by gasping.

He rose up to his full five eight, rocked back on his heels, and considered me. "Tell me about the pain," he said.

I wondered what the right answer was. I wanted to tell him that what I knew about pain was that it hurt, but I'd already established that he had no sense of humor. I settled for description. "It's not as bad as yesterday," I said. "Still bad, but different. Yesterday my whole side was on fire and my head was unbearable. Today it all just aches, unless I try to move, and then my ribs catch fire again. When can I get out of here?"

"She's a real charmer, isn't she, Bob?" asked a voice behind him. I turned my head too quickly, trying to see who was there, and was rewarded with a wave of nausea. I closed my eyes and waited for it to pass. "Going to spring her today, or are you keeping her a little longer?" I didn't have to open my eyes. I recognized Andre's voice.

"I can let her go today if there is someone to look after her. Otherwise no. She needs someone to take care of her." What an awful thought. I was a very bad patient. I couldn't stand being in bed, or being unwell. But I needed to be somewhere where

113

I could get something to eat. I'd die of hunger here, or lack of rest. Hospitals hate to let you sleep. It offends their sense that they should be doing something to help you get well, so they wake you and treat you.

"It's OK, Bob. She's being picked up today and returned to Massachusetts, if she can travel that far."

I opened my eyes. Dr. Bob was shaking his head. "She's young and strong. She could take it, but another day of rest would do her good. Why don't you take her home for twenty-four hours? She couldn't do the stairs, but you could carry her. You and Beezer could really dish out the TLC between you." I felt like a roast again.

Andre laughed out loud. "I tried, Bob. I offered my heart, my life, and my undying devotion, but she said she preferred to sleep alone and went out and drove into a tree."

That brought me up off the pillow in a hurry. "You bastard," I said, "I told you. I didn't drive into any tree..." That was as far as I got in my protest before the pain took my breath away.

"I'm going to have to ask you to leave, Detective. You're upsetting my patient," Dr. Tabor said.

"Why don't you both leave," I whispered. I hated them both passionately and I couldn't even yell, much less stalk out. I hated being helpless. I closed my eyes and waited for them to go. When I finally opened my eyes, they were gone. My body desperately wanted a nap, so I deferred my plan of getting up and leaving immediately. It would have been hard to carry out anyway, since I didn't have any clothes, and the cute little hospital gown had no back.

What woke me was the sound of the door shutting, followed by footsteps. If it was Andre or Dr. Bob, I decided, I was going to throw the water pitcher at him. I opened my eyes warily. Suzanne's anxious face was just inches from mine. "Thea. You poor thing. Are you awake?"

"Suzanne. Please say you're here to rescue me. I couldn't stand another day of this." Some of the anxiety left her face. I must have sounded like my old self. "I hope you brought clothes."

"Of course I did," she said. "You aren't beginning to doubt your partner's competence, are you?"

"I never doubt your competence, Suzanne. I'm just so overwhelmed with gratitude I'm not thinking clearly. How did you know... to come, I mean?"

"Your mother called to say you wouldn't be at work today. Very brisk and efficient. You know your mother. So I asked her what was wrong. She said a little accident. Said she was coming up today to get you. I was trying to get some details when she broke down and had to put your father on the phone. You know, Thea, your mother never breaks down." I did know. Mom prides herself on her control. "So I told your dad I'd be glad to come and get you myself, and he jumped at the offer. Said your mom really wasn't up to it, and he'd have a hard time getting away. So I just hopped in the car and came."

My rescuing angel didn't look like she'd just jumped in her car and gone anywhere. Her gorgeous, naturally straight, naturally blond hair was impeccably coiffed, and she had a tweedy raw linen fitted suit over a pale peach blouse. She looked competent, efficient, and delicious. I knew she'd chosen her outfit carefully to create exactly that impression. I could imagine her analysis. Small local hospital. Not completely familiar or comfortable with professional women. She needed to look both professional and feminine. Just the right simple gold accessories. Nothing large; nothing that clanked or rattled. Unobtrusive heels. A briefcase instead of a purse. "I can't bear to look at you," I said. "You look too nice."

"Thanks," she said. "I wish I could say the same for you. Are you sure you want to leave the hospital so soon? You do look terrible." She seemed doubtful. I couldn't let her leave me here. I had to get out. Another day of Andre's disbelief, Dr. Bob's snide prodding, and trays of pabulum and I'd need a transfer to the mental ward.

"Truth?" I asked.

"What else?" she said.

"OK, the truth is that I feel every bit as bad as I look, but I'm on the road to recovery. And this place is beginning to have a detrimental effect on my health. They don't feed me, they just poke and pry. If you don't get me out of here soon, I'm going to murder the doctor. The jerk treats me like a piece of meat."

"Dr. Tabor?" she said. "I'm sorry to hear that. I was just talking to him. He seemed very nice. Described you as feisty and restless. I wonder what those were euphemisms for? Bitchy and unreasonable?"

"Probably," I said.

"And that policeman. What a hunk! Made me want to have a little accident myself."

Well, everyone can't have my good judgment about men. Besides, Suzanne didn't know them like I did. Maybe they only treated women like meat when they were horizontal. But that's a large part of the male/female relationship. "I don't recommend it," I said. "My nose may never be the same again." I struggled to a sitting position, feeling energized by my nap. "Help me get dressed, will you?"

My contortions and grimaces must have alarmed her. She just stood there, staring at me. "Thea," she said, "I don't think…"

"Don't think," I said, "help. I'm no martyr, you know that. I wouldn't try to leave if I wasn't ready." Which was a lie. I would have left even if I had to crawl out. "Didn't the good Dr. Tabor say I could leave?"

"Not quite," she said. "He said you could leave if there was someone who could take care of you. And I know I can do that, even if you are an impossible patient. I've done it before." She opened the bag she'd brought and became her usual efficient self, laying things out on the bed in the order we'd need them. I said good-bye to the hospital johnny without regret and we went to work. Getting my bra on took both of us and made us both laugh so hard I almost died from the pain, but it felt good to laugh. "Hold still," she ordered. "It isn't easy to corral two wayward cantaloupes if you keep laughing."

"They aren't that big," I said.

"Compared to two fried eggs like mine, dahling," she said, "they're enormous."

She'd chosen black lace underwear. It matched my bruises nicely. My side, where Charlie had kicked me, was a multicolored extravaganza. I was decently dressed in the two black wisps, bent over, holding my side and laughing, when the door opened and Andre and Dr. Bob strolled in. Andre had the grace to stop at the door, but Dr. Bob kept on coming until Suzanne took charge. "Stop right there," she commanded. Dr. Bob looked surprised, but he stopped. "You can see that the patient is dressing," Suzanne said. "Don't you have any manners? Don't people in hospitals bother to knock?" She stood protectively between me and them. She's only about half my size, so it wasn't a total screen, but it was something.

"She's my patient," Dr. Bob began. "I've seen — "

"I'm sure you've seen it all before, Doctor," Suzanne said. "So have I. I'd still mind if you barged into my bedroom uninvited while I was dressing. You might even mind if someone did it to you." She pointed at the door. "Please?"

Andre was staring at the bruise on my side. "Like I told you, Detective," I said, "this is not from any car accident. It was a human foot. Bet you've seen bruises like this before."

He opened his mouth to reply, but before he could say anything, Suzanne interrupted. "Out." They left. "I see what you mean," she said. "A bit pushy, perhaps. Still, Dr. Bob has possibilities. I wonder if he's married?"

"Probably to a prime rib," I said.

After that, getting dressed went smoothly. She even brushed my hair and tied it with a scarf. Then she stepped back and inspected me. "That's the best I can do, without a veil," she said. "You really are a sight. It's a good thing I talked your mother

117

out of coming. She would have been shocked." She pulled a pair of sunglasses out of the briefcase. "Wear these. I've taken care of the paperwork. I'll go and tell them you're ready to leave. They insist on taking you out to the car in a wheelchair." I opened my mouth to protest. Suzanne held up a hand like a traffic cop. "Don't argue about it, Thea, OK?" She knows me so well. Anticipating the trouble spots and smoothing them over. She'd picked the right clothes for me, too, soft and stretchy and easy to put on. She'd even brought my favorite scarf. My partner. She left to secure my release.

CHAPTER 13

SUZANNE WAS NOT pleased when I told her we still had to clean out Carrie's apartment. In fact, she flatly refused to do more than go by to pick up my suitcase. "Don't be silly, Thea," she said. "I'm not dressed for lugging boxes and you can't do anything. We'll just explain that to the landlord. He'll just have to wait. We can offer some extra rent or something. Wasn't Carrie paid up for the month?"

"She was. The landlord's a lady, or at least a woman. And reason is not her strong suit," I said, describing my previous encounters with Mrs. Bolduc.

"I'll take care of it," Suzanne said. Normally I would have argued. I'm bad at delegating. I prefer to do things myself. But Suzanne and I have five years of working together. We've both had to let go when it was hard for us. So I didn't argue. I'd used my day's allotment of energy just getting dressed and leaving the hospital. You know you're hurt when the effort of getting from a wheelchair into a car makes you want to cry.

Suzanne parked outside the apartment. I gave her the key and told her where my stuff was. She was halfway up the walk when Mrs. Bolduc came charging out of the house. "I hope you've come to get the rest of her stuff out of there. I have a tenant who wants to move in this week, and I've got to clean..."

I watched through the window, eager to see what Suzanne would do. She held out her hand, very formal. "Mrs. Bolduc? I'm Suzanne Begner." Mrs. Bolduc stopped talking and reluctantly shook the offered hand. Suzanne took her firmly by the arm and steered her over to the car. "This is Mrs. Kozak, your late tenant's sister." I also shook her hand, enjoying the way Suzanne was taking control. "Mrs. Kozak, as you know, came up to clean out the apartment. Unfortunately, she was in an automobile accident on Saturday. I've just picked her up at the hospital. Her doctor says it will be at least two weeks before she can do any lifting." Suzanne put her hand on Mrs. Bolduc's arm, which was resting on the hood, and leaned forward, lowering her voice. "Such a dreadful series of events for the family."

Mrs. Bolduc stirred restlessly. I'd only seen her behind the curtain. She turned out to be a small, yellowish woman with badly dyed black hair and heavily penciled brows. She had a narrow, mean mouth. "Of course I'm sorry for their problems," she said, "but I've got my own living to think about. It ain't easy to rent a place that was had by a murdered person. Folks don't like that. Now I've got a tenant who don't care, says he'll take it anyway, but he's got to move in soon. Leavin' his wife, see. So her stuff's got to be gone this week."

"Miss McKusick paid her rent to the end of the month, didn't she?" Suzanne asked.

Mrs. Bolduc nodded. "And don't expect to get it back. Not entitled, you know, what with her not giving no notice or nothing."

Suzanne feigned surprise. "There was a written lease?"

"Nope. I just told her, that's all. Two weeks' notice. In writing. So I could plan, see. These girls, they're not real responsible, see, so you have to give 'em some rules."

I could tell Suzanne was trying not to smile. "You can hardly hold it against Miss McKusick that she didn't give notice, Mrs. Bolduc. She didn't expect to be killed, did she? Of course, we'd be glad to give notice. There are still two weeks left in the month. Perhaps, Mrs. Kozak, you should?"

I'd almost drifted off, sitting in the warm car. I uttered the most formal sentence I could think of. "Mrs. Bolduc, please consider this official notice, on behalf of my sister Carrie's estate, that the apartment will be vacated in two weeks, on the last day of September. We'll send written notice tomorrow," I said.

Mrs. Bolduc folded her skinny arms across her chest. "Nope," she said. "Now." I wanted to hit her.

Suzanne stayed cool. She opened her briefcase and pulled

out her checkbook. "What was the rent?" she asked.

"Five hundred a month," Mrs. Bolduc said, automatically. "Security deposit of one month's rent in advance."

Suzanne wrote a check, tore it out, and handed it to her. "Out by the end of the month, and here's another half month's rent for your inconvenience. I think you'll find that's fair. We would hate to have to get lawyers involved in this. That would be needlessly expensive for you, wouldn't it? You did know that Miss McKusick's father is an attorney?" She waited for Mrs. Bolduc's reaction. The landlady hesitated, then snatched the check out of Suzanne's hand.

"Out by the thirtieth or I really will get rid of her stuff," she said. "And I ain't renting to no more single girls. Sluts, all of them. Leading good boys astray." She glared at me. "Your sister deserved what she got." She turned her back and walked away.

"Wow, what a bitch!" Suzanne said, leaning against the door. "What was that all about?"

"Beats me," I said. "I wish I knew."

"Or maybe you don't," Suzanne said. "Let's get out of here before I give in to my desire to burn her house down." She went inside and was back in no time with my suitcase. She put it in the back seat, started the car, and backed out. She handled her BMW with the same easy competence she brought to everything she did, moving it smoothly through the gears.

"Mind if I sleep?" I asked.

"Yes," she said. "I insist you stay awake and make scintillating conversation."

"Right," I said. "Good night." I reclined my seat as far as it would go and went to sleep, confident that this time no one would wake me to take my temperature.

I woke to someone shaking my shoulder and calling my name. I woke slowly, like a swimmer coming up from a very deep dive. When I got to the surface I found Suzanne, looking worried. "Sorry to wake you, Thea," she said. "I didn't want to leave you alone in the car in case you woke up and were disoriented."

"Are we home already?" I looked around. We were in a parking lot. "This isn't home."

"Home is still about an hour and a half south," she said. "I'm too hungry to wait that long. Think you could eat something?"

"I could eat an elephant... if you cut it up for me."

"Good," she said. "This is some sort of steak house. I can't vouch for the quality, but I'll be happy to cut your meat."

The hostess didn't bat an eye at my bandaged nose and bruised face. Just picked up two huge, glossy menus and led us to a nice dark corner. Our waitress appeared promptly and offered us "something from the bar." Suzanne asked for white wine. I wanted something a good deal stronger than that, but I didn't know much about mild concussions or how well the painkillers I was taking mixed with alcohol, and my doctor hadn't given me any advice. I hadn't seen Dr. Bob after Suzanne drove him out of the room. I'd barely noticed him then. I'd been watching Andre. Andre, who had stared at my body like an impassioned artist first seeing the ceiling of the Sistine Chapel. Under other circumstances it might have been very erotic.

"Suzanne," I said, "can I drink?" She shook her head sadly. "Perrier," I said, "with lime." The waitress gave us an appraising look. Maybe she thought we were a couple. "We should be drinking champagne," I said, "to celebrate our partnership."

She smiled. A warm, happy smile. "We will," she said. "The Acton report was very good. You write so well. I'm jealous."

"Thanks. And you manage people so well. Neither Dr. Bob nor Mrs. Bolduc will ever be the same again."

"Poor Carrie. What an awful landlady she must have been. It was a nice apartment, though."

"It was," I said. "But Mrs. Bolduc spied on her. She even spied on me."

"That must have been very exciting for her," Suzanne said, "watching you carry in your suitcase and then carry in some boxes."

"She almost fell out the window when the state trooper brought me dinner." I waited for Suzanne's reaction.

"What?" she said.

"The detective working on Carrie's case. Andre Lemieux. The other guy you threw out of my room."

"He brought you dinner? My, you do work fast. I thought you'd sworn off men for life, after that awful banker?"

"I have, sort of. It was a bribe." I told her about my meeting with Andre, and how he'd shown up later with a peace offering in the form of dinner. Suzanne thought it was wonderful.

"No romance, just business?"

"Wouldn't be very practical, would it? Two hundred miles apart, and in such different professions?"

She just shrugged. Suzanne is very romantic. "I wouldn't let it stand in my way, if it was something I wanted. Now I understand why he was looking at you like you were a hot fudge sundae."

"Right," I said. "That sure is romantic. One of them thinks I'm a sundae, the other treats me like a roast. What about my mind?" I opened the menu. What appealed to me was meat. Steak, baked potato, and salad. Even though the steak house had been her idea, Suzanne had swordfish and salad. She loves fitted clothes, and she's tiny, so she has to be careful about her weight. "Speaking of romance," I said, "who was the deep-voiced gentleman in the background last Sunday, or shouldn't I ask?"

She smiled mysteriously. "You can ask. His name is Paul. Paul Merritt. Headmaster at a certain unnamed private school we've been courting as a potential client. I've been seeing him for a while. He's fun."

There was something she wasn't saying. "Single?" I asked.

"I can't hide anything from you, can I?" she sighed. "Married. Separated about a year. The divorce is in the works, but it's not final. In fact, it's been a real roller coaster. A couple times they've considered getting back together. It's been pretty discouraging. I know better than to let myself get into situations like this, but he's a wonderful man, and we have a lot of fun together. What about your policeman? He single?"

Suzanne was annoying this way. She wanted people to be happy, so she latched on to involvements way too early and then watched them like a hawk. She reminded me of those kids back in junior high who assumed you were going steady if you talked to the same boy twice. "Suzanne, he's not my policeman. Anyway, it's trooper, or detective. I don't know anything about him."

She left me alone after that. We ate our salads in silence and when my steak came she cut it up without being asked.

"Thanks, Mom," I said.

"I'm not sure that's funny," she said. "So far, you're the closest I've come to having a kid."

"Life is long," I said. "Maybe your dream guy is right around the corner."

"He'd better come around the corner soon," she said. "The clock is ticking. You want to tell me about the accident?"

"There was no accident," I said, "or, to be more precise, I didn't have an accident, an accident was done to me."

"Done to you?" she said, sounding puzzled. I told her the whole story, starting with lunch at Leadbetter's and ending when I woke up in the hospital.

She was shocked. "Thea, it sounds like something out of a cheap novel! You must have been terrified. Have the police arrested this Charlie? Is he the same person who killed Carrie?"

"The police think I drank too much and ran into a tree. Or they did think that. I told them what happened and they thought it was all the product of my deranged mind, the result of the concussion." Now that I was neither drugged nor dizzy, remembering how condescending Andre had been made me furious. I wasn't wild about having been seen in my underwear, either, but maybe showing him my bruise might have helped change his mind. It wasn't an injury that would have logically occurred in an accident. I was sure Andre had seen enough bruises in his life to know the difference. "Charlie has disappeared. And I don't know if he killed Carrie. I don't think so. He seemed genuinely surprised to learn she was dead. He's unreadable, of course, but there was something about what he said — that he'd hurt me so that we'd both hurt — that made me think he didn't."

I decided to tell her what I'd been thinking about in the hospital. "The main obsession in Carrie's life was the search for her birth parents. Just before she was killed, she told a woman she worked with that she'd finally had a breakthrough. And someone searched her apartment and took all her papers and diaries. All that was left were some notes the police found in her car. Maybe she found someone who didn't want to be found."

"Did you tell the police about your theory?" Suzanne asked.

The waitress arrived and began to clear away our plates. "Can I bring you ladies some coffee or dessert?" she asked.

"Just coffee for me, please," Suzanne said.

I just shook my head. I wanted dessert, but my face already ached from so much chewing and talking. When the waitress had gone, I answered Suzanne's question. "The police don't think much of my theory. They're still assuming it's a sex crime. But they didn't know Carrie. It's hard to explain to an outsider how significant her adoption was to Carrie. Since they don't see that as an obsession in her life, they can't take the next step, and see how important duplicating her search may be. So I'm going to do it." I hadn't known, until I said it, that I'd made up my mind, but Suzanne didn't seem surprised.

Her eyes gleamed at me over her coffee cup. "Thea will fix it, right?"

"You know me too well," I said.

"Well enough. I ought to, after all this time. They haven't exactly been uneventful years, have they?" She dropped her AMEX card on top of the check without looking at it. "You've chosen a good time. Things at the office should be pretty quiet.

No big deadlines, just some proposals to write. You can recuperate and do a little legwork." She seemed delighted with the idea of me as a detective. Of course, to Suzanne, a quiet period meant we only worked fifty-hour weeks instead of eighty, but I appreciated the support. I was lucky to have such a flexible boss, even if I never took advantage of it. But I was forgetting. I was a boss now, too.

"On your feet, Thea," she said. "We've got miles to go before we sleep." We stopped in the ladies' room, where I almost had to ask for help, I was so stiff. By the time we got to the car, I was wishing the restaurant had sent me out in a wheelchair. Suzanne read it all in my face. "Feeling rotten, huh?"

"Rather."

"Be right back." She was out of the car before I could protest. She came back a minute later with a cup of water. "Hold this," she said, digging around in her briefcase. After a prodigious search she came up with a little brown container. "From Dr. Bob," she explained, shaking a pill onto the palm of her hand and passing it to me.

"What's this?"

"He didn't tell me," she said. "He just handed it to me, followed by a long litany of instructions about taking care of you, most of which were appropriate only to the care of idiots and vegetables. I told him you were neither. He said he had observed that Mrs. Kozak — and he emphasized the words 'Mrs. Kozak' — seemed very able to take care of herself. So I gather you gave him a hard time."

"He's too sensitive. All I did was tell him that if he was Dr. Tabor, I was Mrs. Kozak, not Theadora."

She giggled. "That's all? Well, you made quite an impression. Now you lie back and go night-night and I'll wake you when we're home." I did as I was told. It took about twenty minutes for Dr. Bob's gift to work, but after that I felt just fine.

CHAPTER 14

IT WAS WEDNESDAY before I felt like a normal human being again. A being without a headache, who could take a deep breath without wincing. On Wednesday Suzanne drove me to my local G.P., who pronounced me well on the way to recovery and took the tape off my nose. It was still swollen — to me it looked gigantic and ugly, like a lump of mottled clay — but the doctor and Suzanne both assured me that it wasn't bad. The black around my eyes had faded to a hideous yellow-green. I looked like the star of *Creature from the Yellow Lagoon*, but I felt better without strips of white tape below my eyes.

Wednesday was also the first day I didn't feel feeble and exhausted by midafternoon. I went from the doctor's office to work, despite Suzanne's protests, and put in three good hours before I ran out of steam.

Being without a car was making me crazy. Suzanne was happy to help, but it made both of us feel trapped. I called my insurance agent, who assured me that I was welcome to rent a car, and my insurer would pick up the cost, as long as it was moderate. Moderate, further questions revealed, might get me something off the back lot of Rent-a-Wreck. I was spoiled by my Saab. I wanted it back. If I couldn't have it, I wanted another Saab.

I let my fingers do the walking, searching for a Saab to rent. It wasn't easy. I was afraid my ear would become permanently attached to the receiver. It would have been easier to rent a BMW, but I finally found a Saab for only about twice the cost of an American car. Luckily, money isn't a problem for me. David's company had a good life insurance policy, and I collected the policy limit from the guy who killed him. Plus, Suzanne paid well, and I was too busy working to spend much money.

Suzanne, relieved to have her chauffeuring chores at an end, drove me to the rental agency. After an uncomfortable twenty minutes with a rental agent who couldn't stop staring at my face, I drove away in a shiny red Saab loaded with options. It had a state-of-the-art sound system, a sun roof, an air bag, and a car phone. I felt like a real fat cat. The only drawback was that it was automatic, probably to leave one hand free for the phone. Half the fun of driving is shifting gears. It would take a while for my left foot to stop flopping around hopelessly on the floor.

Thursday I worked until midafternoon and then drove to my parents' house. It was a dual-purpose visit. First and foremost, I went to prove to them that I was truly alive and well, so they would stop calling me every night. Second, I hoped to persuade them to help me find Carrie's birth parents.

The evening was an unqualified disaster.

It began before I even got in the door. Mom opened the door, took one look at me, and burst into tears. Dad tried to calm her down, but it was evident that he was also shocked by my appearance. Before things could settle down, Michael and Sonia arrived, looking tanned and rested, and Mom couldn't resist pointing out that taking a vacation immediately after the funeral was in very bad form. Sonia and Mom get along badly at the best of times, and Sonia didn't appreciate the comment, a fact she made abundantly clear.

Then, when Dad asked what I'd like to drink, Michael said, "Maybe you shouldn't give her anything. We don't want her wrapping that nice red Saab around a tree. I don't think her face could take it."

I tried to pass it off lightly. "Thanks for your concern, Michael," I said. "You can always drive me home if I can't handle it. We're practically neighbors, after all." He scowled at that. Mike hates to put himself out for other people. We do live in neighboring towns, but he never calls to see if I'm OK, or invites me to dinner. "I'll have my usual."

My brother wouldn't leave it alone. He and Sonia must have had a fight on the way over. Michael doesn't know what to do with bad feelings, so he spills them all over everyone. He's always been like that. When he was little, if he broke a favorite toy, he'd try to break one of mine to make himself feel better. He's developed some controls. He no longer indulges in physical violence, but he's still into verbal violence. Between them, he and Sonia had two of the nastiest mouths on the East Coast. "How's everything at that little think tank of yours?" he asked. "You and Suzanne still the happy couple?"

It would have been a good time to mention my partnership. My parents would have been pleased, but Michael was looking for a fight, and he'd find something nasty to say. I wasn't in the mood for nasty remarks. Or a fight. I can give it back just as fast as he can dish it out, if I want to. But it had been a hard week; I didn't have energy to waste on a pissing contest with my brother. "Things at work are fine, Michael," I said mildly. "How is your work going?"

"Michael seems to be suffering from artist's block," Sonia said, "if there is any such thing. In fact, he's suffering from a block in several areas. It's tough on his fragile male ego, isn't it, dear?" She sat back on the sofa, smoothing her glossy hair with hot-pink fingernails, gloating over her remark. The rest of us refrained from comment. Dad came back with a tray of drinks, handed them around, and settled into his favorite chair. Mom came in from the kitchen, bringing with her the faint scent of fresh bread, and sat beside him. Her sherry was waiting. She took a sip and smiled at all of us.

"Dinner will be ready in about twenty minutes. The roast is slow tonight. I hope you don't mind waiting." Dad said he didn't, and the rest of us agreed. I was looking forward to dinner. Suzanne is not a great cook. Mom looked at my drink with undisguised disapproval. "Thea, dear," she said, "are you really feeling all right? Should you be drinking so soon?" She didn't wait for my answer. "I should have come to get you myself, instead of letting Suzanne do it. You're not getting enough rest. I can see that. I hope you're not back at work?"

I guess moms never stop worrying about their kids. "I'm doing fine," I said. "I know I look awful, but that's just the way bruises are. You must know that, with all the time you spend at the hospital. They stay ugly long after they stop hurting."

"That's good news," Dad said. "The whole thing was quite a shock. It's not like you to drink and drive. Was it so upsetting, trying to pack her things?"

I realized I hadn't told them about the accident. "I didn't drink and then drive my car into a tree. I was put into the car unconscious and then the car was allowed to run into that tree."

"Oh sure," Michael said, "and I suppose someone else drank the beer from the bottles that were found in your car?"

He was beginning to get on my nerves. "Get real, Mike," I said. "You know I'd never drive around in my car drinking beer. That's not what happened. It's a long story, but put most simply, our sister Carrie had hooked up with her old friend Chuck again. You remember Chuck, the car thief? One of the waitresses Carrie worked with told me about this guy Carrie had been seeing. She described him. He sounded familiar, so I went to see him, to ask him a few questions. And he welcomed me with closed fists instead of open arms. He beat me until I passed out — at his house, not in my car — and when I woke up, I was in the hospital."

Mom stared at me, clutching her sherry with both hands, her eyes wide with shock. I told them, briefly, what had happened at the camp, and pulled up my sweater to show them my bruised ribs. "This is where he kicked me. I fell down and hit my head, and that's the last thing I remember. The police looked for him, but Chuck, or Charlie, as he now prefers to be called, was nowhere to be found."

I hadn't expected a great outpouring of sympathy — we tended to be a "buck up and get on with it" kind of family — but I hadn't expected this silent staring, either, as though it was my explanation that they found fantastic, not what had been done to me. "I can't believe you guys thought I'd had an accident

because I was driving drunk. You know me better than that!"
Not that I'd never driven in an intoxicated state, but it's rare. If
anyone knew that, it should be my family. These people knew
how cautious I was, but my explanation didn't seem to satisfy
them. They sat staring until I began to feel like something from
a sideshow. "Look," I said, "will you guys stop goggling at me
and tell me what's on your minds?"

Michael's smile was malicious. "That's a hell of a story,
Thea. So why did the police tell us the one about drinking and
driving? It's a bit too convenient, isn't it, Chuck or Charlie, or
whatever his name is, disappearing?"

"Come on, Michael, you can't think I'd make up a story like
that, just because I was embarrassed? I was unconscious. The
police read it the way they were supposed to, until I explained
to them what had happened." Sonia was smirking behind her
hand. "Mom? Dad?" No one said anything. How could they not
believe me? The implication that they didn't made me furious.
Unexpectedly, I felt disoriented, as confused as I'd felt when I
first woke up in the hospital.

I think everyone has a secret fear of being crazy, or rather, a
fear of being sane but unable to communicate it, and being
considered crazy by everyone around them. I felt a little of that
fear now, or like a character in a movie who discovers everyone
else in the room has been turned into an alien. These people, my
loving family, the ones I'd come to reassure, the ones I might
reasonably have expected to cluck over me a bit and clutch me
protectively to their bosoms, had turned into aliens. "Dad," I
said, "do you really think I'd make up a story like this? Why
would I?"

His face was a map of confusion, deeply etched lines leading
nowhere. "Honey," he said, "it's not that I don't believe you.
It's just such a shock, out of the blue like this..."

"Out of the blue! What do you mean by that? Everything's
out of the blue the first time you hear it, right?" The nerve of this
self-righteous crew, letting me do all the dirty work while they

went on with their busy little lives, and then condescending to me because they thought I'd blown it. "Listen," I said, "you guys sent me up to Maine to do the cleanup detail because no one else would go. Mom was too upset. Dad, you were too busy. Michael had to work on his tan, so I was the one who got elected. Good old Thea, the lucky winner."

Mom was horrified. "Thea, please don't..."

I ignored her. "I'm the one who had to spend an afternoon with the police detective, discussing the details of Carrie's sex life. I'm the one who had to look at the pictures of Carrie's body. I'm the only one here who really knows how she died." I had to stop for breath. "If I told you how she died — all the terrible details — would you not believe me because you hadn't heard it before? Because it came out of the blue?"

They might not like what I was saying, but at least I had their attention. "I had to pack up her things and deal with her nasty landlady. And I'm the one — when the police weren't getting anywhere — who found out she was seeing Chuck again." I was out of control, and I didn't care. I wanted to bat the smug look off Sonia's face. I wanted to shock them out of their complacent disapproval. I started yelling. "I know you guys all remember Chuck, the guy who liked to hurt Carrie. We all had a big celebration when he went to jail. You haven't forgotten that have you, Mom? You're the one who used to throw away his letters. He said he was hitting me because he couldn't hit you." I pointed to my ugly yellow bruises. "I got these on family business."

They were all poised on the edges of their seats, waiting for a chance to escape. All except Sonia. She was smiling and swinging her foot like this was all a show being staged for her benefit.

"Michael, do you remember Chuck?" He nodded. "Dad?" A nod. "Mom?" Nods but nothing more. No support. There's a famous line that says home is the place that when you go there they have to take you in. If that was the case then I wasn't home.

These people whom I thought I knew so well were acting like strangers. Drawing away from me because I'd dared to challenge their assumption that I would always be there to quietly do their dirty work. Thea the fixer. Suddenly, as I sat there enduring the scorn of their disapproving faces, I understood better how Carrie, always the object of someone's disapproval, had felt. My perfect, happy, loving family looked suddenly different, like a junkyard glimpsed through a chink in a clean white fence.

Mom drained her sherry and stood up. "I just can't understand why you would take it upon yourself to go and see that awful Chuck character," she said. "That was so foolish of you. I think I'd better check the roast."

"I don't think so," I said, anger at all of them outweighing my usual reticence. "What you'd better do is stay right there until I'm finished. It's no wonder Carrie sometimes felt alienated from all of you, the way you can turn on one of your own. I never saw that until now. She didn't feel safe, and now I understand why. I came here tonight, still hurting from a beating and a contrived accident that occurred because I was trying to help find Carrie's killer, to reassure you that I'm OK, assuming that you loved me and were worried about me. I found a bunch of self-satisfied people feeling superior to me because they think I'm a weakling who got overwhelmed by my feelings, got drunk and ran my car into a tree. I can't believe you're treating me this way."

Sonia had stopped swinging her foot and was making strange mouth motions like a fish out of water. The rest of them were silent, unwilling to meet my eyes. They were astonished, I suppose. I don't usually make waves. "I don't care whether you believe me or not," I said. "I know what's true. I do have strong feelings about Carrie's death, but they aren't driving me to drink, they're driving me to try to find her killer. To keep pressure on the police. Which is what we all should be doing, unless you all think it doesn't matter, that it's OK to let her killer

133

walk away."

"Don't be silly, Thea. Of course we don't want that. And now I really must check on dinner." Mom walked rapidly out of the room. This time I didn't try to stop her. Instead I fed myself some fortifying alcohol, followed by cheese and crackers. The silence was as thick as yogurt.

"The beaches in Bermuda were just as nice as the pictures," Sonia said. She looked tanned and gorgeous. I hated her. "We went snorkeling every day, and once a fish swam right up and bit Michael's finger. It was only a tiny fish, too. Have you ever been there, Mr. McKusick?" Sonia may blame Mom for all of Michael's faults, but she likes my dad.

"A few times," he said. "Linda and I like it a lot. We were talking about going this fall, before Carrie... before all this happened. Where did you stay?" And they were off, making polite small talk, as though the earlier conversation had never happened. As though I didn't exist and I'd never said anything. Bermuda carried us through the rest of cocktails and on into dinner.

Normally, the conflict would have ruined my appetite, but when I sat down and inhaled all the delicious smells, I realized I was starving. I didn't know if it was physical or psychological, but I felt like my body needed meat to recover. Meat and homemade bread. By my second helping of roast beef, I was ready to let go of some of my anger and move on to the second item on my agenda. "The paper that the police found in her car, and some I found in the apartment, suggest that Carrie's death is connected to her search for her birth parents," I said. Mom's fork dropped from her hand, bounced off her plate, and rolled into her lap.

"I know you didn't want her to search, and wouldn't help her, but you can get access to the papers, and no one else can. It can't hurt you now. If I can duplicate the search, and find out what she learned, I believe somewhere in that search is the clue to her murderer."

Mom stood up, clutching the fork like a talisman to ward off evil. "No, Theadora, I forbid it. It doesn't matter now. She's dead. Let the matter lie. No one will be helped... can be helped, now. She doesn't need a mother."

"Not for that, Mom. Not to challenge your position as Carrie's mother," I said. "This is not about finding mothers or fathers anymore, it's about murder. This may be the only way to find her killer. The police don't have any leads."

Dad was hunched over his plate, head between his hands, gripping two hunks of hair. When he looked up, his face was agonized. "Of course we want Carrie's killer found," he said. "You know that, but this is something you can't ask of your mother, after all she's been through..."

"I'm not asking *Mom* to do anything," I said, not understanding why my simple request was getting such a strong reaction. "She doesn't have to have anything to do with it or know anything about it. I'll do it myself. All you have to do is give me a signed authorization, agreeing I can see the records. You're Carrie's parent, too. You can sign it."

Mom dropped the fork again with a loud clatter, glaring at me. "Tom," she said, "make that child understand. There is absolutely no way we're going to get involved in reexamining Carrie's adoption. No way. Innocent people might be hurt."

"But, Mom," I repeated, "it may be the only way to find out what happened."

"Then I guess we won't be finding out," she said angrily. "What difference does it make anyway? Your sister's just as dead. I don't see why you want to hurt me any more than I've already been hurt."

"Mom," I said, "this isn't about you. It's about Carrie..."

She ignored me. "Make her stop, Tom," she said. She grabbed his plate and carried it to the kitchen. He stared sadly after his unfinished dinner, then got up, gathered the rest of the plates, and followed her out.

"Well, sister dear," said Michael, "what do you do for an

encore?"

"I suppose you're with them?" I said. "You don't care if Carrie's killer is found?"

He set his glass down with a thump. "You can cut out the holier-than-thou act, Thea. Of course I do. We all do. But it's not our job. That's what police are for."

"And if the police aren't getting anywhere?"

Sonia snorted. "I don't know where you get this idea you can do anything, Thea. Why should you succeed if the police can't?"

"Because I care more," I said. "I thought we all did. You think it's just a harebrained scheme? A wild-goose chase? Stay tuned, guys, you might be surprised."

Dad came back for Michael's plate. "Thea," he said, "your mother is very upset. Can we just drop this and finish dinner in peace? You can call me at the office tomorrow. We can talk about it then. I don't think you understand the whole situation."

I was glad to drop the subject. He was right. I didn't understand. I couldn't understand how my own family could have treated me so scornfully earlier and I couldn't understand why they were reacting so negatively to my suggestions about Carrie's birth parents. It seemed like they were all eager to sweep the whole mess under the rug. I felt used and abused and had the unpleasant, unsettled feeling that I no longer understood my family. Like Carrie, I was an outsider in their midst.

The acrimonious evening had given me stomach pains. This must be what hell is like — an eternity at a great dinner with so much conflict you get an ulcer. As soon as I'd had some coffee I was getting out of there. And maybe I was overreacting. Maybe Dad's cryptic comment meant he was willing to help. If so, I'd accomplished my goal. I clung to that thought because I needed to, because I needed to take away something good, even though I knew I was fooling myself. "Sure," I said. "I'll call you."

Dessert was a lemon cake, filled with layers of lemon curd

and fresh raspberries, topped with whipped cream. Even Sonia admitted it was good. As soon as I decently could, I grabbed my purse and coat and escaped.

It was a filthy night. Torrents of rain and patchy fog. I was glad I had a Saab. The rental car seemed to already have my own Saab's instincts, which was good, because my mind was on autopilot. Jackson Browne sang song after song to soothe my bruised spirit, while my car took me safely home.

CHAPTER 15

I WOKE ON Friday feeling like someone had performed a root canal on my spirit. The only emotion that didn't seem to have been reamed out was anger — that was intact. I'd been betrayed by my family; now I was outside, with Carrie, in the realm of the orphans.

Dad is usually at the office by eight-thirty — I get my workaholic genes from both sides — and I called him there before I left for work. His secretary doesn't come in until nine, so I knew he'd answer the phone himself. I hesitated when I heard the familiar voice, knowing he'd hoped I'd forget his suggestion. I didn't hesitate for long.

"Hi," I said, "it's Thea. Mom OK today?"

"Thea," he said. "I'm glad you called. I'm sorry about last night. I guess we all got off on the wrong foot." There was a slight pause before he spoke again, being extremely careful about what he said. "I talked with your mother about your plan to search for Carrie's birth parents. I understand. We both understand how upset you are about your sister's death. Of course we all want the murderer to be found. We just don't see how this search can help."

"I can explain that," I said.

"Let me finish, Theadora. Just thinking about someone else as Carrie's mother causes your mother great pain. I know you realize that. Going through the legal steps to get the records released would be much more painful. I'm sure you understand how hard this has all been for her. I cannot support you in an endeavor which would cause her more pain. You can't put your mother through that."

"But it won't..."

He cut me off. "Carolyn is dead. Finding her birth parents now cannot possibly do her, or them, any good. A course of action which benefits no one, and which hurts people in the

138

process, should not be pursued. Surely you can see the logic of that, Thea? What basis do you have for this theory that Carolyn's search is connected to her death?"

I told him about the notes in Carrie's car. About what Lorna had told me. About the papers I'd found in Carrie's closet. I didn't tell him about the dream and Carrie asking me for help. No lawyer would consider that a credible reason for anything. I knew it didn't sound like much, and that's exactly what he said.

"I know it's not much," I said, "but it's the only avenue left. Plus my instinct, or woman's intuition, or whatever you want to call it, tells me that if I duplicate Carrie's search, I'll find her killer."

He swept away my arguments like I was an annoying gnat. "Intuition? Hysteria, more likely. You've had a difficult few weeks, I know. But let a little more time pass and all this will seem silly to you, too." He took an audible breath. "Let it rest, Thea, will you please? For my sake and your mother's."

When I was a teenager, I was a pretty good kid. Michael was the wild one. I didn't do a lot of wild things, and I rarely lied to my parents. I was about to do that now, and I hadn't had enough practice to do it well. "Ok, Dad, you win," I said. "I'll stop bugging you and Mom about searching for Carrie's birth parents." It was a carefully phrased capitulation. If Carrie did it on her own, so could I. I just wouldn't tell them what I was doing. Sure it would be harder, but life didn't seem bent on offering me the easy route, so this was nothing new. Dad thanked me too profusely and hung up. I grabbed my briefcase and went to work.

At noon I went to the library and used the computer to search for books about adoptees. The books confirmed what I already knew — that the agencies were usually uncooperative and the easiest way to search was to have the adoptive parents participating, because they had a right to see the records. I made some calls and located a search group in a nearby town which met on

Saturday mornings. The woman I spoke with was friendly. She invited me to attend and gave me careful directions.

The rest of the day I concentrated on a proposal we were making. At five I took it in and gave it to Suzanne. "I've baited the hook," I said. "Let's cast this one out and see if the fish bites."

"I hardly think a headmaster as tweedy as Throckmorten would appreciate being called a fish," she said.

"I'll try that again." I went out and came in again. "I've released the fox," I said. "Let's see if the hunters will give chase."

Suzanne frowned. "Better, but still not right."

"One more time," I said. "In this envelope I've placed two pages from a rare, illustrated version of the *Story of O*. To see the rest, the recipient must sign the enclosed contract and return it to me."

"You're still no great beauty," she said, "but at least you've recovered your sense of humor. Doing anything interesting this weekend?"

"Thought I'd buy a six-pack and go drive into some trees. Unless I get sidetracked cleaning the oven. What about you?"

"Hiking in New Hampshire," she said, "with Paul."

"Sounds better than driving to Maine to collect a battered colleague," I said. "Hope the weather's good."

She grinned mischievously. "I don't care. If it's not, we'll spend the weekend in our room." She hummed a bit of "White Christmas."

"Looks like you've still got your sense of humor, too," I said. "See you Monday."

"Tuesday," she said. "I'm taking Monday off."

"Unthinkable. You must not be yourself."

She picked up her bag, shoved some papers into it, and locked her desk. "No one lives forever. I've decided to have some fun while I can."

I couldn't argue with that. I hoped things worked out for her, but I wasn't optimistic. A recently separated man is a poor candidate for romance. Not that I was much of an expert on romance myself. Hadn't I been entertaining lustful thoughts about that policeman on Saturday, thinking he was kind and perceptive, only to find him acting like a jackass the very next day?

The rest of the staff followed Suzanne out like ducklings after their mother. By five-fifteen I was alone. I worked until eight, enjoying the solitude, then took my library books and went home, stopping on the way for a pizza. The cute little teenager who waited on me couldn't help staring at my face. "You should have seen the other guy," I said.

I spent the evening in my favorite chair, bourbon bottle and ice bucket by my side, reading the sad, happy, confused, or arduous stories of people who had searched for their birth parents. Beyond noticing how it affected Carrie, I'd never thought much about adoption before. One anecdote after another described how adoption agencies denied adoptees information about their parents, treating them like they had no rights or interest in the matter, doling out bits of non-identifying information like crumbs to the starving. I was furious on their behalf. What right did my parents have to refuse to help Carrie? Just because they had raised her didn't mean Carrie wasn't a separate person with her own needs, her own sense of identity.

It was after midnight when I finally put the books aside and pried myself out of the chair. Bed looked very inviting, but before I quit for the day I wanted to find the notes I'd taken out of Carrie's raincoat pocket. I hoped I'd brought them back with me, and not left them in Maine in one of the boxes. If only I had her diary. I was sure it contained a careful account of the search. But the murderer had her diary.

I found the papers, still in my unpacked suitcase. I took them and crawled into bed, meaning to read through them before I went to sleep. Seeing Carrie's handwriting made me sad. I got up, found a tissue, and tried again, but I was asleep before I got

141

through the first paragraph.

The experts tell you it's a bad idea to drink and drive. These days the warnings are printed right on the bottles. I agree; that's why I rarely do it, whatever my family and the police may think. And though the bottles don't tell you so, it's also a bad idea to drink and sleep. I slept like a crocodile in the sun for the first hour, and then I began to dream. I was dressed in camouflage pants, combat boots, and an olive T-shirt, with a camouflage bandanna tied over my hair, leading a similarly dressed squad of commando adoptees silently through the night in a raid on an adoption clinic. In a mere three seconds, I picked the lock and dismantled the alarm, and then we descended, removing all the records to two red Broncos. We all wore yellow rubber gloves and carried kids' walkie-talkies.

At four-thirty I woke hot and sweaty, with an awful headache. I swallowed three extra-strength painkillers, took a cold shower, and went back to sleep. I slept soundly until my alarm watch began beeping. I cursed it and shut it off. Didn't the damn thing know it was Saturday? Of course it did. One of its jobs was to keep track of the days of the week. Then I remembered the meeting. I set a Guinness-quality record for fastest toilette, threw on some respectable pants and a purple silk shirt, grabbed Carrie's notes and my briefcase, and ran. If traffic was light, I might make it.

CHAPTER 16

CAROL ANDERSON HAD warm brown eyes surrounded by smile lines, and a wide mouth that was made for smiling. Right now, though, she wasn't smiling. She was listening intently to my explanation of why I wanted to search for Carrie's birth parents, and shaking her head. "It's not a good reason for a search," she said. "What are you going to tell her parents, if you find them — that their daughter is dead? You'd only be inflicting hurt on more people, not helping anyone." She sighed. "There are so many people who need help, for more immediate, personal reasons. We're a small group, all volunteers. We just don't have the time or resources to spend on a search for revenge." I'd liked her instantly, and her words really stung.

She spread her hands wide, palms up. "I wish I could help you deal with your sister's death. I wish I could have helped your sister. But with this... and your parents against it, I just can't help. You have to understand how it is for us, here in the search movement. We already struggle to overcome a lot of opposition from the legal system, adoption agencies, adoptive parents, and even birth parents, even though we're constantly seeking to explain and publicize our point of view. Using the search process to catch a murderer may seem very logical to you, but it achieves none of our goals, and a story like yours could be very harmful to the interests of other searchers."

I couldn't let her reject me like this; I needed her help to do what I had to do. "Look, Mrs. Anderson," I said, "I know it's not your usual search, but this is the only thing I have to go on right now. Carrie was searching, and she found something, or someone, and then she was killed. It's the only route I know to find her killer."

"I understand that," she said. "We counsel people all the time to be prepared for disappointment, that they may not like what they find... they may be rejected... or the birth parents may be dead. The birth parents may not be at all what they've been expecting, so it's not that we're incurable optimists here who expect happy endings. For a lot of people, any ending, however unhappy, is better than living with uncertainty. It's still a big jump to go from the search with the unknown ending to the search where your goal is to accuse the birth parents of murder."

We were standing in a church basement. The room was low-ceilinged and dark, with a utilitarian vinyl floor, false-wood paneled walls, and accordion-pleated panels which could be pulled out to divide the room. They were pulled back now to accommodate many rows of chairs. It had been a well-attended meeting, and interesting. I'd felt like an intruder listening to some of the stories. Everyone else there seemed to be an adoptee at some stage in a search, and they were sharing successful methods and techniques. Many people had tears in their eyes when one man got up and said, "I've been searching for four years. This week I found my mother. She has eyes just like mine."

Henry David Thoreau said, "The mass of men lead lives of quiet desperation." It was certainly true for these people. An unhomogenized group, mixed by age, sex, and ethnic back-ground, they shared a common bond, their desperate need to find out who they were. I was astonished, though it was naive of me, to realize how many people were going through these serious personal quests without the world really noticing them. But my own sister had been one of these questing people, and I, who thought I knew her so well, hadn't really noticed or understood, or given her feelings the respect they deserved, and Mom and Dad had simply denied everything and hoped it would go away. But everyone has their secrets. These people lacked identity. I lacked love. It helped me understand.

Before Carol's blunt words, I hadn't thought of my search that way. But I couldn't argue with her conclusion. I did intend to use the search to find Carrie's killer, but where I'd thought of the search in terms of process, she thought of it in terms of people. "It's not as concrete as you make it sound," I said. "I don't know that she even found them... only that she was close. By duplicating the process, I hope to find what she found, and somewhere there is a clue to her death."

"Well, that sounds comfortably vague and distanced," she said, "but there are real people involved here, not just a process. But even the process isn't simple. Don't delude yourself. You heard what people were saying at the meeting. A search can take years." She looked at her watch. "I'm sorry. I've got to go, and I have to lock up first."

I put a restraining hand on her arm. "Mrs. Anderson, please. I heard what people were saying — how important it is to find out who they are. My sister was only twenty-one. She never had a chance to live, or find out who she was, or anything. Someone took that chance away from her. I can't let the person who killed her get away with it. I always promised her I'd take care of her, and I failed at that. This is the only thing left that I can do for her. And I must do it as quickly as I can before clues are lost or memories fade. But to do it quickly, I need someone with experience, like you, to guide me. Please say you'll help me."

I don't know whether she felt sorry for me, or was just worn down by my persistence. Whatever it was, she hesitated, then fumbled in the canvas bag she carried. She pulled out a small booklet and held it toward me. Her set mouth told me how reluctantly she did it. "I've already told you, I can't help. This has the best information we know about how to search. The rest is up to you. Now please, will you leave." I took the booklet and left.

I spent the rest of the day at the library, with the booklet, Carrie's notes, and several books, outlining a plan of attack. My passion for organization has always been a family joke, but it works for me. Michael used to say I wouldn't cross the street without an outline, which is why they were so surprised when I married David so soon after I met him, and without the big wedding Mom had always counted on. So I may strike the world as rigid and cautious, but I have an impulsive streak. This whole search business was an impulse — even if I was taking a methodical approach.

The most important thing, it seemed, was to learn the name of Carrie's birth mother, and, if possible, where she came from. But because of the stigma on illegitimate births, particularly back in the preabortion era, the identity of the birth mother, or of the birth parents, was the fundamental secret of the adoption process. It was usually a closely guarded secret. The rationale was that this allowed the birth mother to return to her former life, put her dirty little secret behind her, and erase the whole episode from her mind. Keeping the secret also protected the adoptive parents from any personal knowledge of the sinful origins of their child, allowing them to bask in the myth that the child was theirs alone, always had been and would be, and that it had no connection with anyone else.

The books suggested several sources of information that might be helpful. If Carrie's mother had been in a maternity home, they might have records which a sympathetic staff person might be willing to share. The original birth certificate, if I could get it, would have the mother's name, unless she'd used a false one, but these were often sealed and inaccessible. The doctor might still be in practice, and still have records, and his name might be on the amended certificate. The name of the hospital where she was born would also appear on the birth certificate, and hospitals, even when they claimed to have no records, often stored decades' worth of records in their basements or on microfilm.

To start, I needed a copy of Carrie's birth certificate. That meant a trip to Boston, if I didn't want to waste a week or two, and that meant that neither Suzanne nor I would be at work on Monday, since state offices are closed on weekends.

Too bad Carrie hadn't kept a copy of her birth certificate with her notes, but then, these notes weren't her working file, I could tell. They weren't complete enough. Her working file, like her diary, was missing. It looked like she'd pursued the same course I was planning, but kept a record of her results somewhere else. She had left me one gem, though: the name of the maternity home. Carrie's anonymous mother had awaited her birth in a place run by the Sisters of Harmony in Braintree, called Serenity House. The reference to Serenity House was crossed out. I didn't know whether that meant it had been an unproductive lead, that she couldn't find it, or only that she'd found it and moved on.

I asked the librarian where they kept phone books. The Braintree phone book had no listing for Serenity House, but the Sisters of Harmony were listed, with a street address. The librarian directed me to a pay phone, and I called the number. The woman who answered asked me to hold, and referred my call to a brusque woman who identified herself as Mrs. Ireland. Mrs. Ireland admitted that the order still ran Serenity House, and asked what the purpose of my call was.

Carol Anderson's reaction had made me cautious. This time I didn't launch into my tale of murder. I told her only that I was interested in information about a child whose mother had been at Serenity House before she was born. But Mrs. Ireland wanted to know much more. I ended up telling her that I was searching for my own birth mother. She was neither friendly nor unfriendly, but neutral and carefully guarded. She explained that it was the policy of Serenity House not to reveal any identifying information without the consent of the adoptive parents. I admitted I didn't have the consent of my parents. She tried to end the conversation right there with a homily about the value of protecting family privacy.

When I persisted, she suggested I make an appointment to speak with their social worker, Ms. Pappas, gave me a different number to call, and terminated the conversation. I was left with the impression that Mrs. Ireland was unhappily familiar with adoptees searching for their birth mothers. Even though it was Saturday, I called the new number, and someone answered,

"Esther Pappas."

I explained who I was, except this time I said I was helping my sister conduct a search, and asked if she could help me. She repeated, almost verbatim, what Mrs. Ireland had said, trying to discourage me, but when I refused to be discouraged, she agreed to meet with me to discuss the matter further if I could be there by four-thirty. By my watch, it was almost three-thirty, which meant that if I exceeded the speed limit, ran into no traffic jams, and could find the place, I might just make it. I said I'd be there, hung up, and ran out of the library.

CHAPTER 17

SEVERAL TIMES ON my way to Braintree I thought I was going to find out whether the air bag on my rented Saab worked, but whoever watches over the foolish and the desperate was watching over me. My mind wasn't on driving. I was rehearsing what I was going to say to Ms. Pappas. The driver of the black BMW in front of me must have been rehearsing for a square dance; he kept changing lanes without signaling and without paying any attention to the other cars. I finally passed him before he gave me a heart attack, and discovered his inattention was due to the animated phone conversation he was conducting. People who talk with their hands shouldn't be allowed to have car phones.

I arrived at Serenity House and found a parking space with fifty seconds to spare. Serenity House was an ugly pile of yellow brick four stories high fronted by a diminutive pillared portico as absurd as a bow tie on a fat man. It was set well back from the street and the lot was enclosed by an unfriendly black iron fence. A few demoralized shrubs tried to soften the outside, but the overall appearance was as inviting as a bed of nails. Perhaps, in a more punitive time, that had been the intent. Three young women, girls, actually, were sitting on the steps. All three were hugely pregnant. They stared at my waist as I went by. Another pregnant girl sitting at a desk directed me to Ms. Pappas. None of them looked happy.

I knocked on the door and a voice invited me to enter. Not an inviting voice, but stern and gravelly, which prepared me for what came next. A prison matron. Esther Pappas was tall and square. She wore sensible, black-rimmed spectacles, sensible shoes, and a sensible gray wool jumper over an unadorned white blouse. The blouse had a tiny, round collar. Her graying brown hair was pulled tightly back in a bun. A plain black cardigan hung over the back of her chair. Her colorless eyes were small, her nostrils large, and her mouth turned down at the corners. She looked like she'd never seen anything in her life that she approved of and never expected to.

She held out a large, blunt-fingered hand. "You made good time, Miss Kozak," she said. "Won't you sit down."

I shook the hand and sat down in one of the world's most uncomfortable chairs. It might have been psychology, to keep those sinful little mothers-to-be, or those poor, precatory, infertile couples, from feeling comfortable. More likely it was simply economics. Whatever the reason, I had to hold on to the arms to keep from sliding onto the floor. I was glad I wasn't pregnant. "It's Mrs. Kozak," I said. Her eyes shifted to my left hand and rested on my ring finger. "I'm a widow."

"I see." She leaned back in her chair and tented her fingers. I could tell she found that inappropriate. Probably, like Lorna, she thought widows ought to be old. "What brings you to Serenity House?"

"Mrs. Ireland suggested I contact you," I said. "My sister, Carolyn McKusick, was born at Serenity House. I'm trying to help find her birth parents."

Her eyebrows rose. I had the impression she and Mrs. Ireland weren't simpatico. "How old is Carolyn?" she asked.

"Twenty-one."

"Why isn't she here herself? It's not usual for a family member, like yourself, to be searching, instead of the adoptee. Except, sometimes, for husbands. Husbands sometimes help."

"Carrie isn't able to do this herself. She isn't very well." I didn't tell her how unwell Carrie was. "She asked me to help her, since she can't do it herself." Which was sort of the truth, if you believed in dreams.

Ms. Pappas didn't seem to know what to make of me. I guess I wasn't her usual sort. She took some time to look me over, her nostrils flaring slightly as her eyes roved over the purple shirt. I wished I'd worn something more conservative. She studied her tented hands again. "Do you have any sort of authorization from your sister? Something which would indicate her approval of this conversation?" I shook my head. I hadn't thought of that. "I mean," she said, "how do I know you are who you say you are, and that you're really related to this person, Carolyn McKusick, if she is, in fact, one of our adoptees?"

I pulled out my wallet, took out my driver's license and the family photo, and laid them on the desk. She picked them up and studied them. "You're not adopted," she said. "The blond is your sister, Carolyn?"

"Yes." I put my license away. I reached for the photo, but she pulled it back and looked at it again.

"Are your parents aware that your sister wants to conduct this search and that you are helping her?"

That was the question I'd been dreading. The standard rule about lies is to stay as close to the truth as possible and don't lie about things that can be easily checked. She seemed like the type to immediately pick up the phone and call my parents. I didn't want her to do that, so I told the truth. Sort of. "Yes, they know," I said. "They don't want to be involved, and they don't want to know what we find out." Her face was unreadable. So far, other than the nostril flare, she'd reacted to nothing. At this she nodded.

"At Serenity House," she said, "we may be a bit old-fashioned, but we believe that the commitment made to the birth mother to protect her identity should be honored. I recognize that times are changing, and many today are arguing in favor of open adoption. We don't do open adoptions here. It's dangerous, almost obscene, really, letting these young girls go shopping for families for their babies. Practically selling them, sometimes." She shook her head sadly. "Those poor desperate parents will do anything to convince the girls to give them babies. But once the birth parents know the adoptive parents, what is to keep some confused young mother from showing up on the doorstep once, or even many times, changing her mind about whether she's willing to give up the baby? How can adoptive parents ever relax and develop a relationship with their child, not knowing when the birth mother may show up again or what she may do?"

I didn't know what to say. But it was more a monologue than a conversation, so I just sat and waited for her to finish. At least I knew where she stood — one hundred percent in my mother's camp.

"That," she said, "is why we have a policy of not releasing any identifying information. What did your sister want to know?"

"Anything you could tell us about her mother and father. Their ages, where they came from, religion, ethnic background, were they married, are there other siblings, is there any history of health problems, who her parents were. I know you're familiar with this kind of request, Ms. Pappas. Carrie wants to know what all adoptees want to know — who she is." I imagined some of the people from this morning's meeting sitting here in my place, in this unwelcoming office with this hard, opinionated woman. No wonder they needed support groups. No wonder they were angry. Adults still required to get their parents' permission to find out who they were, forced to listen to lectures about how indecent their desire to search was.

"In my opinion," Ms. Pappas said, "it is a mistake to tell adoptees anything. It only whets their appetites for more, and leads them along the road to tragedy, but our board has decided we can share nonidentifying information without violating the privacy of the birth parents or the adoptive parents. I'll see if I have the file." She crossed to a bank of filing cabinets, pulled a key from her pocket, and unlocked one. She jerked open a drawer, thumbed through the index tabs, and hauled out a file. She slammed the door shut and came back to the desk. Before she opened the file, she picked up the photo again, studied it, and looked at me. She seemed angry. Well, she'd told me she didn't approve of this, hadn't she? "I hope you have a pen," she said, "and paper? I'm only going through this once. I should have left half an hour ago. I only stayed to accommodate you."

She opened the file.

I pulled out my notebook. "All set."

"Your sister Carolyn was born at Mercy Hospital on June 18, 1969. Her mother was white, eighteen, and a high school graduate. She was not Catholic, as most of our mothers are, but Protestant. She came from a small town. Her father, that is, the birth mother's father, was a businessman. Her mother was a housewife. The birth mother's name was Elizabeth. She was called Betsy. She was unmarried at the time of the birth. She stayed here at Serenity House for five months. She had no visitors during her stay, and received no mail. Her labor was long and difficult, and the baby weighed less than five pounds. The birth mother was extremely depressed during the pregnancy, and once attempted suicide."

She stopped reading and glared at me. "The mother came from Maine. There is no information in this file about the father, which is a little unusual, except where there was rape or incest. There is no indication either of those was the case here. And that is all." She closed the file firmly. "Perhaps now you will follow the advice your search group has given you, and see if you can find the hospital records. They won't help, even if you can find them. All our mothers used false names to protect their privacy. Which is how it should be."

She stood up and came around the desk. "I won't wish you luck, because I don't want you to have it. I've only complied with the rules of our board. Go home and tell your sister to give up and get on with her life, and leave her birth mother's privacy undisturbed." She handed me back the photo. "You can also tell her I remember talking to her when she came in person, and that no, you didn't learn anything new." She was my height, half again as heavy, and smelled faintly of mothballs.

I put the photo away in my purse. Carrie must have wanted to strangle this woman. I could imagine how awful it was to know the file contained all the information she needed, and to have a few random facts uncharitably doled out by this bitter old witch. Unsocial worker would be a more appropriate title. I paused at the door. "Thank you for your time," I said. "Unfortunately, I can't pass your advice along. Carrie is dead." Her nostrils were twitching violently as I shut the door.

The girl at the desk was gone, and there was no one on the steps when I went out. It was after five; perhaps they were all at supper. I hoped the rest of the institution didn't treat these little mothers with the same bitter charity Ms. Pappas handed out. I felt begrimed with a thick layer of her condemnation and scorn. The cheerful red Saab sitting at the curb seemed like a refuge. I climbed in, locked the doors, and turned the music up loud. Don Henley promised I'd spent my last worthless evening. A lot he knew.

I'd skipped breakfast and lunch, nothing new, and I was hungry enough to eat a horse, or the next pedestrian who crossed my path. Luckily, before I saw a likely pedestrian I saw a shiny, fifties-style diner, replete with chrome and neon lights and a few vintage cars out front. Inside, a perky waitress with a poodle skirt and a ponytail told me to sit anywhere I wanted. I slid onto the vinyl bench in a corner booth. There was a little chrome jukebox at each table. I ordered a burger deluxe, fries, a chocolate milkshake, and fed the box a quarter to play "Mr. Blue" and "Blue Moon." The place was pleasant, but I was still feeling blue.

Right now my world was a wallow of murder, violence, and sad women with unwanted babies. Poor Carrie. Poor me. Chocolate is supposed to contain chemicals which elevate moods, and right now mine needed elevating. I listened to the music and wondered if I'd learned anything useful. I pulled Carrie's notes out of my briefcase and spread them on the table. No wonder she'd crossed off Serenity House. I didn't know enough to know whether I'd learned anything useful. The book said write down everything. Any random fact might be important — a name, a date, a place. If this was all I ended up with, what could I do? Erect a huge billboard in Kittery that said, "If

154

your name is Betsy, you once attempted suicide, and you had a baby girl at Mercy Hospital on June 18, 1969, please call me"? No. I had to get more.

After Serenity House Carrie had written *Mercy Hospital* and her birth date. Then just a name, Agnes Deignan, and a telephone number. I didn't want to call the number until I had some idea who Agnes Deignan was. It looked like my next step was Mercy Hospital. I wondered if there was anyone in the records department who might be willing to talk to me on a Saturday night.

I finished eating and asked for my check. It was ridiculously small. I left a big tip for the girl in the poodle skirt and went out to the car. So far, the chocolate was having no effect. I still felt like kicking kittens and babies. I slammed the door with a big, satisfying thunk and sat glaring at the windshield, wondering if I should look for a pay phone. Then I remembered. This was a luxury car. I had a phone right beside me.

I called Mercy Hospital, and asked for the records department. The first person I spoke to didn't even understand what I was talking about. I got her to transfer me to someone else, a woman with such a bad cold she sounded like she should have been hospitalized herself. I asked her if Mercy Hospital still had its records from 1969. She said, "What?" I repeated my question and she repeated her "What?" four times before she said, "I'm sorry. This cold's gotten into my ears and I can't hear a thing you're saying. I'd better transfer you to someone else."

She transferred me to a man with a heavy Boston accent who listened to my question, asked me a few clarifying questions about what I was seeking, and then, just when I'd gotten my hopes up that I might learn something, said, "Sorry, lady, I don't know."

I was getting impatient. Good thing it was a rented car. If it was my own, I might have broken something in exasperation. "Well, sir," I said, "you're the third person I've spoken to who doesn't know. Is there anyone I can speak to who might know?"

"Might know what?" he said.

"Might know if the hospital still has records from 1969," I said, trying to keep the impatience out of my voice.

"Oh well," he said, "you probably oughta speak to someone in the records department."

"I thought you were in the records department."

"Don't know why you'd think that," he said, "I'm just here at the information desk. You shoulda said you wanted records. Hold on. I'll transfer you."

I waited patiently through a series of clicks and silences and ended up listening to a dial tone. I pressed redial and got a bored-sounding voice saying "Mercy Hospital?"

"Records department, please."

"Hold on, please. I'll transfer you." This time the series of clicks and beeps connected me to an answering machine which informed me the department was open Monday through Friday from ten to four and asked me to call back then. I hung up and tried again.

This time I told the bored voice that I needed some information from records right away, and instead of getting the recording I got a real human voice. It wasn't any more helpful than the recording. I persisted, got shuffled around to about seven different people, none of whom knew anything, and finally gave up, sure of only one thing — I never wanted to be a patient at Mercy Hospital. The only useful information I'd obtained was that in the morning Mr. Coffin would be working in records, and he knew everything. I decided to pay Mr. Coffin a visit the next day. It's hard to shuffle someone around or hang up on them when they're standing right in front of you. I started the car and went home to assemble my props.

CHAPTER 18

I FOLLOWED Ms. Pappas's advice and wrote a simple letter from Carrie authorizing people to assist me in my search, tracing her signature at the bottom. I planned to tell people, if necessary, that my sister was sick and we needed her parents' medical histories. After consulting my medical dictionary, I decided that if I was pressed about the nature of her illness I would say that Carrie was pregnant and being tested for diabetes, and I was trying to locate the birth parents to see if there was a family history of diabetes. Thus armed, I showered and dressed carefully for my assault on the unknown Mr. Coffin.

Usually I dress to minimize my figure and subdue my wild hair, but there are times, as Suzanne recognized when she rescued me from the hospital, when a genteel yet sexy approach can be very effective. So today I wore a fitted jersey dress in soft sea green with a demure V-neck, a wide belt, green suede pumps with modest heels, and a simple gold necklace. I left my hair loose, wore a tweedy perfume and gold wedding band earrings. What little bruising was left on my face I covered with makeup. I hate makeup but I could see that at times like this it had its uses. It was cold, so I wore my sexy green leather trench coat and carried a black leather briefcase. I creaked like a saddle when I walked.

Mercy Hospital was a hodgepodge of new and old buildings, perched on a mound of high ground at the edge of the city. I left my car in the garage and followed the signs into the main building. I told the woman at the information desk I was there to see Mr. Coffin and asked directions to the records department. "Down the hall, take your second right, and then take the elevator to the third floor and follow the signs," she said. She didn't seem to find it odd that I was there on a Sunday.

I half expected, after the runaround I'd gotten on the phone, that her directions would lead me to some totally random place

157

like the nutrition department or nuclear medicine, but when I exited the elevator on the third floor, a sign said: RECORDS DEPARTMENT. An arrow pointing left said, OFFICE AND INQUIRIES, one pointing right said, AUTHORIZED PERSONNEL ONLY. I went left. Facing the hall was a glass window with three openings. The sign said, INQUIRIES. I looked through the glass. There was no one interested in answering my inquiry. At the far end of the room, three women were smoking and drinking coffee. I got a business card out of my wallet and knocked on the glass. They stared at me for a while, and finally one woman came over. "We're closed, honey," she said. "Open Monday through Friday, ten to four." She started walking away.

"I'm looking for Mr. Coffin," I said. "Is he here?"

"Down the other way, past the elevators," she said.

I walked past the AUTHORIZED PERSONNEL ONLY sign until I came to a reception desk. A pert little redhead with masses of freckles was reading *People* magazine. She grinned at me. "Authorized personnel only," she said.

I handed her my card. "I'm here to see Mr. Coffin," I said.

She snapped her gum and studied the card. It took her quite a while to read it, even though all it said was "EDGE," which is the name of our consulting group, and Theadora Kozak, with my phone number. "He expecting you? He didn't say anything."

I stepped closer to the desk and leaned forward so that I towered over her. "I don't think so," I said, "but it's very important that I see him."

"Wait here," she said, and bounced away through the door behind her. She bounced back a minute later. "Follow me," she said. The door led to a corridor of small offices. Mr. Coffin's was the first one on the right. She pointed at the door. "Go ahead in." She didn't wait to see if I followed her instructions.

I knocked on the door, and walked in. Mr. Coffin was about my height, with a tight body and well-cut fair hair. His suit pants had pleats, he wore gold-rimmed glasses, and there were impressionist flowers on his tie. Either he was into sartorial splendor or he hadn't gone home last night. He stood up when I came in and held out his hand. "Ms. Kozak?" he said. "Please sit down. What did you want to see me about?" He gave me the same once-over I'd given him, and seemed equally impressed.

I took off my heavy coat and sat in one of the visitor's chairs. "I'm sorry to bother you on a Sunday, Mr. Coffin," I said. "I understand you are the senior person in the records department today. I need your help locating records from 1969."

"We don't keep records that long," he said automatically, but his curiosity got in the way of his brush-off. "Why are you looking for records from way back then?"

I pulled out Carrie's letter and a tissue, and handed him the letter. "My sister Carrie is very sick, Mr. Coffin. Her doctors think the condition may be hereditary, and they'd like to get her family medical history. But she is adopted, you see, so I'm trying to find them — her real parents, I mean. I don't really know what I'm doing here, I'm just trying to help, and I don't know much about this search business, but I read in a book that hospitals sometimes keep their records a long time, and I was hoping you'd have a record of her birth and I'd find some information there which would help me." I delivered my speech with as much conviction as I could muster, and dabbed at my eyes with the tissue. "Are you sure there are no records?"

He handed me back the letter. "I'm afraid, without permission from the trustees, that we really cannot let you see those records."

"You mean you do have them?" I said, giving him my best smile and the full benefit of my green-eyed gaze. I leaned forward and seized his hand in both of mine, pulling my elbows together. The forward-lean-and-elbows trick filled my V-neck with cleavage. A cheap trick I'd learned in high school. Learned it accidentally, when I pulled my elbows together to hide the chest I was still shy about and my breasts almost popped out of my sweater. His eyes went to my chest, my face, and back to my chest again. It was a cheap, sleazy trick, and I was ashamed to be using it. I embrace the basic Superman virtues, truth, justice, and the American way, but if I got what I wanted here, the end would justify the means. That was also a tried and true part of the American way.

"We both know how committees work," I said. "Getting the trustees' permission could take weeks, Mr. Coffin, and I'm just at the beginning of my search. Carrie might die before I find her parents. Please help me." Feeling like an actress in an afternoon soap opera, I squeezed his hand and sighed. "Don't send me away empty-handed. That lady at the adoption agency was so terrible. You'd think it was a crime to be adopted. Don't say you won't help me either."

I bent my head and checked the cleavage. Positively blooming. I sneaked a look at Mr. Coffin. His eyes were locked on my chest. I raised my grief-stricken face. "No one would know you did this except you and me, and I'll always be grateful. Please say yes." I waited. I sensed that he wanted to help, but felt bound by the rules. Still, his tie told me he wasn't entirely conventional. I brought my elbows closer together and waited while he struggled with his conscience. Justice had better prevail soon. My arms were getting tired.

Suddenly he rose out of his chair. "Oh, rules be damned," he said. "Of course I'll help you. We'll go down there right now and look for those records." I grabbed my briefcase and followed him. As we passed the redhead he said, "We're going to get some coffee, Kim. Back in twenty, OK?" She nodded and snapped her gum. Bored and uncurious. We took the elevator to the basement. I followed him through a maze of corridors to a door marked RECORDS. He pulled a key out, unlocked the door, and snapped on the lights. It was an awesome sight. A warehouse-sized room jammed with seven-foot metal shelves bulging with manila files.

"Quite a sight, isn't it?" he said.

"I'm glad I'm not alone," I said. "It would take a lifetime to search through these."

"You're luckier than you think," he said. "The records you want are on microfilm. Over here." I followed him to a table with a microfilm reader. At the back of the table, and on many more tables along the wall, were drawers of film. "Do you know the birth mother's name?" he asked.

I shook my head. "Only the birth date, and her mother's first name. Her birth date was June 18, 1969. Her mother was at Serenity House."

He was scanning the rows of drawers, looking for the right date. "Serenity House, eh? You've already been there? Of course, you said you had. So you've met the delightful Esther Pappas?"

"Yesterday," I said. "It was brutal. You know her?"

"This city is really just another small town," he said. "Serenity House is still in business, you know. We still have their girls delivering here. And she's their social worker. A superb example of a person totally unsuited for her job. Besides," he said, smiling, "you aren't the first person to come searching for birth records, you know. Did she tell you not to bother?"

"She did. She said all the girls used assumed names and the records wouldn't tell me anything. What do you think?"

"You're here, aren't you? So you didn't believe her." His eyes stopped roving. He opened a drawer, pulled out a roll of film, and began threading it into the reader. "You ever use one of these things?"

"I used to be a reporter, briefly," I said.

"Great," he said. "I'm beginning with the records for the seventeenth, when she might have been admitted. Serenity House always had a slightly punitive attitude toward their girls..." He paused. "I hope you don't mind if I say girls. Most of them are very young."

"I had the same reaction myself," I said.

"So they used to let them labor a while to punish them for their sins before bringing them in. Poor little things. All alone and scared and in pain." He stood behind me as I scanned the film, looking for a patient named Elizabeth or a woman who'd had a baby girl on June 18. I came to the end of the roll and shook my head. "Nothing on this one." He put it away and brought another. And then another. It was on the third film, but I almost missed it.

"Wait," he said, "go back to that last one."

Together we stared at the record. On June 18, a woman named Elizabeth Alden had been admitted from Serenity House and given birth to a female infant weighing only four and a half pounds. "I'll bet this is it," I said. "You've done this before, haven't you?" He nodded. "What am I looking for?"

"Clues. Names, addresses, places, other people or organizations that might have records," he said. "Don't you have that handy booklet?"

"I do. But it still seems mysterious. How will I know what's important?"

"You'll know," he said. "Things just jump out at you." He checked his watch. I felt like we'd been there for an hour, but it had been less than ten minutes. "I shouldn't be doing this," he said. "Hospital policy is that when someone other than the patient wants to see the records and they don't have written consent from the patient, they have to fill out a request form stating the purpose of the request, which is then reviewed by the hospital board to determine whether access will be granted. The board is very conservative — that is, they share the Pappas view that access should be restricted."

"So why did you say yes?"

He put his hand on my shoulder. "How could I say no to a lady in distress?"

I felt the warmth of his hand through my dress. I turned around and looked at him. His eyes were twinkling behind the academic glasses. He looked as impish as my brother Michael used to look when he was plotting a raid on the cookie jar. He'd seen right through my sexy-damsel-in-distress act. So why was he helping? "You believe in helping people like my sister, don't you?" He nodded. "Do you ever say no to helping people search for their birth parents?"

"Often," he said. "I have to. I'm not usually alone in the department. And there's usually an old battle-ax guarding the door. A real stickler for rules and regulations. The lovely Kim only comes in and snaps her gum on weekends. But I'm on your sister's side. I believe people have a right to information about themselves." He dropped his hand. "Let's see what we've got." Slowly we scrolled through the pages. There wasn't much. As I interpreted the information, which was scrawled in barely comprehensible medicalese, the labor had been long and difficult, just as Mrs. Pappas had said, and the birth normal. The baby was small but healthy. The mother had no appetite and no visitors. Mother was returning to Hallowell, Maine, and social services notes indicated she had been encouraged to seek counseling there. Not a word about the father. Bills were to be sent to Dr. Peter Deignan.

I made a note about Hallowell, Maine, and wrote down the birth mother's own birth date, as possible identifying information, but I didn't see how it would be useful if I didn't know the mother's surname. I turned to my guide. "Mr. Coffin, do you know who Dr. Peter Deignan is?"

"Bill," he said.

"Bill?"

"Call me Bill, please," he said. "Coffin is a pretty grim name, you'll have to agree. Dr. Deignan was a local OB. Delivered most of the babies for Serenity House. And much of the rest of town. A real nice man. Grandfatherly. Probably one of the only truly nice people those poor girls encountered around here. It was a real loss to the community when he died. Practiced right up to the end, too."

The tide of optimism I'd felt when I saw Dr. Deignan's name in the records ebbed away. Then I recalled Carrie's notes. "Did he have a wife named Agnes?"

"He sure did," Bill said, checking his watch again. "She lives right around the corner. You ought to go and see her. She might still have his records around, and she loves company." He pointed at the screen. "You done with this? I'd better get back upstairs, before someone comes screaming for a record." He put the film away, and gestured toward the door. "After you, Theadora," he said. He followed me to the door, pausing with his hand on the light switch. "Are you married?"

"No."

"Good," he said. "Call me callow, or rapacious, or a sexist pig, or whatever you want, but I can't end a half hour alone with a woman as gorgeous as you with a handshake." He put his hands on my shoulders, drew me toward him, and kissed me. A nice kiss. Gentle and friendly, and offering better things to come. I enjoyed it. "That's what you get," he said, "for flashing those breasts at me. I'm only human." He locked the door behind us and we walked to the elevator. The car that came was empty. "You take this one," he said. "I'll wait for the next one. Good luck with your search. I hope things work out OK for your sister, and if you ever need more records, or... or anything... you know where to find me." The door closed slowly on his boyish grin. I stood staring at the fingerprint-smudged door, grateful for his kindness, and feeling slightly guilty for not telling him the truth.

CHAPTER 19

UPSTAIRS IN THE lobby I found a pay phone and called Mrs. Deignan. The phone rang so long I was about to give up when a faint, breathless voice said, "Hello." I explained who I was and why I was calling. Mrs. Deignan confirmed that she was indeed the person I wanted, and insisted I must come for lunch. "I've just made a big pot of split pea soup," she said. "I'll never be able to eat all of it alone." My watch said it was after twelve, and as usual, I'd skipped breakfast. My stomach told me that Mrs. Deignan's offer was too good to refuse. She asked me where I was, and laughed when I said I was at Mercy Hospital. "Why, you could walk from there, dear," she said, and gave me directions.

Outside it was cold and gloomy, and I shivered in my thin jersey dress. I was halfway across the dimly lit parking garage, looking through my briefcase for the keys, when I remembered that I'd left my coat in Bill's office, and the keys were in the pocket. I turned back, feeling like a bird dog called away from a falling pheasant. I hadn't gone far when I saw a blond man coming toward me waving something in the air. Bill. He was waving my coat and his arms, and yelling, "Theadora!" Unusually uninhibited for a man, I thought.

"Over here," I called, waving back. We met between a battered Chevy Nova and a shiny red Toyota. He gallantly held the coat for me. I slipped it on and checked in the pocket for my keys. "Thanks, Bill. You're a prince," I said. "I'm on my way to Mrs. Deignan's for lunch."

He grinned. "You'll like her." He hesitated, as though about to say more, then turned and walked away.

Mrs. Deignan lived in a perfect grandmother's house, gingerbreaded, with a peaked roof and a wide, inviting porch, surrounded by gardens and shrubs. From her voice, I'd been expecting a feeble old lady, but the woman who answered the door was maybe midsixties, small and vibrant, with rusty red hair and apple-pink cheeks. She wore cinnamon-colored sweats with streaks of mud on the knees and Wellington boots. She held out a callused hand. "Are you Theadora? Nice to meet you. Come on in. I was just out back dividing up some daylilies. They get their little toes intertwined and get in each other's way and stop blooming, so I had to thin them, but now I've got enough extras to plant a couple acres. You wouldn't like some daylilies to take home, would you?"

"I wish I could take some. I love daylilies, but I don't have any gardens. I live in one of those cookie-cutter condos with managed plants — neatly trimmed shrubs and borders of boring annuals, and that's all. Do you do all these gardens yourself?" I asked. I was jealous. I enjoy gardening, and while the condo is extremely convenient for a workaholic, it is rather sterile.

Mrs. Deignan smiled. "Yes. I do. I have a high school boy for some of the 'strong back' work, but otherwise it's all mine. Being a doctor's wife, I found out early on that I needed to keep busy or I started feeling sorry for myself with him being away so much. When the children were little, they kept me busy, but children grow up. Flowers are nice, you know. They always need some kind of attention. And in the winter I knit. I've probably knit enough mittens in my life to cover all the hands in Braintree. What do you do to keep busy? Do you work?"

Mrs. Deignan didn't stand still while she talked; she moved. I followed her past a wide staircase with a gleaming banister, down a hall carpeted with an Oriental runner, through the dining room and into the kitchen. Somewhere on our journey from the front door to the kitchen, I shed my coat. The kitchen was big and old-fashioned, with tall glass-fronted cupboards and a polished oak floor. A big oak worktable stood in the middle, waiting to be photographed for some home magazine. On it were a clay-colored bowl of apples, a green marble pastry board, and a freshly baked apple pie. "I must be in heaven," I said.

"Not too many people confuse Braintree with heaven," she said. "Does that mean you're hungry?"

"Starved," I said. "I keep forgetting to eat. But I'm sorry, you asked if I work. Yes, I do. I'm a consultant to independent schools. I know consultant is a dirty word to a lot of people. But I'm a consultant who really does work. I work most of the time, so it's a good thing I enjoy what I'm doing. I advise private schools about admissions issues, things like how to change their image and how to attract the type of students they want."

"Sounds interesting," she said. "But why do you work all the time?" She picked a stack of magazines and newspapers off a chair. "Sit down, please."

"It keeps my mind off other things," I said.

"I see," she said, nodding. Her expression was curious, but she wasn't about to pry. "But you aren't here to consult about private schools. I assume you're here to look at some of Pete's old records. Are you another one of our adopted babies?"

"Not me, Mrs. Deignan," I said. "My sister Carrie was adopted. I'm trying to find her birth parents." I pulled the family photo out and showed her. "That's Carrie. I think she came to see you."

"Call me Agnes," she said, taking the picture. She took it over to the window, squinted at it, then pulled a pair of half-glasses out of her pocket, put them on, and looked again. "The little blond girl?" she said. I nodded. "Yes," she said, "your sister came to see me. A lovely girl. We had such a nice visit, and I believe she found some very useful information in Pete's files." She turned on the gas under a large tea-kettle. "Sit down, Theadora," she said again. "You look tired."

"I'll call you Agnes if you'll call me Thea," I said. "Theadora is just too much name." She nodded as though she knew exactly what I meant. I was too restless to sit down; instead I circled the kitchen, watching Agnes fix lunch. Things seemed to be moving too fast. Only a few days ago I'd known next to nothing about what Carrie meant when she said she wanted to search for

167

her parents. Now I was completely immersed in it. It was like riding on a roller coaster — the rush of anticipation, the stomach-dropping plunge, the slow, anxious climb to the next peak, and then another flying rush down again. It was hard to stay here and be polite, even to someone as nice as Agnes, knowing that in a nearby room another vital clue might be waiting.

"Did your sister ever find her birth parents?"

I saw no reason to lie to Agnes, which was a relief. Lying is exhausting. "I don't know if Carrie found her birth parents. She was murdered a few weeks ago."

Agnes almost dropped the two bowls she was holding. "That sweet girl? I can't imagine anyone wanting to hurt her! These are terrible times we live in. Who would do such a thing?"

"That's why I'm here," I said. "The police don't have a suspect. They're assuming it was a sex crime, either a boyfriend or a stranger. They could be right, but I think her death is connected to her search. She told a friend at work that she'd finally had a breakthrough, and some notes they found in her car suggest she may have gone to meet someone connected with her search, but no one knows who she met. Carrie kept a diary. If we had it we'd know what was happening in her life, but whoever killed her took her keys and searched her apartment. All her personal papers have disappeared."

She was still holding the bowls, listening intently. "Neither the police nor my family understand about Carrie and her search, so they don't believe me when I tell them it could be connected. My family says I'm just having crazy ideas because I'm upset, and I should just let the police handle it. The woman who runs the search group I contacted for help said it was an inappropriate reason to search, and refused to help me. Every-one tells me not to stir things up. I feel like I'm out here all alone..." I realized that I was pouring my heart out to a virtual stranger. "I'm sorry, Agnes," I said. "I'm babbling. I don't usually go around with my heart on my sleeve." Behind her, the bright copper kettle was sending up a cloud of steam. She set the bowls down beside the stove and turned off the gas under the kettle.

"So," she said slowly, "you're duplicating her search so that you can find out what she found out or find the person she found. Aren't you afraid of what you might find? Whoever killed your sister might do the same to you."

For a minute I was speechless. I'd never considered the possibility that I might be putting myself in danger. As Carol Anderson had pointed out, all my focus had been on process. On whom to see and what to ask. On what facts might be important. It had simply never occurred to me that what I was doing could be dangerous. I admitted as much to Agnes. "To be honest, Agnes, I never thought about that. But it's a risk I'm willing to take. I can't let someone kill my sister and get away with it."

It sounded melodramatic, even to me. I tried to explain. "That sounded pompous and theatrical, didn't it? And I'm neither of those. I'm a terrible actress. But I am willing to take some chances, if necessary, to find her killer. You had to know Carrie to understand, I think. She was sort of a lost soul. Someone who inspired a desire to protect her and fix things for her. She was eight years younger — my baby sister. In a way, this is just part of taking care of her, which I didn't do so well these past few years. This is the last thing I can do for her now — make sure that someone doesn't triumph over her in death, that her killer doesn't make her life, her quest, futile or insignificant by killing her." In my mind I saw the picture of Carrie lying sprawled there on the dirt. I wondered if I'd ever be able to get that image out of my mind.

"Someone tossed her life away like she was garbage, when she was a special, beautiful person. If it was one of her parents, then they tossed her away twice. She deserved more than that." Suddenly my legs got weak. I sat down quickly. "I'm sorry," I said. "I don't know what's the matter with me, running on like this." I was mortified at the way I'd been babbling. I don't

169

believe in sharing my troubles with strangers.

Agnes poured hot water into two large mugs, dropped in tea bags, and set one in front of me. "Sometimes people just need to talk. I don't mind at all. Would you like honey with your tea?" She lifted the lid on a pot and stirred the soup, sending up a cloud of fragrant steam. "Almost ready," she said. "Why don't you make a salad while I set the table? All the stuff's in there. From my garden, every bit of it."

Relieved to have something to do, I took a deep breath and stood up carefully, hoping my legs were steady again. I opened the refrigerator and pulled out a collection of veggies, including a huge yellow onion. "You want onion in it?" I asked.

"I'm not planning to kiss anyone, are you?" she asked.

"No," I said, remembering Bill. She handed me a bowl, showed me where the knives were, and left me to it. It was pleasant working in such a nice kitchen, and Agnes was easy to be around. I made a strong mustard vinaigrette, applied the black pepper liberally, and set the bowl on the table. She ladled up the soup, sliced some warm homemade bread, and said, "Let's eat."

The food tasted as good as it smelled. I was voracious, and was relieved to see that Agnes was too. Between us, we ate half the loaf of bread, four bowls of soup, and all the salad. Agnes raised her eyebrows when she first tasted it, but then she dug in happily. "You aren't a subtle person, are you?" she said.

"I can be," I said, "but your vegetables cried out for something strong. Anyway, I hate insipid salads."

"Yes," she said, "I imagine you have little interest in insipid things." She got up and cleared away our plates. She set out clean dessert plates and a wedge of cheddar cheese. "Pete always used to say a foolish rhyme when we had apple pie. Apple pie without cheese is like a hug without the squeeze. I don't even know if I like cheese with my apple pie, but I've served them together for so long the pie would seem incomplete without cheese." She cut two huge slices of apple pie. "You

170

want cheese with yours?"

"Please." She cut a big wedge of cheese and set it beside my pie. "My dad has chocolate ice cream with pie," I said, "usually with blueberry pie, but he also likes it with apple."

Agnes made a face. "Cheese I can handle, but chocolate ice cream sounds awful." We ate our pie in companionable silence. By the time I set down my fork, I was contentedly full and feeling very grateful for a homemade meal that didn't come with strings attached. Agnes hadn't slowed down a bit. She leapt up and finished clearing the table, sliding the plates into a sinkful of soapy water. "There," she said, "we'll just let those soak while we take a look at Pete's records." I followed her back down the shiny hall, past the stairs, and into a large room near the front door. It still looked like an office. Along one wall were shelves lined with medical texts. Along another stood a bank of filing cabinets. Two upholstered chairs sat facing a wide oak desk. Behind the desk, a big leather chair was turned toward the window, as though someone had gotten out of it just moments before.

Agnes looked sadly at the big chair. "He was sitting there when he died. He'd seen his last patient and was catching up on some reading. I went in to call him for dinner. I'd made a boiled dinner for St. Patrick's Day. I hate them myself, can't stand the smell of cabbage in the house, but it was one of his favorites and he only asked for it that one time every year. His book had fallen on the floor, and he was slumped over in the chair like he'd fallen asleep. I touched his shoulder to wake him, and I knew." There were tears in her eyes. "We were good friends, Pete and I, for thirty-five years. I miss him. The children say I'm foolish to keep the office like this, but it makes me feel closer to him." She shrugged. "It's a big house. I don't need the room."

"I know how you feel," I said. "When my husband died I wouldn't even wash his dirty clothes. It made him seem close, having them around. His smell was all I had left of him." We stood together a moment, remembering our men, and then

171

Agnes shook off the memories and went over to the filing cabinets.

"Do you have the birth mother's name?" she asked.

"It's in my briefcase." I got the case and took out my notes. "Her name was Alden. Elizabeth Alden. The social worker at Serenity House said that it wouldn't be her real name."

"It probably wasn't. The girls usually didn't use their own names. Having a child out of wedlock was a real stigma twenty or thirty years ago. Now it seems to be fashionable. Did your visit to Serenity House include Esther Pappas?" I nodded. "I've often wished I had the courage to shoot her," Agnes said. "She's inflicted misery on so many poor young girls. She once told Pete he treated the girls too well. As though you could ever treat people in that unfortunate situation too well. Ah, here we are." She reached in and pulled out one of the files. "Let's take it over to the desk." She opened the file and gestured toward her husband's chair. "I'll get out of here and let you get down to business."

She walked out and shut the door behind her. I sat down in her husband's chair, opened my notebook, and read the file. It was much like the hospital record, except it covered a longer period. Full of clinical details without much personal information. It began when she was about five months pregnant and ended after her postpartum exam. She'd been about seven months pregnant when she attempted suicide, cutting her wrists with a broken bottle. I felt like a voyeur, peering into the poor girl's unhappy life, and I hadn't found anything useful. I'd almost given up when I found it, a small penciled notation on the inside of the file jacket: *Send bills to Omar Norwood, 121 Water Street, Hallowell, Maine.*

I almost shouted, I was so excited. I copied the information down in my notebook, imagining Carrie sitting in this same chair, making the same discovery. For a moment, I felt very close to her, planting my inelegant size nine where her little sixes had so recently been. "I'm getting there, Carrie," I

172

whispered. Now all I had to do was find someone named Elizabeth Norwood, probably named something else by now if she was even still alive, somewhere in the state of Maine. First, of course, I had to find Hallowell. I closed my eyes and rested my head against the cracked leather. Things seemed to be happening too fast. Better, I knew, than spending four years like that poor man I'd listened to yesterday, but I needed to pause and get my bearings before I went on. I closed the file and went to find Agnes.

She was sitting in a rocking chair by the kitchen window, knitting, looking so peaceful and content I hated to disturb her. "Agnes," I called softly, "I found it." She set down the knitting and stood up. "Don't get up," I said. "I can find my way out."

"I'm not a feeble old lady yet, dear," she said. She led the way back to the front door, found my coat, and watched as I put it on. She didn't even come up to my shoulder, but she was a forceful presence. "I've been thinking about what you said, Thea, and I'm worried," she said gravely. "I don't see how you help your sister by getting yourself killed. You shouldn't be doing this alone. You say you haven't thought about risks, but if your intuition is right — and I'm a great believer in intuition — there are risks. I thought about volunteering but it isn't practical, even if you could imagine a little old lady as your sidekick, but there must be someone who can help you. What about someone in your family? Your boyfriend?"

I shook my head. "Not really. My family thinks I should forget the whole thing, and I haven't got a boyfriend. The police detective on the case might be helpful, if I could convince him that I know what I'm doing. He's the only one I can think of."

She put a hand on my arm and spoke very seriously. "Then you must promise me you'll try to persuade him to help you. Promise me, Thea." Her concern touched me. I'd only known her a few hours, yet she seemed more concerned about me, and interested in what I was trying to do, than my own family. I promised that I'd get in touch with Andre Lemieux before I tried to contact Carrie's birth mother. She hugged me. "Be careful, Thea," she said, and pressed something into my hand. I looked down. It was a pocket-sized container of Mace. "A present from my son. He worries about me living here alone. I hope you won't need it, but you never know."

"Thank you, Agnes," I said, "for everything." There were tears in my eyes as I stumbled down the steps. They mingled with the rain that had begun while I was inside. But despite the rain and my tears, I felt a vague excitement. Like a hunting dog that's picked up a scent, I was on the trail that Carrie had been following, and wherever it went, I would follow.

CHAPTER 20

I DROPPED MY keys on the counter and threw my coat over a chair. It was a relief to be free of it. It looked nice, and I felt sexy in it, but it weighed a ton. I leaned wearily against the wall, wishing I could just slide down onto the floor and go to sleep. The light on my answering machine was blinking frantically, demanding attention. But after a long day walking in Carrie's footsteps, I was wrung out. I didn't even want to listen to anyone, let alone talk to them, even though there is something compelling about the phone. The night was young, but I felt old.

Meeting Agnes and Bill had been bright spots in the gloom. Both of them had been wonderfully helpful and kind, but all the kindness and goodness in the world couldn't change the reason I'd gotten into this search. Carrie was still dead and her killer was still at large. And now there was a new figure in the picture. As I followed Carrie's lead, and learned what she had learned, I was seeing what she had seen — the lonely, suicidal woman who had been her real mother. A burden Carrie had borne in silence. Maybe that was why she'd call me, because she needed to talk about it. But I hadn't returned her calls, so I would never know. I could hear the harsh voice of Esther Pappas, "Tell your sister to give up and get on with her life..." Perhaps if Carrie had taken that advice she'd still be alive. But Carrie's real mother had been an issue all her life. She couldn't have walked away from the search having learned so much and just lived with the specter of that elusive, unhappy woman.

Now that I'd put myself in Carrie's shoes, I couldn't walk away either. I'd started this search because I felt I had to do something tangible to help solve the mystery of her death. I hadn't reckoned on how emotionally draining it was going to be. My head hurt from the crash of the wipers on the rainy drive home, and from the anticipation of the task that lay before me. I hadn't completely recovered from last week's assault, and after the long day, my side hurt and I was bone-tired.

Thank goodness Agnes had fed me. Now that I was home I wasn't going out again, and the cupboards were pretty bare. I was too tired to fix something anyway. I made myself a drink, changed into a cozy velour robe and warm socks, curled up in the chair, and pushed the message button. The first message was some anxious breathing followed by a click. Some machine phobic. The second was David's old friend Larry, who liked to call and leave me jokes. Without preamble he said, "Hey, Thea. Did you hear the one about the agnostic, dyslexic insomniac? He sat up all night wondering if there was a dog." I laughed so hard I inhaled my bourbon and almost missed the next message.

"Hi, Thea. It's Dad. Your car is fixed and you can pick it up anytime. The deductible is two hundred fifty dollars, plus fifty for the towing. You need to call and let them know when you'll pick it up. Erikson Saab in Thomaston. I don't have the number. Hope you're taking it easy. Give us a call."

Silence, followed by a ring, a click, and a new voice. "Thea? It's Andre Lemieux, the state trooper you suspect may not be human. I hate these machines." There was a long silence. "I called to apologize for not believing you. I asked Bob about your blood-alcohol level. You remember Dr. Bob — good medical training, lousy bedside manner? They had tested it, and it was virtually nil. So I took your advice and checked the bottles for prints. Like you said, you never touched them." Another long pause. I could hear him breathing. "So I'm sorry I was such a horse's ass. When are you coming up to get your car and clean out the apartment? Give me a call when you do. Or if you need to be picked up at the airport, or something. I want to see you. Please." A click, then silence.

There was a message from the headmaster of Acton Academy, asking if I could meet with his board on Thursday to go over our report and recommendations. A message from another school, wanting to set up a meeting to discuss a proposal we'd made. Two dinner invitations. A cold call from an agitated broker. And last, but not least, a shrill call from Mrs. Bolduc, wondering when I was coming back to clean out the apartment and reminding me that time was passing.

I turned the machine off, thinking about Andre. It was nice of him to call. Generalizing from my prejudice against the police, I'd judged him too macho to consider an apology. It would be nice to see him again, sometime when I wasn't too busy doing his work for him. I took my glass to the kitchen, switched from bourbon to diet soda, and sprawled on the couch, remote control in hand, giving myself up to the wasteland of television, too tired to think. Don Johnson and company obligingly entertained me with the stubble, sweat, a rain of bullets, and much masculine angst.

Despite the rampant sweat and testosterone on the screen, I fell asleep. The doorbell woke me about an hour later. I stumbled sleepily to the door, puzzled by the intrusion. No one drops in on me on Sunday nights. First of all because I'm usually at the office anyway, but even when I am home, Sunday night is reserved for mending clothes, ironing, doing laundry, conditioning my hair, and watching mindless television. I peered through the spy hole. An attractive brown-haired man was standing there. I had never seen him before. "Who is it?" I called.

"Let us in, Thea," Suzanne said. I looked again. She was standing behind the man, so I hadn't seen her at first. I undid the latch and opened the door.

"Hey," I said, "I thought you were in New Hampshire for the weekend."

"It has been raining," she said. "Didn't you notice? No, you probably didn't. You haven't been in the office all weekend, have you?"

"No," I said, "Detective Kozak has been on the case. Is this Paul?" They both looked glowing and healthy and outrageously happy. I hadn't been hiking since David died. We used to do a lot of it, taking the less traveled trails so we could detour to make love in mossy glades off the beaten path. I recognized their healthy flush. Sex. They'd found their own bed of moss.

Suzanne waved a bottle of champagne. "We wanted you to celebrate with us, Thea. Paul and I are getting married."

I bit back the first three comments that came to mind. I didn't need to point out that he was already married. Suzanne knew that. Nor that he was a bad risk, being caught on the rebound. Instead I hugged her, and kissed Paul. "I'll get some glasses," I said. I went into the kitchen, got the silver champagne cooler and three flutes, filled the cooler with ice, and took it all back into the living room on a tray. I poured a jar of macadamia nuts into a dish, dug out some cheese that wasn't moldy and crackers that weren't stale, and put that out, too. Paul deftly popped the cork without blinding anyone and filled our glasses. I raised my glass. "To happiness," I said. The doorbell rang. I touched my glass to theirs, drank a sip, and set it down. "Be right back."

Once again I peeked through the spy hole. This time I recognized the man on the doorstep. Andre Lemieux. I opened the door and stepped back so he could come in. His quick eyes took in my bathrobe, Suzanne and Paul, and the champagne. It probably made no more sense to him than it did to me. "I'm sorry," he said. "I don't want to interrupt your party."

"It's not a party," I said. "You remember my friend Suzanne?" He nodded. "She and Paul stopped by to tell me they're engaged. We were just having some champagne. I'll get another glass. Coat closet's over there." I gave him a gentle push. "Go ahead. You're dripping on the floor."

We sat in chairs across from Suzanne and Paul and drank champagne. They looked good together, sitting there on the sofa, Paul big and graying, the lines in his face etched by good humor; Suzanne petite and neat and outrageously happy, with eyes only for him. I was all in favor of happiness, even if I was a bit jealous. The bottle vanished quickly. Suzanne waved the dead soldier at me. "Got any more of this stuff around, Thea?"

There was still a bottle in the refrigerator left over from my dates with Steve, one I'd put there in anticipation of a romantic evening. That was before I discovered that romance wasn't in his vocabulary, at least not in his physical vocabulary. "I'll get it," I said.

Andre followed me to the kitchen. "Are you sure I'm not intruding on something private?" he said.

"No more than they are," I said. "This was a real bolt from the blue. I was asleep. They took me completely by surprise. I didn't know they were this serious." I stripped off the foil and unwound the wire.

He took the bottle out of my hands. "Here, let me do that."

"I'm not helpless, you know, Trooper," I said.

"Andre," he said. "I hear trooper enough when I'm working." He removed the cork, and set the cork and bottle down on the counter. He backed me up against the refrigerator and pinned me there with his body. "I realize that you're not helpless, ma'am, but I sort of wish you were." He gently took my face in both hands and kissed me. Not a sweet, gentlemanly kiss like Bill's, but the kiss of a man with more than just kissing on his mind. "I've been looking forward to that," he said.

"I think that's the first time I've ever kissed a horse's ass," I said.

His inquisitive eyebrows rose. "As long as it's not the last." He picked up the bottle and walked out. Paul and Suzanne were necking on the sofa. They broke apart with embarrassed smiles when we came in. Kissing in the kitchen, necking on the sofa — it could have been a high school party except I never went to those in my bathrobe. We drank the second bottle and made small talk. Andre, it turned out, had come down to pick up Carrie's medical records and interview her doctor. He'd stopped by to see if I needed a ride to Maine to pick up my car.

Maine was the next stop in my search, and I needed to get my car anyway, so I decided to take him up on his offer. "Looks like I'm going to Maine, Suzanne," I said, "so neither one of us will be at work tomorrow."

"Oh, I'll be there after all," she said. "Paul has his kids tomorrow. You coming in on Tuesday?"

"I'm not sure. Maybe. Maybe not on Wednesday either. But I'll definitely be back on Thursday for the meeting at Acton Academy. Do you mind calling tomorrow to confirm that?"

"Not at all," she said. "Should we both go?"

"I think so. It will make them feel more important if they get the head honcho. And that's you. But I'll set up a meeting with the Willis School. They want to talk about our proposal. Mrs. Pettigrew sounds very eager to start working with us."

Suzanne smiled. She liked being head honcho. But she was also fair-minded. "We're both head honchos now," she said.

"As long as we don't turn into a pushmi-pullyu, I guess we'll be OK with two heads. Seems odd, though, that as soon as I'm a partner, I stop coming to work."

"I'm assuming assaults, accidents, and murder investigations aren't going to become a chronic condition," Suzanne said.

"What's a pushmi-pullyu?" Andre asked.

"I hope not," I said. "I don't think my aging body could take it."

"Didn't you ever read Dr. Doolittle?" Paul said.

"What does that have to do with aging?" Suzanne asked.

It was all beginning to sound a little bit like who's on first. Paul pointed at Andre. "I was talking to him," he said. "Dr. Doolittle is a character in children's fiction who started off as a people doctor and decided he liked treating animals better. His house gradually became a menagerie including an animal with a head at each end called the Pushmi-Pullyu, which had trouble deciding what to do because the heads couldn't agree."

"And he had a parrot, and Jip the dog, and..."

I signaled for a time-out. "All right, you guys. Enough. We can talk about children's fiction some other time. I hate to be a party-pooper, but I've put in a hard day of sleuthing and it's worn me out."

Suzanne was already on her feet. "Sorry, Thea. We need to get going anyway. Laurie is dropping Amy and Jeremy off at eight tomorrow morning. I have to be packed up and out of there before she comes." She wrapped an arm around Paul's waist. "Now that the divorce is final, I don't have to worry so much about my presence in Paul's apartment being an issue, but I'd rather get to know the kids a little better before I start greeting them in my bathrobe." She wrapped her other arm around my waist. "Not that there's anything wrong with entertaining in your bathrobe. You do it very well. See you Wednesday. Or Thursday. Let me know which, OK?" I hugged her back, but I was feeling confused. It seemed like there was a whole chapter of the Suzanne and Paul story that I'd missed completely. When I got current matters settled, I'd have to tackle that mystery.

Andre and I walked them to the door and watched them dash away through the rain. I shut the door and faced him. "I'm not leaving," he said. "At least, not yet. I promise not to talk about fictional animals."

The combination of alcohol and exhaustion was impairing my ability to be cool and rational. I wanted him to stay, and I wanted him to go, and I didn't know which I wanted more. He took charge before I could decide, taking me by the hand and leading me down the hall to the bedroom. He sat me down on the bed, sat beside me, and took me in his arms. I could feel his body trembling as his weight forced me back against the pillows. I was trembling, too, but not with passion. Sex with David had been satisfying, intoxicating, honest, and fun. My experience with Steve had been so bad I didn't trust my instincts anymore. I wanted to sleep with Andre, but I was scared.

He reached over to unzip my robe, but I put a hand over his. "Wait, Andre," I said. "I'm not sure I'm ready for this."

I watched his face anxiously for signs of scorn or rejection, but there were none. He was smiling. "I'm afraid I'm too ready," he said, "except for the shoes. My mother told me never to put my shoes on the bedspread." He bent over and took off

181

his shoes and socks, rolling the socks up neatly and tucking them into his shoes. He walked around the bed, propped two pillows up against the headboard, and lay down on the other side, leaving a wide expanse of bed between us. "What aren't you ready for, Thea? Sex? Involvement? Undressing in front of a stranger? I'm afraid I'm guilty of assuming that because I want this so much, you must want it, too. I didn't mean... I don't mean... to rush you. We can take things as slow as you want."

Already it was clear this man was no Steve. I sat cross-legged on the bed, facing him. He was wearing a blue shirt with rolled-up sleeves and tan cords. He looked comfortable and sexy and friendly, waiting patiently for me to speak. I looked down at my hands, clenched in my lap. "I haven't done this for a long time," I said. "There's only been one man since David. It was a disaster. He made me feel like trash because I had needs and desires of my own. I don't want to get into something with a man I can't talk to. I'm afraid to trust my instincts. Oh, I don't know. I can't seem to say it right."

He was watching me, his eyes shining. "I'm listening," he said. "Please try to overlook the lust in my eyes. I can't help staring at you. You're even more gorgeous than I remembered. I've dreamed about you, Thea. Endless wicked, erotic, incredible dreams. And woken up and kicked myself because I was cruel to you at the hospital. Jumping to the conclusion I was supposed to reach. Judging you, when I had no right to, and when I was wrong anyway. Doubting you after you explained. So I know I have no right to be here with you like this, but I couldn't help myself." He gently unclenched my hands, and took them in his. "Talk to me, Thea. We can go back to the living room, if that would make you more comfortable."

Maybe I could talk to him. He wasn't ashamed to apologize, and he was willing to listen. I took a deep breath. "OK," I said, "here goes. I want to sleep with you, but there are some things holding me back. I'm afraid I'll blow it again. I'm afraid I won't be satisfied. And I'm even afraid that I'll like it, and I've learned to live without sex." I shrugged. "I'm doing OK, you see. Why rock the boat?"

"Because life without sex is like champagne without bubbles. Sure, you can drink it. But it's not the same," he said. "Whew. Now I'm getting nervous. There's nothing like performance anxiety to kill desire."

"I'm sorry," I said. "I didn't mean to..." He took my hand and guided it to his body. His desire wasn't dead yet.

"I want you so badly I'm shaking," he said, "but I don't want to do anything that isn't right for you. Let's just take off a few of these clothes, climb under the covers, and see what happens. We can take it as slow and easy as you want. We don't have to do anything you aren't comfortable with. Scout's honor. We can even stop right here and just cuddle. And I promise not to call you a tease or moan about blue balls or anything else to make you feel guilty. OK?"

"OK," I said, beginning to relax.

He unbuckled his belt, took off his pants and shirt, and folded them neatly on a chair beside the bed. I sat on the bed, watching him. He stood before me in his underwear, uninhibited. "What you see is what you get," he said. He held out his hands to me. "Come here."

I took them and let him pull me to my feet. Slowly he unzipped the robe and slid it off my shoulders, down my body and into a pool at my feet. I stepped out of it and stood there in my underwear, feeling shaky. He didn't touch me; he just stood there, admiring. After a minute, he reached out and touched the fading bruise on my side, where Charlie had kicked me. "Does it still hurt?"

"Only when I laugh," I said, "or lift heavy things."

"I'll be careful," he said, reaching past me to pull down the covers. "Jump in. It's cold out here."

My bed is a big mahogany sleigh bed, with a high curving head and foot. It's always felt like a big ark, or fortress, where I'm safe and secure. Steve was never in this bed, so it isn't tainted. Andre held up the covers. I slid in and he slid in after me. A quiver went through me when our bodies touched. He turned out the light and put his arms around me. His body was hard and muscular. I buried my face in his warm chest, feeling the crisp rough hair under my cheek. He smelled like soap.

"I'm going to kiss you from head to toe," he said, starting with the side of my neck. He nibbled on my ear, and then found my mouth. We stopped there for a while, exploring, and then his lips traveled south. Along the way my remaining clothing got in the way and was discarded, and so was his.

I forgot about being afraid and surrendered to the pleasure of being with a man who liked women's bodies. Suddenly he pulled away and sat up. "Thea," he said, "what about birth control? Are you protected?"

"Yes," I said. In one smooth, quick motion, he rolled me onto my back and lowered his body onto mine. He started slowly and gently, as though afraid he'd hurt me, but my body jumped to meet his and we gave ourselves up to the ancient, satisfying art of love, our bodies showing none of the hesitation that had been in our heads, reaching a dizzying, mutually satisfying crescendo that literally rocked the bed. And all the time he was careful to keep his weight off my cracked ribs. Afterwards we lay in a sweaty, panting heap.

"Was it good for you?" he asked, finally. I could hear the satisfaction in his voice. He wasn't experiencing performance anxiety.

"My worst fears have been realized," I said. I felt him stiffen beside me. "Do you think we could do that again?"

CHAPTER 21

IT WAS A night for the record books. For my personal record book, at least. I hadn't realized how much I'd been missing. I'd felt restless stirrings, and the occasional stronger urges that had driven me to the banker. In that relationship — and it really glorified it to call it a relationship — I'd felt nothing but frustration. After that I'd pushed it all away, burying my frustrations in aerobics and work. Now it was like a dam had burst, and all my stored-up passion let loose. We spent the night like starving people at a banquet. It was insane, delirious, and fantastic. It was dawn when we finally fell asleep. When I woke, my watch said nine. Andre wasn't in the bed, but I could hear the shower running. I snuggled back down under the covers, lazily watching the patterns of sun and shade on the ceiling as I slowly woke up, feeling sore and bruised, the way you do after an excess of pleasure, but also very content.

Drawn by the appealing sound of running water, I went into the bathroom and opened the shower door. Startled, Andre whirled to face me, trapped without a weapon. "At ease, Trooper," I said. I stepped in and shut the door behind me.

I'd been too nervous last night to notice his body, the body I now knew so intimately. This morning I took the time to study it. He was very different from David. Andre had a heavier, sturdier body, comfortably furry, with big shoulders and strong legs. His bristly hair was beaded with water, and he needed a shave. His eyebrows rose slightly when I picked up the soap and began washing his chest, but he was smiling, and the smile broadened as the soap traveled lower. We ended up making slippery, soapy love against the shower wall. He rinsed and got out, and I stayed in to wash my hair, letting the hot water pour over me, wondering idly what this was all leading to..

When I arrived in the kitchen, clean, combed, and dressed, breakfast was ready and Andre was pouring out the coffee. He

hadn't shaved, and the stubble made him look slightly de-
bauched, but he also looked relaxed for the first time since I'd
known him. His quick dark eyes traced me from top to toe, as
though I was being memorized. "I've never spent a night like
that," he said. "I've heard about them, but I didn't believe it.
You're incredible."

I removed the coffeepot from his hands, set it on the stove,
and wrapped my arms around him. He smelled faintly of soap,
and felt so good. "Or insatiable," I said. "Oh, man, Andre
Lemieux, I am sore and sated and I feel like the cat that
swallowed the canary."

"Hey, lady," he said, "watch who you're calling a canary."
His grin was positively wicked. "Not too sore to sit, I hope.
We'd better eat before this gets cold." I let go of him reluctantly,
and went to the table. It was a perfect day. A few fat white clouds
were floating in an otherwise clear blue sky. The treetops
swayed gently. The thermometer said sixty-five. Some of the
leaves would have turned, along the turnpike. Too bad I was
going to miss it. Before the evening had turned into a party, I'd
been ready to sleep for a week. I'd probably slept about four
hours. I needed a clear head for the next part of my search and
I felt like a zombie. A contented zombie. A zombie who was
going to sleep all the way to Maine.

I sighed audibly as I looked at my loaded plate. There's
nothing like exercise to give you a healthy appetite. I was
ravenous. Despite my lack of supplies, Andre had managed to
make us a huge breakfast — toast and eggs, fried ham, and home
fries. My refrigerator must be completely empty now. Between
us we ate every scrap on our plates. I reached for the last piece
of toast just as he did, so we divided it. "So, what's for dessert?"
he asked, leaning back in his chair.

"This is breakfast, Lemieux," I said. "People don't eat
dessert at breakfast. I might have a frozen coffee cake."

"I could eat another whole breakfast," he said, "if you had
any more food, which you do not. Don't you worry about

starving to death?"

"I don't eat at home very much. I'm usually at work. Speaking of work, don't you have to be at work today? When do we have to hit the road?"

"I am at work," he said.

"You call the last twelve hours work?"

"Your eyes are getting greener," he said. "That's a danger signal, right? Doesn't anyone ever tease you, Thea? I already told you the last twelve hours were heaven on earth. If I died now, I'd go happy." He said it lightly, but I knew he meant what he was saying. "All I meant was that I set my own hours and go where work takes me. Speaking of work, how about being a little domestic and seeing if you can find that coffee cake. I really *am* still hungry."

"Domestic I'm not," I said, "but even I can't resist a hungry man." I rooted through the freezer, pulled out the cake and nuked it. I carried it and the coffeepot back to the table. "More coffee?" I asked.

He held out his cup. "Please," he said. He also took about half the coffee cake and put it on his plate. It vanished before I finished pouring my coffee.

"Gad, woman," he said, "what have you done to me? I never eat like this."

"The same thing you've done to me, I think. I usually have just a little birdlike appetite."

"Vulturelike, maybe," he said. I threw my napkin at him. It landed in the coffee. "I hope you understand this means war," he said, slowly getting up and coming around the table. "No one throws napkins at me and gets away with it."

I stuck out my tongue. "I ain't 'fraid of you, mister," I said. I slid out of my chair and circled away from him so that the table was between us. We circled warily around it. He had a danger-ous look in his eyes. I was afraid he was going to dive right across the table, smashing the coffeepot and half my dishes, when I was saved by the bell. The telephone bell. I went into the

187

living room and picked up the phone. The detritus from last night's celebration was still there, looking seedy in the bright light. Something else I had to take care of before we left, or I'd come back to the sour smell of old champagne. Mrs. Bolduc was on the phone, complaining before I even finished saying hello.

As soon as I could get a word in I said, "Relax. I'll be there today. The apartment will be empty by the weekend. Now, if you'll excuse me, I'm busy right now." I hung up without waiting for her reply. Andre pounced just as I set the phone back in its cradle, picking me up and tossing me over his shoulder. I landed squarely on the two cracked ribs, and the pain brought tears to my eyes. "Put me down," I gasped.

I leaned against the wall, hugging myself, waiting for the agony to subside. He stood beside me, hands thrust into his pockets, dancing from one foot to the other, the picture of abject misery. "I'm sorry, Thea," he said. "I forgot."

"Don't worry about it," I said, when I could talk again. "It was an accident."

"Why don't you pack while I clean up," he said, escaping into the kitchen.

I got out a small suitcase and began to pack, trying to take as little as possible. I included the green knit dress and a jacket in case I needed to look grown-up, and some jeans and stuff for packing up Carrie's apartment. An oversized T-shirt to sleep in, in case it got cold, though, if Andre was going to be around, I probably wouldn't need it. He seemed to be one of those people who are always warm. Besides, when we were together, we didn't sleep.

Last night was the first time since she died that Carrie hadn't been foremost in my mind. Now that I was getting ready to go back to Maine, I was on track again. Suzanne and Paul had interrupted me before I had a chance to plan just how I was going to find someone named Elizabeth Norwood who had lived in Hallowell, Maine, over twenty years ago. As soon as I was alone, I'd have to sit down and think about that. I had to be back at work on Thursday. I didn't have much time.

I snapped the suitcase shut, picked it up, and started for the door. Even that slight effort hurt. I'd let Andre carry it. Suddenly I was crying. Sitting on my bed soaking tissue after tissue, when Andre came in to see what was taking me so long.

"What is it, Thea? What's the matter?" He sat down beside me and very carefully put an arm around me.

"It's so silly," I said.

"Tell me anyway."

"It hurt to lift my suitcase, so I just thought, well, you could do it. And suddenly I was crying, because I felt so pitiful."

"Pitiful? I don't understand."

"Because I was so grateful. That there was someone around who could do things for me. That I didn't have to do everything myself, even if I was hurt, or tired. And suddenly I saw myself as needy, and it seemed pathetic that I should be so moved by having someone to do me a simple favor. Look, forget it. I can't be making myself clear..."

"I think I understand," he said. "You're the fixer. The strong one. But that doesn't mean it's not OK to want a little caring for yourself." He brushed back a strand of hair that was hanging across my face. "I'd be happy to carry your suitcase." And he got up and picked up my suitcase. No more speeches. No more questions.

I went to the closet and got out the black leather bomber jacket with the fur collar David had given me our last Christmas together. It makes me feel like a million dollars every time I wear it. When I took it off the hanger, something in my leather coat clinked. Curious, I reached in and found the little can of Mace Agnes had given me. I pictured her worried face, asking if I wasn't afraid whoever had hurt Carrie might also hurt me. I'd promised her I'd be careful. I wasn't expecting trouble, but I dropped it into my pocket. It never hurts to be prepared.

I stuck my head in the kitchen to see what still needed to be done before I left. Andre was just wiping the counters. The coffee table was spotless, the sink was empty, and the dishwasher was slurping happily to itself. "Ready when you are," I said. "You're pretty domestic for a tough guy."

"My wife trained me well," he said, watching closely for my reaction.

"Wife?" I said. "Current or ex?" If he said current I was going to whip out the Mace and let him have it. I wouldn't be made a fool of. My fingers closed around the little can in my pocket.

He read my unsubtle expression correctly. "Ex. Ex. Long time ex," he said quickly. "You aren't a very trusting person, are you?"

"No, I'm not," I said. "I can't believe I've been to bed with you, and that's a pretty pallid euphemism for what we did last night, and I don't even know if you're married. What's the matter with me?"

He came closer, tilted my face up to meet his, and stared searchingly into my face. "Nothing is the matter with you. People have to take things on faith, go with their instincts, sometimes. Like we did last night." His eyes narrowed. "Maybe you were just screwing, though I don't believe it, but I was making love to every glorious inch of you. You can think what you want, but I don't jump into bed every chance I get. I'm picky." He released my face and stepped back. "You feeling OK? Still up for a long drive?" He drove a fist into his other palm. "Damn. I know how bad ribs can be. I can't believe I did that to you."

"Shut up," I said. "I'll be fine. I'm no fragile blossom. I just can't carry my suitcase." I could worry about how I was going to finish packing when I got there. There were several hours of rest and some prescription painkillers between me and that problem. I got my briefcase and the car keys, he grabbed my suitcase, and we went out. He followed me to the rental agency and waited while I turned in the car, and then we hit the highway. On the way to Maine I slept. It didn't seem fair, he should have been just as tired as I was, but while last night's exertion was beginning to make me fade, he seemed energized. Besides, someone had to drive.

He let me sleep until we got to the Saab dealer, then he shook me gently. "Thea, wake up. Time to get your car." Sometimes a little sleep can be a bad thing, especially in the daytime. Waking up can be so hard. I felt like I was swimming through a sea of murky water; even when I got my eyes open, I still felt submerged. I couldn't seem to wake up, and my dull brain refused to work. I nestled into his shoulder. "Can't do it," I said. "Can't wake up."

He took his shoulder away, gently propping my head against the side of his seat. "I'll be right back," he said. I pushed myself upright in the seat and opened the window, sucking in the crisp air. Then I got out of the car and leaned against it, moving my arms and legs in a little warm-up dance. By the time he came back with a cup of coffee, I was beginning to show signs of life. "That's more like it," he said, handing me the cup. "I was afraid I was going to have to throw cold water on you."

I took a sip. Not bad coffee for a car dealer. "You aren't having any?" I said.

"Mine's inside," he said. "I didn't know how long it would take to revive you. I expected to have to pry you out of the car."

"You're a jerk," I said, "but a very nice jerk."

"Thanks," he said, "I guess. I hope you brought your checkbook or a major credit card. The vultures inside are waiting to feast on your bones."

"Yuk. I hope I'm not ready for vultures yet. If I throw fistfuls of greenbacks at them, will they give me the car and let me go in peace?"

He took me by the elbow and steered me toward the door. "One look at you, sweetheart, and you'll have them eating peanuts out of your hand."

The metaphors were getting very mixed, but I was having fun, so I said, "The dealership is run by elephants?"

"You might say that," he said, opening the door. Watching us from behind the counter was one of the fattest men I'd ever seen. He wore a parody of the car salesman's loud plaid jacket in bright rusty red and green that was the size of a VW beetle, and white shoes. He had close-cropped reddish hair and a voluminous red beard. He waddled toward us, hand outstretched. I stuck mine out; it was engulfed in a hand the size of a ham. "Tiny Erikson, this is my friend, Theadora Kozak."

Tiny's bright blue eyes twinkled in his fat red face. He took his time looking me over, then chuckled approvingly. He punched Andre in the arm with one of his giant fists. "So, Detective, this was one accident that was no tragedy, eh? Finally found yourself a woman. About time, too, though all the waitresses will weep and the colonel will have to look for another prospect for his daughter. She looks a handful, this one. No wonder you look like something the cat dragged in. You had quite a night, eh?"

I couldn't believe this. I could feel the red rising into my face. I looked at Andre to see how he was handling it, wondering if he'd set me up. He was grinning, but it was a puzzled grin, like he'd gotten more of a reaction than he expected. "That's enough, Tiny," he said.

Tiny nodded. "Sure thing, Detective. Didn't mean to offend Miss Kozak." He lumbered back to the counter. "If you come over here, miss, I'll get your paperwork." I followed him back to the counter. There were several guys behind the counter trying to stifle grins. "Get to work," Erikson bellowed at them. "Harry, your desk is buried in papers. Shorty, you go get the lady's car, and make sure it's clean." He searched through a mass of papers on the counter, pulled out one with my name on it, and spread it out in front of me.

"Any other car," he said, "and you wouldn't be standing here now, you know that? You should see what you did to that poor tree." He stared boldly at my face and shook his head. "I see the tree struck back. But your car is as good as new, you'll see. We do specially careful work for friends of the detective."

"Just tell me how much I owe you," I said, taking out my wallet.

"Oh, now you're mad at me, aren't you?" Tiny said sadly, turning the form around so he could see it. "The deductible is two hundred fifty, plus you owe me fifty for the towing, and two hundred for expedited repairs. So, altogether, five hundred dollars."

I'd been about to write the check, but I stopped. "Expedited repairs?" I said. "Since when does it cost extra to get things repaired promptly?"

He looked at the sheet again. "Not promptly. Promptly you'd get it maybe next week, if you're lucky. I said expedited. That means we gave it priority over other repairs. Costs extra," he said.

"But you can't charge me extra for some service I didn't ask for unless I signed something. That's outrageous. There must be some sort of consumer law that prevents you from doing that. Andre," I said, "is this legal?"

Tiny was dancing with mirth behind the counter. "Oh, it wasn't you who requested it. It was your daddy. He insisted I fix it right away. I told him it would cost extra, and he says go ahead, he'll pay the extra, his daughter needs the car. Guess he just forgot to tell you." He leered down at me, a grotesque folding of his fat. "Oh, she's a hot one, Andre," he said. "You are going to have your hands full. She a lawyer or what?"

"Will you please," I exploded, "stop discussing my attributes so that we can finish this business transaction. I'm in a hurry." I wrote a check for five hundred dollars, wrote *paid under protest* on the memo line, tore it out, and handed it to Tiny. He stuck it in a drawer and gave me a copy of the repair sheet. "Shorty's just brought your car around to the front." I grabbed the papers and stormed out the door. "Don't be a stranger, beautiful," he yelled. Behind me, I heard him say to Andre, "So, you never told me, is she good in bed?"

"What do you think?" Andre said. "See you, Tiny." He followed me out.

I was still steaming. "I can't believe you went along with that asshole," I said. "He's a dirty cheater and a sexist pig. How can you stand him?"

"Does a good job fixing cars, though," Andre said. "Look at this baby." He patted the hood. "Of course you didn't see it before, but it was a mess. And he is allowed to charge for expedited repairs, even if it does seem outrageous, if your father approved the transaction."

"And what was all that bullshit about the colonel's daughter, and the weeping waitresses?" I was getting angrier by the minute. Shorty had gotten out of the car and stood watching us, a moronic expression on his face. I swung around and pointed at him. "Get back to work," I said. "This is a private conversation, not a sideshow." He ducked his head and walked sheepishly away. "And you," I said to Andre, "how can you call that cretin a friend?"

"I didn't say he was my friend," Andre said mildly.

"You sure acted like it," I said.

"Look, Thea, you have to understand the way it is. A trooper doesn't really have friends, except other troopers. It's kind of a closed society. So he's not a friend, though maybe he wants to think he is. He was just being a guy." He sighed, exasperated with me. "Maybe we should forget about it, OK? Maybe it's something you just can't understand."

"Because I'm not a member of the club, you mean? Not a cop? So I can't understand. Cops only sleep with cops and marry cops? Must be a pretty lonely life, with so few women."

He made a face. "You're a hard woman, Thea." He set my suitcase down beside the Saab. "Going to your sister's place?" I nodded. "Maybe I'll see you later," he said. "I've got some work to do now, if, to quote a woman I met recently, I can get my mind back above my belt."

I thought I knew who that woman was. And appreciated that

it was wise of him to give me time to cool off. I opened the trunk and put my suitcase in. It hurt a little, but I didn't want him to think I was a wimp. I put my briefcase on the seat and climbed in. The engine roared to life with its comforting throb. The seat felt right. I adjusted the mirrors. Everything was fine again, but I couldn't help finding it all slightly shopworn after the fancy red number I'd been driving. Maybe it was time for a new car.

Andre tapped on the window. "I'll be over around eight to help you move boxes," he said. "Maybe you could feed me?"

I gave him a mock salute. "To hear is to obey."

"Get out of here," he growled. I left before his good humor deserted him, and stopped at a market in Camden to get supplies. Baking potatoes. Bluefish and mustard. Bacon and eggs and bread. Salad stuff. Sauerkraut and sausage and sour cream. The ingredients for Thea Kozak's earthshaking raspberry-chocolate mousse. Visions of sugarplums, or at least hot food, danced in my head as I drove up Main Street, turned on Mountain, and parked in front of Carrie's door. Good old reliable Mrs. Bolduc watched from behind her curtain as I unloaded the groceries and carried in my suitcase. I gave her my best smile and waved. The curtain twitched and she disappeared.

I put the food away, made myself a cup of tea, and sat down at the table with Carrie's notes, my notes, and the search guide Carol Anderson had given me. I had a vital piece of information now, her birth mother's name. There were several ways I might be able to find her. I could look in the phone book for Omar Norwood if he was still alive. I could search the marriage records at Hallowell Town Hall to see if anyone named Elizabeth Norwood had been married in Hallowell, to learn her married name. I could look through phone books and see if I could find a listing for Elizabeth or E. Norwood. The first two seemed most promising.

Carrie's phone was still working, so I called directory assistance. They had no listing for an Omar Norwood in

Hallowell. I called the state library and asked if they kept phone books for the whole state. They did. Tomorrow I would go to Augusta and read phone books.

CHAPTER 22

MY MAP SAID Hallowell was just below Augusta on the Kennebec River. Bright and early the next morning I was washed and shined, dressed in my success clothes, and tooling along Route 17, the road leading from the coast over to the capital city. The first part of the road was wide and smooth, swooping along past rugged hills and placid lakes, up steep inclines and through tiny villages. It was pretty country. Fat, fluffy clouds hovered along the ridge tops, while down in the valleys, the ground fog was slowly burning off, revealing fields of pumpkins, squash, and golden corn, and the blazing orange and red beauty of maple trees.

I was enjoying the best part of the day, while Andre was still sound asleep back in Camden in Carrie's bed. Mrs. Bolduc was probably having a coronary. Not only did her latest tenant have a male guest, the guest was a state trooper.

After I passed through Union, a "road narrows" sign appeared. "Road disintegrates" would have been a fairer description. I shuddered and bumped along for about ten miles, past a number of chronic yard sales, until I swept up a bumpy hill and encountered good road again. I passed a curious group of large wooden statues standing by the road, followed closely by a display of birch reindeer planters with little red noses, a flock of woolly wooden sheep, and a house under attack by a horde of wooden butterflies. On this road there were only a few bent-over ladies. Their popularity must have been waning. Now I knew how people in Maine kept busy during the long cold winters. They didn't knit, like Agnes. They went in for wood-working in a big way.

I felt Carrie's presence very strongly today, wondering how she had felt, making this same drive, knowing that at the end of it she might find what she'd been searching for. I had a such a clear picture of her. She would have been driving too fast,

197

because she always did, the music turned up too loud, the ramshackle little Chevette banging and clattering. She would have had the windows down, because it was still warm, her curly hair blowing in the wind. Like me, she would not have eaten breakfast. Carrie could never eat when she was nervous. And she would have had her notebook, because even though she was moody and impulsive, she was also a fanatic about order.

I had an advantage because I had her notes, but I was still nervous. I didn't know what I was going to do if I found her birth mother. I couldn't exactly call up and ask the woman if she'd met and murdered Carrie. I needed some reasonable explanation of why I was seeking her out. I stopped admiring the handicrafts dotting the landscape, put my driving on automatic, and tried to think of a plan. By the time I crossed the Kennebec River and approached the traffic circle near the statehouse, I'd given up. I'd just have to wait and see what I learned.

Because the state library came first, I stopped there. The librarian told me where I could find Maine phone books. They were so different from the ones I was used to, more like the size of magazines than like Massachusetts phone books. But even with little phone books, the job wasn't easy. Norwood turned out to be an awfully common name, not just in the Augusta-Hallowell area but all over the state. I found a Perry, a Percy, and a Paul; an Otto, an Oliver, and an Oscar; an Alcide, an Elmer, and a Crispin, as well as an A., E., I., Y., and U. Norwood, but no O. or Omar and thirteen Elizabeths. By the time I'd finished the whole state, my knees ached from crouching so long on the floor, and my eyes blurred from scanning so much small print.

It was time to stimulate my dulled faculties with coffee and then move on to Hallowell. I could have gone to the phone, instead, and tried the thirteen Elizabeths, but I was following Carrie, and Carrie had been to Hallowell. Besides, it was awkward enough to make one blind call to one Elizabeth, trying to determine if she'd given a baby girl up for adoption twenty-one years ago. The prospect of doing it thirteen times was too awful to contemplate. OK, so I'd do it if I had to. No one had ever suggested this search would be pleasant, and it was no one's idea but my own, but I'd try the easier alternative first. I asked the librarian where I could get coffee, and she said there was a small stand in the basement of the statehouse across the parking lot. "Just past the moose," she said. "You can't miss it."

The moose in the diorama were majestic. The liquid I was sold was not. The best that could be said was that it was brown. I consoled myself with a chocolate doughnut and an instant lottery ticket to test my luck. I won five dollars and got the front of my jacket covered with sugar and crumbs. I left unsure whether I was lucky or not.

The strip between Augusta and Hallowell ran along the Kennebec River, but you couldn't see the river. You could see almost any make or model of automobile you might be inclined to buy. It reminded me of how pleasant it had been driving the fancy rental Saab. As soon as I got the rest of the world in order, I was going to go car shopping.

I was halfway down the main street before I realized I was in Hallowell. The car dealers had given way to two- and three-story buildings, some brick, some wood, crowding the sidewalks. They all seemed to be antique shops. Behind the row of stores on my left was the river. On my right, the land rose sharply uphill. Suddenly the rows of shops ended and the land opened up into a little park along the river. I pulled in and parked, and walked back to the shops to ask directions. In the first shop I found a helpful, motherly woman dusting a shelf of beautiful old bottles. I asked her how to find the town hall.

"You can't miss it, dear," she said. "Just go back down Water Street until you come to the blinking light and turn left up the hill. It's one block up on your right."

"Thank you," I said. "Are those bottles old?"

"Older than I am," she said. "My husband digs 'em up. That man's idea of a good time is to spend the afternoon digging up the yard around an old cellar hole." She chuckled. "He probably knows more about old New England trash than anyone. Last week he found this, down near St. George." She pulled out a small, eight-sided bottle in deep amethyst glass. "Can you imagine anyone throwing this away? It's very old."

I took the bottle and held it up to the light. She was right. It was beautiful. "Is it for sale?" I asked.

"It sure is. If I kept everything I thought was pretty, I'd need a mansion," she said. "But it's a fine bottle. A real collector's item. Can't imagine anyone throwing it out." She shook her head. "You want to buy it? It would be real pretty on a windowsill with the sun shining through it."

We agreed on a price. She wrapped it carefully in many layers of newspaper and put it in a bag. I carried my treasure to the car, turned around, and headed back down the street. I hadn't even noticed a blinking light before but now it seemed very obvious. I turned left, went up one block, and parked in front of the town hall. The road climbed steeply up for another five or six blocks and disappeared over the top. I wouldn't want to try it in the winter. Lovely houses decked the hills rising up from the river. Across the street a patchwork Victorian was practically buried under a mass of staging. I climbed the steps and went inside. Carrie's notes had been in a Hallowell envelope. I hoped that meant she'd found something here, that this wasn't going to be a dead end.

I approached the counter labeled TOWN CLERK, and explained my request to a tall, dark-haired woman who asked if she could help. "I'm interested in the marriage records beginning in 1969," I said.

"For a specific person?" she asked.

"Elizabeth Norwood," I said.

She pulled a fat ledger off a shelf and laid it on the counter. "This book has the names of the bride and groom, the date, and where they were married. If you find the party you're looking for, we can look up the license application and the license. It's five dollars for a copy of either of those." She pointed to a table and chairs in a corner by the window. "You can take it over there if you want. Just don't take the book out of the building." I picked up the book and carried it to the corner. It weighed a ton. "Good luck," she called after me. "There are a lot of Norwoods in that book."

She wasn't kidding. I started in 1968, the year before Carrie was born. That year there were three grooms and two brides named Norwood. In 1969, there were two of each. In 1970, only two Norwoods got married. In 1971, only one, and in 1972, a record seven Norwoods went to the altar. I reached 1980 without finding a single Elizabeth Norwood, and there were none between 1980 and 1990. I closed the book with a thump and slumped in the chair, massaging my aching neck. Maybe Elizabeth Norwood's family had moved out of town while she was away curing her disgraceful condition. Maybe she'd never married.

My head was beginning to throb and my stomach was openly growling. The doughnut hadn't helped at all. Someday I would have to break this bad habit of not eating breakfast. I always ended up paying the price. I needed to take a break, get some lunch and figure out what to do next. Discouraged, I lugged the book back to the counter.

"Any luck?" the woman asked.

"No," I said. "Dozens of Norwoods, and not a single Elizabeth."

"Well, that's too bad," she said, pulling the book toward her. Then she stopped and pushed it back. "Did you look at middle names?" she said. "Because a lot of the Norwood girls are named after their mothers, and go by their middle names to avoid confusion." She pushed a wayward strand of hair away from her face. "I don't know why," she said, "but I feel like I've had this conversation before." She shrugged her shoulders. "I guess that happens when you serve the public. You have the same conversations over and over. You want to take this back

201

and try again?" she asked, thumping the book. An older woman behind the counter gave her a dirty look.

"I do," I said, hefting the book again. "Wish me luck." I carried the book back to the table and began again in 1968. In December, 1969, a woman named Anne Elizabeth Norwood had married Jonah Isaac Davis at the Calvary Baptist Church in Hallowell. I wrote down the names and dates, marked the page, and checked the rest of the Norwoods. Anne Elizabeth was the only possibility. Once again I carried the book back to the counter. The friendly woman was gone, and this time the elderly woman who had scowled at her came to the counter.

"I'd like to get a copy of a license application, please," I said. I opened the book and pointed to the entry for Anne Elizabeth and Jonah. "For this couple." She turned the book around, squinted at the page and back at me and then at the page again.

"Cost you five dollars," she said, holding out a plump, chapped hand. I took a ten-dollar bill out of my wallet and handed it to her. She stared at it like I'd given her Hungarian forints. "You got correct change?" she said. I dug through my purse, found four ones and four quarters, handed them to her, and took back the ten. She studied the money carefully to be sure it wasn't counterfeit, then put it slowly in a drawer and consulted her watch. "I'm going to lunch now," she said. "Come back at one and I'll have that application for you." She scribbled the names on a piece of paper, stowed the book under the counter, and sauntered away, her tentlike garment flowing behind her. A typical public servant. I wanted to argue with her, to say something mature and persuasive like, "If you don't give it to me right now, I'll stand here and scream," but I restrained myself, sublimating my rage in a quest for food.

Luckily, I didn't have to search long. In my weakened and enraged state, I might have collapsed on the sidewalk, but there was a restaurant directly across the street. I had a lobster salad sandwich, a chocolate milkshake, and a mound of french fries. Then I further sublimated my rage by having raspberry pie à la mode. By the time I retraced my steps and reentered Town Hall, I'd let my belt out a notch and was in a much better mood. The friendly woman was waiting for me with a copy of the license application.

She handed it over with a flourish. "There you are," she said. "Hope it's what you want."

I scanned the page. Anne Elizabeth Norwood was nineteen years old at the time of her marriage. Had never been married before. She listed her occupation as student. Her birth date was the same as the one on Elizabeth Alden's hospital records. Jonah Isaac Davis was twenty-nine, also previously unmarried. He listed his occupation as minister. I wondered if he was Carrie's father, and decided probably not. Had he been, the two of them would probably just have gotten married when the pregnancy occurred. A transfer to another congregation would have taken care of any problem with scandal.

Carrie's presence was almost tangible now. She'd stood here in this same room, with a copy of this same paper, another step closer to her mother. I followed Carrie's trail out of the building, back to the car, and back up the road to the state library.

I settled myself on the floor by the telephone books and began again, this time searching for Jonah Davis. My streak of luck continued. I found Reverend Jonah Davis in the first phone book I checked. Intuition, which had been my primary source of inspiration so far, told me to look in the Camden area book. And my intuition was right. A very modern listing — Davis, Rev. Jonah and Elizabeth — it even acknowledged that Jonah had a wife. I stifled the impulse to disturb the dozy afternoon peace of the library by leaping to my feet and shouting "Eureka!" Instead I carefully copied down the number and address, and returned the book to the shelf.

I didn't expect Andre to be there when I got back. It was only midafternoon, and he had more important things to do than wait around for me. The morning had gone more slowly than a crippled snail, but the afternoon had flown. I was looking forward to telling him what I'd discovered. Until now, he hadn't shown much interest in my theory that the key to Carrie's murder was to duplicate her search, but to be fair, I hadn't tried very hard to explain it to him.

Since Sunday, when he'd appeared on my doorstep, we'd been busy with other things, and I'd done my reading and learning since I'd first told him about Carrie's search. I'd left him asleep this morning. He needed it. The novelty hadn't worn off — once again we hadn't gotten much sleep — and I'd left him only the briefest of notes. Over dinner I'd tell him the whole story. I wondered if he liked sauerkraut. He'd better. That was what he was going to be eating.

I stopped at a roadside stand on the way back and got a bag of apples and some last-of-the-season tomatoes. This morning the drive had seemed endless; but now I flew, not to Camden, but to nearby Rockport, to visit Carrie's mother.

CHAPTER 23

I DROVE STRAIGHT to Rockport, stopping at a gas station to get directions to Shore Drive. Shore Drive turned out to be a road looping off Route 1, running along a peninsula separating Rockport and Rockland, along a broad inlet called Glen Cove. The road separated the houses from the shore, but the view was nice. Number 124 was a neat Victorian cottage with gingerbread trim and wide porches. There was a car in the driveway. I parked behind it, climbed the steps, and rang the doorbell. In my mind I saw Carrie parking her battered little Chevette and climbing these same steps.

The door was opened by a small woman smiling the rigid smile of Christian charity. "Yes?" she said. I could only stand and stare at her, speechless. Unquestionably, this was Carrie's mother. The resemblance was uncanny. She looked more like a sister than a mother, but she'd only been eighteen when Carrie was born. Her face was still young and attractive, but it wasn't happy. Marriage to a minister, it seemed, had brought her neither peace nor joy. Her small body drooped in the same dejected way Carrie's sometimes had, but here the dejection seemed chronic. "Can I help you, miss?" she asked in Carrie's voice.

I pulled myself together. "Are you Elizabeth Davis?"

She nodded. "Betsy," she said, waiting for me to state my business. Still smiling, but wary now, uncertain.

"My name is Thea Kozak," I said. "Carrie McKusick was my sister."

She jumped like a startled deer, looked back over her shoulder, then grabbed my arm. "We can't talk here," she said. "My husband's home. You wait. I'll get my coat. We'll go down to the beach."

She shut the door in my face. Down to the beach, she'd said. I looked at my shoes. Expensive Italian leather, with small heels. Very grown-up and elegant, but useless for scrambling over rocks or striding along the sand. This was where men had a real advantage. They might not want to expose their expensive wing tips to the elements, but at least they could walk in them if they had to. The door opened again, and Elizabeth Davis came out, wearing a puffy blue ski jacket. She shut the door carefully behind her, then hurried past me and down the steps. "This way," she said.

I followed her across the road and down a grassy slope to the shore, hitching up my narrow skirt to climb over the roadside barrier. She walked rapidly across the sand and rocks to the point where the beach ended and a rock ledge sloped sharply up the left, climbed without hesitation up the ledge and sat down in a spot halfway up, where a broken shelf of rock made a natural seat. "Come on up," she called.

I slipped off my shoes and followed. The sand was cold and the barnacle-covered rocks shredded my stockings. Away from the beach, the sea was a cold grayish blue. Closer to shore it was dark gray, and the wind was driving waves up onto the beach, the dark tendrils of foam-flecked water hissing up over the rock-strewn sand toward the base of the ledge. At a distance, the sea had looked inviting, but close up, it seemed cold and unfriendly. Across the cove, late afternoon sun glinted off the cars on Route 1. The temperature was dropping as the sun sank. I clambered up the ledge and sat down cautiously a few feet away.

"How did you find me?" she demanded.

"The same way Carrie did," I said.

Elizabeth Davis nodded slowly. I almost couldn't bear to look at her, she was so like Carrie, the same delicate bones, even the same soft curls. Her head was bent over her clenched hands, hiding her face. When she raised it, she looked at me with Carrie's challenging stare. "Why did you come here?" she said. "Why can't you people leave me alone?" I started to speak, but she held up a hand. "Wait. There's something I need to say first." I waited, wondering if she was going to confess.

"When I was eighteen," she said, "I became pregnant. My family sent me away to Massachusetts, to a home for unwed mothers. I had the baby. I gave her up. I came home and tried to put all of that behind me. Soon afterward, I met Jonah Davis and we were married. We have a family — two sons. My husband is a minister. He is also a community leader. People look up to him. I'm proud of Jonah, and I love him very much. He doesn't know about Carrie. You probably think that's odd." Her angry eyes dared me to say so.

"I've never told him about the pregnancy or the baby. He could never have accepted that about me. My husband is a good man, loving in his own way, but he is also a strict man. A religious man. A moral example for others. It's been hard, but I've learned to live with my secret, with my guilt, and I've gone on to make a good life. This may be hard for you to understand. Your sister couldn't seem to understand it, but people here have a certain image of us — of me. It would destroy both of us, and our family, if it were ever known that I had had an illegitimate child. That's why we couldn't talk at the house." She brushed back some curls that had blown into her face. Carrie's hair. Carrie's hand. How odd it must have been for Carrie. Seeing this woman, so like her, I almost couldn't concentrate on what she was saying, despite the desperation in her voice.

"Since your sister called my life has been a nightmare. Her call and her visit have completely destroyed my peace of mind. If the fact that she was my daughter became known, my life would be ruined. Perhaps I could handle my own disgrace, I've lived with it a long time, but I couldn't face the pain of my husband's disgrace, or my children's scorn. I have two teenage sons, one in high school and one in college. We've raised them in a strict, moral home." She hesitated. "I don't know if you can appreciate how serious I am. I don't know whether finding me was important to you for some reason, or it was just a lark. I'm not sure I even care. I'm telling you so you'll know the whole story. Then I want you to go away and leave me alone. I have a right to be left alone! It was bad enough that she came. I don't see why you had to come."

"I can explain that, if you'll let me," I said.

"When I'm finished," she said quickly. "I thought when I gave up the baby that I could leave all of that behind me. They told me I could close the door on that chapter of my life. That my secret would be protected. They told me to go home and put it out of my mind. And that's what I did, as best I could, until your sister showed up." She shook her head angrily. The slanting sun lit her face. Now I could see the lines around her eyes and mouth. She looked bone-tired.

"Lies," she said. "All lies." She stared out over the cove, choosing her words carefully. "I believed that I was safe. Those people who think that they have a right to know who they are, who insist on their right to find their birth parents, don't realize how much they may be hurting someone else." Her voice sank to a whisper. "Ever since she died, I've lived in dread, waiting for the doorbell to ring. I don't sleep. My appetite is gone. I wait like a hunted animal. Waiting for the police to appear on my doorstep. Waiting for this life, these good people that I love, to be destroyed. All because your sister wasn't content with her own fine parents, but had to come find me and ruin my life again."

I stared at her. "How did you know that Carrie was dead?"

Elizabeth shuddered, either from the cold or fear. "The newspapers, of course." She paused. "I guess your dad didn't get his money's worth after all, did he?"

"What do you mean, he didn't get his money's worth?" I burst out. "You sold Carrie?"

"Not exactly," she said, "not me. I had no say about anything in that place. None of the girls did. We were in disgrace. Your father bribed the social worker to approve them as adoptive parents, even though they didn't meet the agency criteria, because he wanted my baby."

"What are you talking about? Mom and Dad got Carrie through a legitimate adoption agency."

"The agency was legitimate. Proper. God, were they proper!" Her stare was vacant, far away, remembering. I thought about the files I'd seen. All those months with no visitors, no friends. "But your parents weren't. They were too old. And they already had two healthy children. But your mother saw me, when they were there at the agency, and she wanted my baby. So your father arranged it and I agreed. I hated the baby I was carrying, but it was a life. I was glad it was going to a good home."

"So, when Carrie came to see you, you told her all this and rejected her again?" I said. "Maybe you should have thought before you got pregnant in the first place!" I couldn't help it. It was wrong to be cruel to this poor unhappy woman, but it was so callous, rejecting Carrie because it might disrupt her nice little life, when Carrie's life had always been disrupted because of this woman's rejection.

"If only it had been that simple," Carrie's mother said. "Does every pregnancy happen by choice? Have you ever been pregnant?"

"No," I said, wondering what was coming next. This whole thing was nothing like I'd imagined. I'd expected to conduct a deft interrogation to discover if Carrie's birth mother had been her killer. Instead here I was sitting on a rocky cliff with this woman who was so disconcertingly like Carrie, my emotions swinging like a rope in the wind.

"Maybe someday you'll understand better," she said. "I've had three children, including your sister. I hated being pregnant, having my body taken over by another being. But that's the way humans have children." Her blue eyes bored into me. "Your sister was not the product of a teenage affair. She was the result of a rape, and every moment I was pregnant with her, every movement, every kick, was a loathsome reminder of my degradation. I can see that you don't like hearing this, but you need to hear it to understand. I hated the baby I was carrying, and I counted the minutes until she was born and I could get her out of my body."

I wanted her to stop. I couldn't bear to hear this, knowing she had also said it to Carrie. I covered my ears. "Stop it," I said. "I don't want to hear any more."

"Look, I didn't invite you here," she said. "Like your sister, you insisted on coming, and now you're going to listen. When I was seventeen, I was raped by my uncle. When I told my parents, they confronted him and he said that I had seduced him. They believed him and blamed me, insisting it must have been my fault. When I told them I was pregnant, my father beat me with his belt until I bled, hoping I might lose the baby. Does that shock you?"

I remembered my interview with Esther Pappas. No wonder Elizabeth had been depressed when she was in the home. No wonder she'd thought about killing herself. "Yes," I said, "it does. I'm sorry. I shouldn't have assumed... Look, you don't have to tell me all this personal stuff."

"Yes," she said, "I think I do. You came here like your sister did, disrupting my life and intruding on my privacy, forcing me to remember again, and now you'd like to walk away, because it's not a happy ending, but a sordid story, right? Well, you can just sit there and listen." The sun was nearly gone, and the temperature was dropping rapidly. I wished I'd brought my coat, but it was in the car with my briefcase. It had been warm when I was driving.

"Things are different now, even here in Maine," she said. "Having an out-of-wedlock baby is no longer such a disgrace. But twenty years ago, things were different. In a small town, people talked. You got labeled. Your family really felt the disgrace, people made sure of that. And once you had a reputation for being sexually available, no man respected you. You were fair game for any sort of abuse. My family was desperate to avoid that. They sent me to Serenity House, and pretended I had gone away to school."

Her thin fingers twisted her wedding band. "You can't imagine how bad it was. From the time I discovered I was pregnant until I left for Serenity House, they made me sleep in the shed so I wouldn't corrupt my sisters." She smiled, a bitter, humorless smile. "Sounds like something out of Dickens, doesn't it? Well, it's true. It was winter. The shed was unheated. I was sick and I was scared. I was afraid I'd die from the cold and sometimes I wished I would. And then they sent me to Serenity House."

"At first, I thought I was better off. At least I was warm. And the other girls were in the same boat. But, like my own family, the staff let us know how worthless we were, a disgrace to our families. And all the time, I was swelling up with my uncle's child, a hideous, wriggling little thing that kicked me and made me sick and distorted. With his child inside me, I couldn't forget about my uncle and what he'd done to me. His filthy hands. His awful breath. His gross body pinning me to the floor. How much he hurt me. My shame when I couldn't stop him. I hated that baby so much I tried to kill it by killing myself."

I didn't want to hear any more. It was too wrenchingly sad and depressing. In everything I'd read about searching for birth parents, would-be searches were cautioned that they might not like what they found. The birth parents might not be as imagined. They might be disappointing or not receptive. They might even be dead. Carol Anderson had tried to warn me, but nothing could have prepared me for this. This woman was supposed to be nothing to me but a source of information. My search was for Carrie's killer. Now I was torn. I didn't like her. She wasn't likable. Yet I felt a deep sympathy for this woman who had been victimized by everyone around her. I could also imagine twenty years of festering anger fueling the kind of violence that had killed Carrie.

The sun was almost down below the horizon, illuminating her face with its last golden streaks and coloring all the shadows purple. The water was eating up the beach below us. As I watched, a wave rolled over my shoes. My beautiful, expensive shoes. But if I went after them, I'd break the flow, and she might stop talking to me. "You told Carrie all this?" I asked.

"Yes," she said, "I did. Just like I'm telling it to you. Except we were in my living room. Jonah wasn't home. She called first and told me who she was. Asked if I would see her. I told her I wouldn't. She pleaded with me, begged me to see her just once. Swore if I did she'd never bother me again. I agreed. And my life has been a living hell ever since."

"So you killed her?"

"I considered it," she said. "But I'm a religious person, and I've been a minister's wife for twenty years. I believe in the commandments. I believe it's wrong to take a life. It was not through my own sin that I became pregnant. But I have lived a deceitful life by not telling my husband. I thought that Carrie's visit might be a punishment for my sin. God was testing me by sending her. I used to think about killing my uncle, too. Sometimes, during those long dismal nights at Serenity House, the baby would kick me awake and I'd lie there in the darkness devising ways to kill him. Maybe he knew that, because he never came around when I was home after that. He didn't come to the wedding. A few years later he died of cancer. A dreadful, lingering death. And I was glad." She shook her head firmly. "No, I didn't kill her. I thought I'd be relieved if she was dead, but my life has been more terrible since, waiting for someone else to discover my connection to Carrie, and reveal my secret. Are you going to tell anyone about me?"

The sun had gone. Below us, the water had now completely covered the beach and crept up the rocks so that the waves were lapping only a few feet below us. There was no way back to the road unless we climbed up the ledge. "The tide comes in fast here," she said. "Are you going to tell anyone? When your sister came, I knew how I felt about killing. After the agony of the past few weeks, I'm not so clear about things anymore. I could push you into the water, wait until you were dead, and then run for help, pretending you fell. But then someone else might come and ask questions. I couldn't go on forever, killing the people who came to ask questions."

She wasn't talking to me anymore. She was just thinking out loud. I'm not easily intimidated, but the look on her face was frightening. She hated me for being there. I knew that. And no one knew where I was, which was on a rocky cliff beside a surging ocean. I was bigger and younger and stronger. Even if she did push me in, I'm a strong swimmer. The water would be cold. The water in Maine is always cold, but I could probably handle it. Still, this woman was distraught and under a lot of stress. I didn't want to wait around to see what she'd do next.

I studied the rocks above us, looking for the best way up. I wasn't looking forward to scrambling over the rocks in my bare feet, but my shoes were under water. I'd miss them. Behind me I heard a loud splash. I whirled around. Elizabeth Davis was no longer on the ledge beside me. Below I could see her bright head, bobbing in the water. She was struggling to get back to the rocks, but the parka she was wearing was pulling her down.

I stripped off my belt and dove in, making a shallow racing dive that brought me to the surface a few feet from her. The frigid impact of the water took my breath away, but I didn't have time to wait until I adjusted to the cold. Carrie's mother had gone under. I dove down, feeling with my arms. Touched something. Grabbed it and pulled her to the surface. As soon as her head was out of the water she panicked, grabbing me and pulling me under. Every lifeguard knows that a frightened swimmer can drown herself and the guard if she panics. I couldn't get a grip on her if she kept flailing like this. I stunned her with my fist, gripped her head under my arm, and hauled her back to the rocks.

She lay limply on the ledge, waterlogged and pathetic, making no effort to help herself. I didn't dare leave her there while I went for help. She might jump in again. I leaned down close to her head, speaking slowly and clearly. "Betsy," I said,

"I'm going to take you to the house. Can you walk?"

Her blue eyes stared dully at the sky. She wouldn't look at me. "I don't care," she whispered.

"We've got to get you back to the house and out of those wet clothes," I said. "Can you stand up?" She didn't answer and she didn't move. I stopped trying to rouse her. Instead I pulled her to her feet, wrapped an arm around her waist, and began to climb up the rock, dragging her along. She made a feeble effort to cooperate, but she was limp as a rag doll. By the time we got to the road I felt like I'd climbed both Everest and K-2, and the rocks had made mincemeat of my feet.

I led her, limp and shambling, across the road, up the driveway and onto her front porch. At the door she balked. "I can't go in there," she mumbled.

"You haven't any choice," I said. "You can't stay out here. You're freezing. You'll get sick." I bent down until my eyes were level with hers. "Here's our story. I stopped on an impulse to ask about real estate because the cove is so pretty. You invited me to walk on the beach, to talk about the area. Just being friendly. We were walking and you slipped. The jacket weighed you down so I had to jump in and pull you out." She didn't say anything, just stared at me, her eyes wary, but she didn't try to run away when I knocked.

I heard footsteps coming. Before the door opened, she said something in a low voice. I bent down so I could hear her. "Get out of here and don't come back," she said. Her voice was cold as ice, and her blue eyes — Carrie's eyes — were just as cold.

The man who answered was tall and gaunt, with unruly graying hair. He might have been handsome if he hadn't looked so severe. His eyes widened in disbelief as he took in my wet hair, bare feet, and clinging dress. "Your wife had an accident down on the beach," I said. His eyes shifted from me to Betsy. He darted forward, nearly knocking me over, and picked her up as though she were a child. "Come in, please," he called over his shoulder. I stood dripping in the front hall while he disappeared upstairs with his wife. From behind the closed door I could hear muffled voices and then the sound of a tub running.

Humanitarian impulses might have gotten me into this mess, but they had abandoned me now. I was chilled, soaking wet, and my feet hurt. Where was that famous Christian charity now that I needed it? It seemed Reverend Davis's charity extended only to his wife. I didn't expect Betsy to think of me. She wanted me gone and that was all.

A noise behind me made me turn. A teenage boy stood in the doorway, staring at me. Yet another version of Carrie, a masculine one this time. I didn't waste my breath asking what he was staring at. My dress clung like a mermaid's skin. To his still raging hormones I was a weird, wet vision. But I was in no mood to be anyone's wet dream. "You could stop staring and bring me a towel," I said. He detached himself from the door frame and slouched past me up the stairs. He was tall, like his father, with the awkwardness of a boy who finds himself suddenly inside a man's body. "Have you got some clothes I could wear?" I asked his departing back.

"I guess so," he muttered. At the top of the stairs he disappeared through a doorway. I half expected that, like his parents, he would stay disappeared, but a minute later he came out carrying a bundle of clothes, got a towel from a closet, and tossed them down to me. "There's a bathroom under the stairs," he said. "You can change there." He stood silently, watching me. I took the clothes and went into the bathroom.

I stripped off my dress, slip, and shredded stockings, dropping the dress and slip into the sink and the stockings into the trash. He had given me a pair of worn Levi's and a high school sweatshirt. I blotted as much water as I could from my underwear and slipped them on. Good thing he was tall. If he'd been built like his mother I never could have worn the pants. As it was, my hips filled the jeans in a way his bony adolescent body never had. I dried my hair, ran my fingers through it, and confined the clammy strands in a rough braid.

He was waiting in the hall when I came out. "Thanks," I said, holding up my wet clothes. "This is a lot better. Have you got a plastic bag I could put these in?"

"In the kitchen," he said, walking toward the back of the house. I followed him, waited while he fished one out of a closet, and stuck my clothes in it. He wasn't exactly a dynamic conversationalist.

"I feel awful about this," I said. "I rang your doorbell on an impulse, to see whether anyone knew about any land around here for sale. It was just so pretty. Your mom invited me for a walk on the beach, so I could really see how nice it was. And then she slipped and fell into the water. That heavy coat pulled her down, so I jumped in to pull her out. Lost my shoes." He stood silently, watching me. I felt like I was babbling, but I wanted to tell someone the story I'd prepared, to protect Betsy, even though I didn't fully understand why I wanted to protect her when I didn't even like her. His staring made me uncomfortable.

"I'd better be going. Please tell your mother I'm sorry for the trouble and thanks for the clothes. Do you want them back?"

"No, that's OK," he said. His look said he'd never wear them again anyway, not after I'd worn them.

I held out a hand. "Good-bye, then. My name is Thea Kozak. What's yours?"

He took it reluctantly, an expression of undisguised distaste on his face. "Chris," he muttered.

"Well, good-bye, Chris Davis," I said. "Please thank your mother for me." I let myself out — Chris didn't even bother to come to the door — threw my clothes in the back seat, and headed back to Camden, uncertain about what I'd learned, and sadder than ever about my sister Carrie. Sorry that I hadn't been there for her, hadn't had any idea what was going on in her life, when her life was full of disasters like Charlie and Betsy Davis. Such a wretched, sordid end to the search she'd put so much hope and faith in.

I turned on the heat to see if I could stop shivering and stepped on the gas, racing north toward a hot bath and a stiff drink.

CHAPTER 24

ANDRE WAS BENT over, taking something out of the oven, when I came through the door. He dropped it hastily onto the stove top and came to meet me, taking in my wet hair, strange clothes, and bare feet. "I've had it, Lemieux," I said. "I'm giving up. No more playing detective for me. You've got to find the person who killed my sister. I can't take any more of this ferreting out suspects and having death-defying adventures." I started out kidding, changed in midsentence to anger, and ended up in tears, running the full gamut of emotions in less than a minute.

"I was worried about you," he said. "I see that I was right to be. You've been on another of your adventures. What was it this time? I thought you were just going to Augusta to read records."

"I did. I went to Augusta, to Hallowell. Read records. Read phone books. I found Carrie's mother. We had a long talk on the beach across from her house, leading to an involuntary swim in Glen Cove when she jumped into the water and I had to jump in to pull her out. Boy, that water was cold!" I threw the bag of soggy clothes over toward the stairs. "I lost my favorite shoes." I'd been running on emotional energy ever since I climbed out of the sea; now that I was here, and safe, exhaustion hit me like I'd been sandbagged. "I'm awfully glad you're here," I said. "I'm tired. I don't want to be alone. I'd hug you, but it would be like the embrace of the swamp thing."

He hugged me anyway. I sagged against him, savoring his warmth and his bulk. His shirt smelled faintly of cigarettes and whatever he'd been cooking. The intensity of his embrace told me things about his caring and concern that his taciturn style left unsaid. When he finally released me, my bra had made two wet circles on his shirt. "Gotcha," I giggled, pointing at them. He grinned and pointed right back at me. I looked down at the circles on my sweatshirt. They were positively obscene. "Is there anything to drink around here? I'm seriously in need of fortification."

Lightly, he touched my face and felt my hands. "You're freezing, Thea," he said. "What you're seriously in need of is a hot bath." He took me by the shoulders, turned me around, and gently propelled me up the stairs. I didn't mind letting him taking charge. I needed a little looking after. It was a welcome change from my usual aggressive independence. I wasn't going to lose it because once I let someone run me a bath.

It was nice to have someone to take care of the physical things, like baths and food, because my mind was elsewhere anyway. Since I'd first had the idea that Carrie's death was connected to her search for her birth mother, I'd been charging forward with my own search, certain that when I found Carrie's mother I would have found the answer to her murder. I knew more than I'd ever dreamed of knowing about Carrie's origins but I didn't know how to evaluate what Betsy Davis had told me. I could see how the impetus to kill could have come from twenty years of festering anger about Carrie's birth, coupled with her fear of discovery. I wanted to find the killer so badly that I wished I could think she was guilty, but I believed that wretched woman when she said she didn't kill Carrie. She'd seemed so honest and so hurt herself. She admitted she was willing to kill me, but in the end it was herself, not me, that she tried to harm.

So what did I know? What conclusions could I draw from my latest foray into detective work, other than that I was not cut out for it? My thoughts about Carrie's mother were depressingly similar to my conclusions about Charlie. Carrie's mother had good reasons to kill her, and she could have acted out of a murderous rage, yet I didn't think she'd done it.

I might as well face it. I'd come to a dead end, out of energy and out of ideas. I didn't know where else to look or whom else to talk to. Carrie was still just as dead. I'd promised that her killer would be found, and I didn't see any way I could fulfill that promise. I remembered Sonia's infuriating smirk; heard her saying, "I don't know where you get this idea you can do anything, Thea. Why should you succeed if the police can't?" What I had said then was still true — because I cared more. But caring didn't seem to be enough, and that was all I had left.

Unpleasant as my encounter with Betsy Davis had been, my main reactions were pity and disappointment; for Carrie, it must have been devastating. To find the mother she had dreamed about for so long, who so vividly confirmed Carrie's physical identity. The books I'd read helped me to imagine how it had been — after a lifetime of being a misfit among us giants, suddenly Carrie had found that there was someone else in the world who looked just like her, sounded just like her. I'd gone to meet Betsy Davis expecting to find some answers to the mystery of Carrie's death, but Carrie had gone with a lifetime of emotional baggage. She must have pinned so much hope and expectation on that encounter! For her it was the fulfillment of her life's quest — the end of being disconnected and the beginning of belonging. She had met with complete rejection; flatly told the whole sordid story of her origins; told, without qualification, how unwanted, even hated, she had been, for Betsy Davis would not have been gentle with her unwanted daughter. I was heartsick at the image of Carrie, sweet, hopeful Carrie, fulfilling her dream of finally finding someone who was like her, and discovering that she had been conceived from rape and incest and hated and rejected from the moment of conception.

I lowered the toilet lid and sat there staring dully at Andre's back while he put in the plug and started the water. I felt as though a giant had picked me up and wrung me out like a used washcloth. My feet hurt. My side hurt. I couldn't stop shaking. I was too wretched to care. "OK, stand up," he said, pulling me gently to my feet. I stood and held up my arms so he could take off my sweatshirt. Then he undid my jeans, tugged them down, and took off my soggy underwear. "Into the tub," he commanded. "I'll fix you a drink, and then I'll wash your back and you can tell me what happened."

It sounded absurdly domestic, I thought, as I slid down into the steaming water. What a life we could have, Andre and I. We could go off every morning confronting murderers, drug dealers, child abusers, hostile admissions counselors, and frantic headmasters, spend the day asking pointed or dangerous questions, and reunite at the end of the day, everything spent, for bourbon and back washing. I floated on my back, feeling the heat penetrate to my bones. The bath felt good even if nothing else in life did.

Andre came back with two drinks. Bourbon. He must have bought some. There hadn't been any here. He took my place on the toilet seat. I sat up and took the glass from his hand, gulping it down like I'd just staggered out of the desert. "Hey, take it easy," he said. "That's not water, you know." The alcohol did a slow burn in my stomach. I drank some more. In my dilapidated state, it hit me like a ton of bricks, sending my anxieties into another dimension. I stopped obsessing about what to do next and began to relax. I was beginning to feel human again, depressed but human.

"I'm glad you're here," I said again. I could have shared some of the other things I'd been thinking, about how nice it was to have someone to come home to, how good it felt to be cared for, but all those things smacked of commitment and if I knew one thing for sure, it was that I had a severe allergy to commitment and the pain that could result from it. David and I had been like an intricate weaving. When our individual threads were blended together, the result had been something special and complicated and unique. I used to wake up early just so I could lie there and watch him sleep. When he died and those threads were unraveled, I was left tattered and vulnerable. I'd mended myself as best I could and I was afraid to risk myself again. Andre and I were attracted, but even if we got past the prickles and quirks of each other's personalities, there was geography. A longterm relationship was impractical. "I'm not ready to talk

221

about my day," I said. "It was too rotten. Maybe you should tell me about yours."

"I had a rotten day, too," he said. "Never even got to talk with Mrs. Bolduc. I caught a new sex abuse case, spent the day talking to neighbors of a couple — divorced mother and her new boyfriend — who reportedly are prostituting her two young daughters to pay for drugs. It's a sick situation, and the heart-breaking thing is that it isn't surprising or unusual even though the girls are only nine and eleven. Their teachers reported suspected abuse when the girls' behavior became strange. And the neighbors won't talk to me. They're like a bunch of goddamned clams. They think they should protect this couple." His face was tight and angry. I put a soapy hand over his. "I talked to four different people today," he said, "each of whom insisted they'd noticed nothing unusual and said they didn't want to get involved. As if we shouldn't all get involved when the welfare of children is at stake."

"People even less cooperative than I was?" I said. I lay back against the tub, watching his face, remembering the first time I'd seen him, and then the interview in Thomaston. How formal and unyielding he'd seemed, yet how passionate about solving the terrible crimes that came his way. I didn't know him much better now, despite our intimacy, but I knew enough. He didn't open up easily. We hadn't had time to exchange stories and maybe we never would, but there was a goodness about him, and a gentleness, I never expected to find in a policeman.

He almost smiled. "They made you look like a paragon of cooperation, even when you were at your most prissy."

"You still think I'm prissy?"

"Lady," he said, "I know better now. I know your most intimate secrets. I've seen you black and blue and bloody. Unconscious. Enraged. In your underwear. Out of your under-wear. And in the throes of passion." His eyebrows rose to a quizzical peak, asking an unspoken question.

"Anytime," I said. "With respect to passion, only, that is.

222

I've given up black and blue and battered." If he hadn't been there I would be hitting bottom by now, compulsively examining everything I knew and obsessing about what to do next, probably well into a bottle of bourbon. Well, I was doing that, wasn't I? I wondered how he knew bourbon was my drink. "I thought you were going to wash my back?" I said.

"I thought you were going to tell me about your day," he countered.

He rolled up his sleeves, knelt down beside the tub, and picked up the soap. He washed my back and massaged the tight muscles in my neck and shoulders while I told him about my trip to Augusta and my meeting with Betsy Davis. "I'm so confused," I said. "Each time I track down the person I'm sure killed Carrie, I come home convinced I was wrong. I have to find out who killed her. I have to."

"I know what you mean." The irony was unmistakable. "You're convinced Betsy Davis didn't kill your sister?"

"Not convinced," I said. "People lie so easily. But she seemed to be telling the truth. And she didn't try to kill me, she tried to kill herself. Do you think disclosure would really ruin her life?"

"It might. People around here are still pretty conservative. People like Reverend Davis especially," he said. "But I've got to go and talk to her. The connection is too important to ignore. Ready to come out?" He held out a towel.

"I suppose you do have to talk to her," I said, "but try not to let her family know, at least until you've seen her and formed an opinion. She's kept it a secret from them and she's very frightened they might find out."

I stood up and he wrapped the towel around me. He took my hand and led me into the bedroom. "Dinner is almost ready," he said, unbuttoning his shirt. Dinner was cold by the time we got downstairs.

CHAPTER 25

WE BOTH SLEPT badly. For me, it was not because I wasn't tired. I was. My feet hurt and my body ached from the effort of rescuing Betsy Davis, but sleep eluded me. My mind wouldn't be still. I lay in the dark, going over the events of the last two weeks, searching for something I'd forgotten, some last lead I could pursue. I tossed restlessly, repeatedly bumping into Andre. He was just as bad, troubled by his new case. Whenever I dozed off he would start abruptly and begin muttering. At four-thirty I gave up and went downstairs to make some tea. He appeared a few minutes later, fully dressed. Wordlessly he accepted the tea I handed him and wandered off to stare out the window. "Something bad is happening with those kids, I can feel it," he said. "I've got to get over there. Do you mind?"

The silence of our unspoken thoughts lay heavily between us. Our failure, despite our goodwill and determination, to solve the puzzle of Carrie's death. What was unspoken was not recriminations, but for each of us a sense of personal failure and shared regrets. Carrie had been our link. Now I was going home, once again to bury myself in work, and Andre was moving on to new, more immediate problems. He wasn't giving up on Carrie but she was being moved to a back burner. I wanted to scream and rage and complain but it wouldn't have done any good. Not even Andre could make something out of nothing.

"I'll be OK. If you can put the boxes I've packed into the car, I'll only have a few things to pack down here, and then I've got to go. I have an important meeting tomorrow, and I can't go unprepared." It was odd. Work had been central to my life for so long, and now it all seemed so remote. That would change when I got home.

He walked slowly back from the window, his big shoulders hunched. "I wish you didn't have to go," he said. I didn't say anything. I didn't have to. We both knew how we felt. He got his jacket from the closet, and held out his hand for my keys. He went in and out, silently putting Carrie's things in the car. "I'll call you tonight," he said, giving me back my keys, and went out into the gray morning. He was lost in fog by the time he reached his car.

I went back upstairs, dressed, stripped the bed and tied the sheets into a bundle, and carried the rest of Carrie's things downstairs. I tuned the radio to an oldies station and started packing up the last of Carrie's things, ignoring all my little aches and pains. I did fine until I got to the books. I didn't know which were Carrie's and which had come with the apartment. From what little I'd seen of her, Mrs. Bolduc didn't seem like the type whose taste ran to books, but they might have been part of her decorating scheme, bought by the foot at a yard sale.

It was too early to bother her, so I took a break and made myself some breakfast, wishing I had a paper to read. The restless feeling persisted, like a premonition of disaster. It was the feeling I'd had before exams — the knots in my stomach, the tightness in my chest. Today there seemed to be no reason for it. Too restless to sit still, I did the dishes and put on my shoes, wishing my feet didn't hurt. The only way I knew to get rid of this feeling was to get some exercise — a brisk hobble downtown to get a paper.

I grabbed my jacket, and stuffed some money in my pocket. Where was the door key? I found it in the pocket of the jeans I'd borrowed from Chris Davis, which I'd balled up and stuffed into one of the boxes. On my way out I checked Mrs. Bolduc's window, but the curtain was still. I limped off into the gloomy morning, the frost-crisped leaves crackling underfoot.

Downtown, a minor traffic jam was building as sleepy Mainiacs, trying to rush to work, found themselves in a peasoup world. I bought a copy of the *Boston Globe*, found a bench down by the harbor, and sat down to read it. There was a damp chill in the air today, but I didn't want to sit inside somewhere where I'd have to be around people. The foggy solitude suited my mood perfectly.

According to the paper, the world was in its usual state of decomposition. In the poor sections of Boston, black children were killing each other with depressing regularity. Elsewhere in the world, politicians were trying to deliver their social philosophies in thirty-second sound bites. The man who loved children unless they grew up to be women; the man who wholeheartedly embraced the AK-47 as a friend. People of all religions were fighting bitterly to prove that theirs was the one true faith. Life as usual. There sure wasn't much to be optimistic about. A few dedicated people doing good deeds while everyone else wallowed in self-righteous acquisition.

What had made me think I wanted to read this stuff? Was this restlessness a sign that it was time for a change in my life? A little voice inside reminded me that the last few weeks had been a time of immense change; maybe instead it was time for a return to normal, time to get back to business as usual. Time to put this futile quest behind me, to grow up and accept that I couldn't do everything. The fact that I wanted to fix things for Carrie didn't guarantee that I could. It was a depressing thought. I still like to believe that I can do anything, that I don't have to accept limitations.

For the first time, I wondered if my mother had known about Betsy Davis. Had she known what heartache awaited Carrie if her search was successful? Was that why she'd been so opposed? Why they'd forbidden me to search as well? It would have been comforting to believe that, but I thought not. Then the simplest thing would have been to tell Carrie the truth, or part of it, instead of flatly forbidding the search. No. Mom's motives had been more selfish, or at least more self-protective. She hadn't wanted Carrie to search because she wanted to be Carrie's only mother. After all, if what Betsy Davis had said was true, they'd bought Carrie fair and square.

I felt this infuriating helplessness and rage, remembering yesterday, knowing now what Carrie had had to go through all alone, with no one to confide in, to help her deal with her feelings. And now I was experiencing my own despair and failure. Why couldn't I just accept this dead end, give up, and go home? I wished Suzanne were here. I could have told her all this and she might have helped me make some sense of it. But Suzanne was busy running a business — our business — while I was brooding beside a picturesque harbor half-smothered in fog, watching the huge ghostly windjammers shift restlessly in the light wind, chains clinking, slapped by the waves. Sailboats are never quiet.

The chill was beginning to penetrate the parts of me that weren't protected by my leather jacket. It would be stupid to get chilled again after yesterday. I rolled up the paper, stuck it under my arm, and headed back up Mountain Street. I'd have my chat with Mrs. Bolduc, finish packing, and go home. Back to my familiar world of interviews, assessments, and reports. Back to someone else's problems — problems that had solutions. It seemed very inviting after a week and a half of beating my head against walls. Safer, too.

Sure enough, the curtain twitched as I came up the walk. I swung around, changing course, and rang Mrs. Bolduc's doorbell. It took her a while to get downstairs, and when she did open the door, her face was unwelcoming, thin mouth pursed, and her stenciled eyebrows quizzical against the yellow skin. "Yes?"

"I'm almost finished in the apartment," I said. "But there were a few things I needed to ask you about. Could you come over for a minute?" I could tell she wanted to say no, just because she hated to be agreeable, but her eagerness to have the apartment free was greater. "Just for a minute," she said. "I'm busy."

Not too busy to spy on me, I almost added, but I held my tongue as I led the way to Carrie's door. Her sharp eyes darted around, taking in what I'd already done, as she sniffed the air. "Smells like cigarettes in here," she said. "I don't allow smoking."

I sniffed, but I couldn't smell anything. No one had smoked in here since the night Lorna had been here, and that was ages ago. I shrugged. "I don't smoke," I said.

"What about your friend?" she snapped.

"Detective Lemieux? He doesn't smoke either. What I wanted to ask about was the stuff in here." I led her into the living room. "These books and knickknacks. I don't know which ones are hers and what was already here."

She walked slowly around the room, pointing to things. "That was here, and that, and that." I moved the things she indicated to the coffee table. She stopped at the bookshelf and studied the titles. She picked out about six books and handed them to me. "These stay. The rest are hers. I'll just check the upstairs, while I'm here. And I expect the place to be left clean for the new tenant, including the refrigerator."

Clean? I hadn't thought about that. She didn't really expect me to waste my time vacuuming rugs and defrosting the refrigerator? She could worry about it after I left. She came back downstairs and went into the kitchen, sticking her pointy nose into every drawer and shelf. "All the kitchen stuff was here, except these things," she said, dumping an armload of kitchen tools onto the counter. "And them blue glasses over the sink. And this ashtray." She set it down too hard on the countertop, where it broke into many pieces.

I stared at the broken ashtray, took a deep breath, and plunged back into the mystery of Carrie's death, the quest I'd put firmly behind me only an hour before. "Why didn't you like my sister?" I asked.

"Who says I didn't like her?"

"Everything you say about her. The way you touch her things," I said. "Why?"

"All those men she had coming and going," she said. "It was disgusting." She'd said the same thing when I stopped with Suzanne to get my suitcase. It hadn't fully registered then.

"How many different men?" I asked.

"Three," she said quickly. "I mean, at least three. Three that I noticed."

And Mrs. Bolduc didn't miss much, so probably there hadn't been others. "Did you tell the police about the three men?" I asked.

She nodded. Then hesitated. "Well, I told them there was some men. I don't know if I gave 'em a number."

"Did the police ask you for descriptions of the men?"

"The police," Mrs. Bolduc said pointedly, "was that guy who stayed here last night. You and your sister, you're two of a kind."

I resisted the urge to grab her by her skinny throat and shake her. "What did they look like, the three men?"

"I don't remember," she said, "and I've got to go now. You finish up here nice and quick, and don't forget to clean up before you go." She scuttled toward the door, showing her yellow rat's teeth in a forced smile.

"A moment, please, Mrs. Bolduc," I said. She hesitated, the forced smile collapsing into her usual tight-lipped frown. "You're anxious to have this apartment vacated, and I'm anxious to find out who killed my sister. So here's how it is — I'm not leaving until you tell me about the men, everything you can remember about them. We can stand here and play verbal tennis as long as you want, but if you want to speed things up, you can just tell me."

She gave me a look that was meant to be withering, but I don't wither easily. I waited patiently, once again resisting the urge to throttle her. Then, quite abruptly, she ended the glaring contest. "We better sit down, then," she said. "I ain't as young as I used to be. And you can fix me some coffee. Instant is fine." She sat stiff and silent until I set the coffee in front of her. I took the chair facing her. She stirred the coffee and tasted it before she spoke.

"At first," she said, "there was just two of them. A big dark guy. Handsome and mean looking. He drove one of those

229

Bronco-things. Red. And this other guy, a young boy. Too young for her, I mean. Sometimes he'd come with the guy in the jeep, and sometimes by himself. He — the kid, I mean — had a real nervous way of acting. Always looking over his shoulder. Jumpy. Like he knew he shouldn't be here, which he shouldn't have. But I knew him, so I told his mother, and then he stopped coming. Then it was just the big guy. I didn't like him. He used to do rude things..."

"Hold on," I said. "You knew who the young kid was?" She nodded. "Who was he, then? Did you give his name to the police?"

"Of course not," she said. "I told his mother. She wouldn't want her son mixed up in something like this. A sex crime."

"What's his name?"

Her smile was sly. "I ain't telling you," she said.

"Yes, you are," I said. "Either to me or to the police. Your choice. And I can tell you that the police aren't going to be too pleased that you withheld information about a murder." I headed for the phone. "I can call them right now."

She clawed the air, summoning me back. "Don't do that. I don't want the police coming around here. I don't like 'em. Not that I like you, either. It was Kevin. Mrs. Harrington's boy." She sank back on the sofa, sulking. I'd met Kevin. And I knew who the big dark guy was. That left the third.

"What about the third guy?" I said. "Did you know him?"

She shook her head. "Nope. Never saw him before."

She wasn't volunteering anything now. She was too angry at what she'd already been forced to disclose. She sat there glaring at me, daring me to ask her any more questions. Any information I got I was going to have to work for. Which was OK. I had plenty of experience with reluctant people, admissions directors and other staff members who viewed our presence as a threat to their jobs and their competence. Naturally they weren't forthcoming. I enjoyed the challenge. "Describe him for me," I said.

"I didn't see him very well," she said quickly. "I don't remember."

"Of course you do, Mrs. Bolduc," I said. "Take a few minutes and search your memory and I'm sure it will come to you. I can tell, from the way this apartment is decorated, and from the speed with which you picked out the things which don't belong here, that you have a very good eye for detail. Maybe it would help if I asked you some questions."

She tried glaring at me again, forgetting that I was glare-proof. Her glare was becoming chronic. It was an odd personality trait, this refusal to cooperate just for the sake of not cooperating. Lorna had it, too. Maybe it was something in the water. It must have been a lifelong habit, too. The scowl lines were etched deep in her face. Ignoring the message she was trying to send, I began the game of twenty questions. "Was he tall?"

She nodded. "About as tall as you, maybe taller," she said.

"Light hair or dark?"

"Light."

"Curly or straight?"

"Sort of curly." Each response was minimal. Nothing volunteered, the words spat out through tight lips. I'd never wanted to hit someone before, at least not since Michael and I stopped using physical force to resolve our differences, but I was having a hard time restraining myself now.

"How old?"

"I can't say. Young. Her age. He always kept his face down. I never saw him clearly. She must of told him I was watchin'. And why shouldn't I? I gotta know what my tenants are doin'. My property, ain't it? That's all I can tell you," she snapped. "I've gotta go. Finish up and get out of here. I don't want you around. No more of you disgusting young girls, goin' around acting all holier than thou all day and screwin' your brains out all night. Don't think I don't hear things." She stood up and marched purposefully toward the door.

231

I could picture her, yellow face pursed, her ear pressed to the wall of Carrie's bedroom. It was pathetic. "One more question," I said. "How did he get here? Did he have a car?"

"I never saw one," she said. "They came in her car."

"Did he spend the night?"

"No. He'd stay late, but not all night. Not that I noticed anyway. No. They'd just come in and do their dirty business. Then they'd both come out together, and she'd drive him somewhere and come back alone. That's all I can tell you," she said, and was out the door before I could ask anything more.

It wasn't much, but it was more than I had before. Maybe Lorna would know who this guy was, if I could find Lorna. If she'd talk to me once I found her. Otherwise, all I knew was that Carrie had had a young blond boyfriend. And I had no more time to spend tracking him down, even if I knew how. I had to get back to the business of running a business. The best I could do was pass the information along to Andre and let him carry on the detective work. He'd have a good time with Mrs. Bolduc. I didn't imagine he'd have a lot of patience with her rude remarks about our disgusting physical relationship. I was disappointed that I'd failed Carrie, but that was just the way it was. I couldn't think of anything else to do. Today, driven by emotion, I'd been changing my mind like a traffic light. It was time to get back to work, back to discipline and routine. In the struggle between good and evil, I'd lost, and I didn't like it one bit.

I got another box and vented my frustration by throwing her books into it. I piled trash novels, feminist tracts, Jane Austen and Thoreau — why is it all college students read Thoreau? — haphazardly into the box. In went the complete set of Poe, a gift requested during her most morose period of adolescence. Two coffee-table cookbooks. A Reader's Digest condensed book, which seemed an odd choice for Carrie. As I tossed it in, it fell open, spilling a wad of papers into the box. It was a fake, a hollow book in which Carrie had stored some papers. Papers the murderer hadn't found. I gathered them into a pile and dumped

them on the floor. With trembling hands, I picked up the top
sheet and began to read.

CHAPTER 26

I SAT CROSS-LEGGED on the floor reading Carrie's diary, my schedule forgotten, certain that here, finally, she would give me the information I needed. The first entry was from mid-July, meticulously dated and recorded in her small, neat handwriting.

July 17th. Hello, new diary. I'm starting you today and I've got a great hiding place — inside this dumb hollow book I found yesterday at the bookstore. Why am I hiding you? Because that pointy-nosed snoop of a landlady comes in and prowls around, looking through my things when I'm at work. It's bad enough being spied on. I won't have her reading this as well. So, the hiding place. She won't find it. She is allergic to books. Bet she hasn't read one in years.

My feet hurt! Glad I don't plan to make waitressing my life's work. But sometimes good things happen, like today. Today a real neat guy came into the restaurant looking for a job. They didn't have anything for him, and he looked depressed, so I gave him a Coke when Mr. Hoggins wasn't looking, and told him I'd heard they were looking for a busboy at the Homeport. He left to check that out, but he was waiting outside when I finished my shift, and asked if he could see me sometime. He looked sort of young, so I asked him how old he was. He said he bet he was the same age as me, and asked how old I was. I said 21. He said so he was right, we were the same age. We went walking by the harbor and had ice cream. We both like black raspberry. If Charlie knew about this, he'd kill both of us.

July 21. Today, my day off, I met my new guy again. I'm not even going to write his name here, just in case Mrs. B does find this. She loves to cause trouble for people, like she did with poor Kevin. My guy says his parents wouldn't like it if they found out he was seeing me. They like to choose the girls he goes out with, girls who are the same religion. Parents sure can be a bore. Even parents that choose you, like mine.

Tonight Charlie wants to take me someplace nice for dinner. I have a sexy new black slip dress that will drive him wild. He likes it when I look sexy and innocent at the same time. He's been like that ever since I really was innocent. In a way, if it weren't for him, I'd still be innocent. Him and a few other guys. Sometimes I wonder why I bother with men. They aren't very nice. Maybe this new guy will turn out to be nicer.

Charlie's changed a lot since he came out of prison. Sometimes I think he really loves me and this relationship might go somewhere. Then he knocks me around or ignores me or treats me like shit to impress his friends and I know deep down he's the same old Chuck. So why can't I stay away from him? I called Thea for advice but she didn't call me back. I guess she's fed up with me unless maybe she's still mad at me because I wouldn't agree to give up searching for my real mother. She never meant any of that anyway. She was just being the good daughter. Sometimes I wonder how someone as smart as Thea can be so dumb about the family. They say jump and she says how high and doesn't even realize she's doing it. I feel sorry for her, though. She's so sad. Makes me wonder if it's worth it to fall in love.

It was hard to keep reading. Carrie's diary was so much like her, written the way she talked. I had the eerie sense that she was here, telling me this. That I wasn't reading at all, she was right here, and I was listening to her. But I had to face facts. I was only reading Carrie's words; she'd never again be here to talk to me. Maybe that premonition I'd had this morning that something

235

was about to happen had been about finding this diary.

I unfolded my stiff legs, got a box of tissues, and went back to the diary, skipping the next few entries, which were full of details about life at the restaurant. She and Lorna might have been friends, but she didn't have a very high opinion of Lorna's character. It seemed that Lorna had her priorities very clear — herself first, last, and always. And Lorna also had her eye on Charlie, though he didn't seem to be looking back. There was a casual reference to Kevin. Carrie felt sorry for him, amazed to find someone even more lost than she was. Kevin's parents, by treating him like a helpless baby, had made him unable to think for himself. Embarrassed by this, Kevin solved his problems by taking drugs.

I didn't see Kevin as a killer. Like Carrie, I found him too helpless. I scanned the entries for references to Charlie and the third guy. A few days later they both popped up again.

July 24. The shit hit the fan today all right. Mr. Hoggins put his hand up my skirt while I was putting ice in some glasses, and Mrs. Hoggins saw him do it. She took one of the glasses of ice, poured it down inside his pants, and said maybe that would cool him off. I thought she was going to fire me, but she didn't. She just told Lorna to take over my tables and told me to take the rest of the day off. I must have looked worried, because she said I wouldn't be fired, she just needed some time to straighten Mr. Hoggins out. I would love to have stuck around to see what happened, but I want to keep the job, so I grabbed my purse and left. Hated to lose those tips to Lorna. I'd got my lunch crowd eating out of my hand. Literally.

Over by the library I met my friend coming out with a stack of books. He is taking some summer courses, but he said it was too hot to study and suggested we go swimming. We walked home to get my car and drove

236

out to Megunticook Lake. It was the first time I'd seen his body. He's not a hunk exactly, he's a little too thin and lanky, but he's so young and perfect it almost makes me cry. He swam like a pro. I loved watching him. Afterward we came back here and made love. I told him to hide his face so Mrs. B. wouldn't see it. He won't tell me who his family is, just that they are prominent and wouldn't want us dating.

It was the first time for him. He didn't say so, but I could tell. I found it very sweet. I tried to make it nice for him, but I didn't have to worry. Men are born to screw. Lying there, after, we looked just like twins, with our flushed faces and wet blond curls. I asked him when his birthday was. He said November. So he wasn't 21 yet, only 20. But at least he isn't my brother, even if we do have the same weird longer second toe and love the same music. I worry about stuff like that sometimes. When you don't know who you are, you don't know who your relatives are, either.

I had to meet Charlie later, so I offered him a ride home, but he would only let me drive him down to Rockport, where he said he was meeting his father. What a pair we are! My identity is a secret, and he wants his to be. We're the mystery twins!

July 26. Mom and Dad are coming to see me. I just hope I can get through it without a fight but it won't be easy. She doesn't even know that she treats me like a slightly inferior moron and always has. It's as though, despite all that "chosen" bullshit, she somehow got an inferior product and can't help showing it. Dad doesn't see it, either. She has him so cowed.

I'll bet even Thea doesn't notice. She sees the world through rose-colored glasses. She notices a lot of other things, though. That's why she was always running interference for me — because she could tell Mom and

I couldn't get along. Yeah. Thea loves me like a sister. She's the only one of them who does. But she's one of them. Sometimes I wonder if she'd still love me if she knew what I'm really like. If she knew how bad I am. Well, I've got some really good dope Charlie gave me. A few puffs of that should mellow me out enough so nothing Mom says will bother me. Wouldn't she just die if she knew I was screwing three different guys, including Charlie?

I read on. Carrie got through her family visit, though it was painful to read about. I didn't like what she was showing me. About the family and about herself. I wanted to keep seeing through my rose-colored glasses, and Carrie, even in death a determined iconoclast, wouldn't let me. She kept seeing her mystery guy, and Charlie, and mothering Kevin, but she didn't give me clues about his identity. Mrs. Hoggins had straightened out Mr. Hoggins, so he wasn't bothering her anymore. Lorna was being difficult at work and alienating the customers. Carrie was spending her spare time searching for her birth mother, and on her next free day she was going back to Massachusetts, to Serenity House. Poor girl. I knew how that was going to go.

I sat on the floor, lost in remembrance, following Carrie through her last month. I'm not prissy, nor the prude Andre accused me of being, but I meant it when I said I was uncomfortable talking about Carrie's sex life. I was uncomfortable reading about it, too. Part of me was thrilled to have her diary, for the information she was giving me and for the closeness I felt. Another part of me was a little disturbed. The Carrie I was seeing here wasn't always a very nice person. I had an idealized picture of her, because she was my sister, because she'd been such a sweet child. As a confused young adult, she sometimes shocked me. I had to admit that the things she said about me really hurt, too. And I couldn't say, "But Carrie, I don't want to know all this," because I might need to know it. Worse yet, I was going to be giving it to the police.

Under August 29th I found the sentence that broke my heart. I'd followed in her footsteps so I knew what she was going to learn, and the diary led her to all the people I'd seen. Like me, Carrie had wanted to hurt Esther Pappas and had found food, comfort, and the vital clue at Agnes Deignan's house. As I got closer to the point when she would meet her birth mother I almost couldn't make myself read on. Even now, when it was too late, I instinctively wanted to protect her from what I knew was coming. I could see her sitting alone here, writing it, and a terrible grief seized me.

August 29. They bought me. That's what my mother said. They bought me. My mother. There's no doubt about who she is. It's like looking at myself in the mirror. Even though they warned me, back home in my search group, that you don't always like what you find, I couldn't have expected this. How much she hates me. Has always hated me. No wonder I'm no good and can't be happy. I was conceived in violence, hated, rejected, and then sold.

Carrie's handwriting trailed off into an illegible blur, and from the smudges on the page I could tell she'd been crying. I was crying, too. In shame for the phone calls I hadn't returned, in sorrow for all that she had had to face alone, impotently angry with the family for the way we'd all let her down.

The shrill of the phone jarred me back to the present. Something else I'd forgotten — to disconnect her phone. I assumed it would be Andre, but the voice on the other end was unfamiliar. A strange man who knew my name.

"Mrs. Kozak? This is Chris Davis. You borrowed some of my clothes yesterday." With difficulty, I shifted my mind back to the present. Who was Chris Davis? I vaguely remembered borrowing some clothes. Oh yes. From Betsy Davis's son. "I need to talk to you... about my mother and your sister. Please," he said. He sounded scared and determined. "We can't talk here at the house. Will you meet me somewhere?"

I was intrigued. Why the son and not his mother? She said she had kept all this a secret from her family. I looked at my watch. I'd dreamed away a lot of time, and I did have to get back tonight, but if this was important, I'd make time for it. "I could meet you in about half an hour," I said. "Where?"

"Do you know where the public boat landing is, near the Wayfarer Marine yacht storage buildings?" he asked.

I said no, and he gave me directions, which I scribbled on the back of an envelope. It took me almost the whole half hour to finish packing and get everything stowed away in my car. I was moving in an emotional fog. Reading the diary had left me feeling hollow and depressed. I called the Thomaston barracks and left a message for Andre that Carrie's brother had called and asked me to meet him at the public boat landing, and that I'd found Carrie's diary and would stop in and give it to him on my way back to Massachusetts. They promised to give him the message.

The last thing I did before I left was call the phone company and arrange to have the phone disconnected. It turned out to be harder than I'd expected. Carrie hadn't had the phone changed to her name when her roommate moved out and I didn't remember her roommate's name. Fortunately, the service rep was able to work from the phone number and we got things straightened out in the phone company's own special way. She agreed to close the account and send a final bill to me as soon as she received a letter from the former roommate. Another thing to take care of when I got back.

As I carried out my suitcase, I saw the curtain twitch one last time. I wondered if Mrs. Bolduc would rush right over and check the apartment and see that I hadn't cleaned. I pictured her chasing me down the street, yellow teeth bared, her skinny arms churning frantically in the fog.

It was foggier than before, and chillier. A bone-deep chill that made me appreciate the heated seat. Hard to believe it was only the end of September. It felt like December today. Switching on my lights, I crept down Mountain Street through the fog, trying to follow his directions to the public boat landing. He'd said it was right beside a row of new condominiums, which would normally make it not too difficult to find, but today I could see only about ten feet in front of the car.

Suddenly a vast blue building loomed up on my left. I drove past it, peering through the fog for the boat launch parking area, and almost launched my car. The tiny sign marking the spot would have been more suitable on a peanut butter jar. I had stopped at the very edge of the lot, or street, or whatever it was. Ahead a wad of lumpy tarmac, riddled with fissures and craters, sloped sharply down to the water. I backed up and moved the car farther to the right, where a ragged patch of weeds provided at least a visual barrier between my car and the beach. There were no other cars around.

Farther right, a rank of gray condos looking like highstyle beehives marched away into the fog. They looked uninhabited. No lights shone out into the gloomy afternoon. I cut the engine, stuck the keys in my pocket, and got out. The keys clinked against something metallic in my pocket. Curious, I reached in and pulled out the little can of Mace Agnes had given me. I stuck it back in my pocket and walked slowly around the car, looking for Chris Davis.

I could hear the faint scrunching of shoes on gravelly tar, and then, as I watched, he emerged from the shelter of some big dark evergreens, walking toward me with an odd smile on his face. Once again I was struck by his resemblance to his mother. The same blond curls, now wet with fog and plastered against his forehead, the same blue eyes. Carrie's eyes. His sister's eyes. The nose and mouth must have come from his father along with his height.

As I watched him approach, a remark Lorna had made

flashed across my mind. A remark I'd ignored at the time. "…she was seeing two guys, this cute blond guy, I never heard his name, looked like he coulda been her brother." And something from Carrie's diary. She'd written "lying there, we looked just like twins." I'd been too stunned yesterday to notice, or I would have seen it then. But I hadn't seen it. Hadn't thought of it when I was reading her diary. Hadn't wondered how he could call me at Carrie's when she wasn't listed, unless he already knew the number. Hadn't put it all together until now, as Carrie's killer came toward me, an unpleasant smile on his face.

CHAPTER 27

I'D DELIVERED MYSELF right into his hands, even let him choose the spot. I reached into my pocket for the car keys, but it was too late. He was too close. I turned and ran down onto the beach, heading left away from the condos, stumbling down the rough, slippery ramp and onto the rocky sand. I could hear him following behind me, calling as he came, his voice distorted by the fog. "Mrs. Kozak? It's me. Chris Davis. Don't run away. I just want to talk to you."

"Yeah, right, brother," I thought as I ran, "and after that you've got a bridge to sell me." I scrambled on blindly, trying to run quietly, an impossible task on this rocky beach. My feet crunched through the sand and squelched over the rocks, scraping over barnacles and sliding over seaweed. It was like running an obstacle course — a deadly one. Magnified by the fog, my footsteps and his sounded unnaturally loud in the otherwise silent afternoon. We were sealed in a thick, gray world, isolated by the intangible blanket around us. I couldn't see more than ten or fifteen feet ahead, not far enough to plan an escape. In the distance, a foghorn called its deep-throated warning across the invisible sea.

If only I knew where the big blue building ended. It would have been easier to lose myself on land or go to a house for help, but I didn't dare head that way, fearing I'd be trapped between the beach and that unending wall of blue metal. Ahead of me a groin of boulders, meant to stop beach erosion, rose up. There were deep crevices between some of the rocks where they'd been shifted by storms. I found one big enough to hold me and crawled into it, pulling my sweater up over my face to muffle the ragged sound of my breathing. I loosened my hair and pulled it forward to cover my face, trying to make myself only a dark blur.

His fair head appeared out of the fog, swiveling left and

right. He stopped about eight feet away and listened. I held my breath. He turned and began walking up the beach, peering down among the rocks. "Mrs. Kozak, what's wrong?" he called softly. "I didn't mean to scare you. Please come out. I just want to talk to you."

He sounded so kind, so friendly, so trustworthy. Lucifer, I thought. God's favorite angel. So innocent. So perfect. So profoundly evil. An innocence and perfection that had made Carrie cry and then done so much worse. I saw the pictures again. Saw again what he'd done to her. Poor Carrie, who had wondered if this was finally the guy who would turn out to be nice. He made Charlie's sadism seem benign. I was as brave as a barrelful of bears, but what I was facing now chilled me to the core. Absurd as it was, his evil seemed more extreme, more frightening, because it was so at odds with his boy-next-door appearance.

He started to walk away and I felt my panic begin to subside, thought I might begin to breathe again. Knowing I would have to stay here for a while, I shifted into a more comfortable position, accidentally knocking one rock against another with my foot. He whipped around and headed back toward me, walking along the top of the rocks, peering left and right, his sandy shoes grating loudly on the granite. I pulled myself as far back as I could, cowering in my chilly cave, clinging to the irrational hope that he might not see me. The footsteps came closer, then paused, and I knew he'd spotted me. Reluctantly I shook back my hair and raised my eyes to meet his. They glittered with triumph. "Found you," he said simply. "Come on out of there."

Reluctantly I crept out and faced him.

"Why did you run?" he said.

"I don't know," I said. "Everything suddenly seemed so strange. This place. The fog. I'd been thinking about my sister. You were a stranger. I guess I was spooked. I'm sorry. It was silly. Let's go back and talk in the car where it's warm. This

244

place gives me the creeps." I started walking.

"No, wait, don't go," he said, his voice suddenly harsh. "We can talk here."

"I'd rather go back to the car. It's raw and damp out here, the fog is turning to drizzle, and I'm getting cold," I insisted, edging sideways onto the next rock. I didn't dare turn my back on him. Carrie had been hit from behind. He jumped past me, blocking my way. "Don't move," he ordered, sounding uncertain.

I pressed at that uncertainty. "Why?" I asked, moving sideways to go around him. "What's the matter with you? Why talk here, when we'll be more comfortable at the car? Why shouldn't we be comfortable?" I moved again, but he lunged at me and grabbed my arm.

"I told you not to move," he said, his voice shaky. "You're making me nervous. I need to think, to figure out what to do. You stay right there."

I shook off his hand and took another step sideways, glancing back in the direction of my car. There was nothing to see but rocks and fog. I was taking a risk. He might be paralyzed by fear or he might try to stop me. But I couldn't see what I had to lose by trying to get somewhere safer. This wasn't your everyday pissing contest to see who could get the upper hand, or even about whether I got a few bumps or bruises. This guy had killed once and obviously was planning to do so again. There was a shuffling of feet and then he rushed at me and shoved me down onto the ground. "You... stop... here," he said.

I landed hard, jarring my ribs on a rock and scraping my hand on some barnacles as I tried to break the fall. I rolled over into a crouch, fumbling for the can of Mace. "What did you do that for? Why do you care where we talk?" I yelled. "You stay away from me! You must be crazy." I got up slowly, backing away from him, and brought up the can. He grabbed my arm and we swayed there, locked in our struggle for possession. I managed one squirt toward his face and heard his surprised yelp, but he was strong and determined. I couldn't twist the can enough to give him a decent squirt. My shoe slipped on some seaweed, knocking me off balance. As I swayed, struggling to regain my footing, he tore the can out of my hand and blasted me.

He wasn't the only one who was strong and determined. Despite being blinded, I struck out at him, knocking the can out of his hand, and kicked out at him, breaking his hold on me. The can clattered away into the fog. My eyes were on fire, my face stung like I'd been attacked by bees, and I couldn't breathe. I tried to crawl away and lose myself in the fog. I didn't dare stand because I couldn't see. I got only a few feet before his foot slammed down between my shoulder blades, flattening me on the sand and taking my remaining breath away. I lay there, spitting sand out of my mouth, furious and helpless as he jerked my hands roughly behind me and tied them together. I didn't make it easy for him, but he had one knee on my back and the other on the back of my neck, pressing my face down into the sand, so there wasn't much I could do. When he finally let me raise my head, my lip was bleeding. I had sand stuck to my face and in my nose and I couldn't use my hands to wipe it off.

"What was that stuff?" he said. "It hurts like hell." I didn't bother to answer. He pulled me up and tried to lead me along. I couldn't see anything through my streaming eyes and immediately fell over the nearest rock. "Hey," he said, "watch where you're going!"

"I can't see anything, you idiot, and it's your fault," I said. "What's the matter with you, anyway? You said you wanted to talk and now you're acting like a maniac." I might be bound and blinded, but I was staying on the offensive. "What are you going to do with me now?"

"I don't know," he said. "Get rid of you. Somehow. I have to think." His words came in short bursts. I could hear the fear in his voice. He'd led me here without a plan and I didn't want to give him a chance to make one. "This whole thing is so confusing," he said. "I need to tell someone about it. About everything," he said. "I have to tell you about her. About what happened."

The agony in my face was not going away and I couldn't buffer the pain by burying my face in my hands. My ribs ached, I was sure he'd left a footprint on my back, and the sand on my face was driving me wild. I wanted to scream and shriek and cry, but I was fighting for my life here. I had to stay calm. Also, little as I wanted to hear what he had to say, the longer I kept him talking, the longer I stayed alive. Right now I was helpless. If I could make it until the Mace wore off, until I could see again, I'd have a better chance of surviving. And if I kept him talking, he couldn't be thinking about what to do with me.

"That's a good idea," I said, "We'll sit down right here and you can tell me what happened," I said. I dropped down on my knees and wriggled around until I was leaning against a rock. It wasn't comfortable, but it wasn't bad, given the choices. He sat down near me on a rock.

"I had to kill her," he said, as if he expected me to understand.

"Why?" Like a pot of water coming to boil, a small bubble of anger floated up through my fear and exploded. What was wrong with the world, that someone could see killing someone else as the only possible solution? How had human life become so devalued? How could this monstrous boyman expect me to understand why he "had" to kill my sister? How absurd and macabre that he should choose me to hear his confession. But then, whom could he tell, except someone he already planned to kill? An involuntary chill went through me.

"From the first moment I saw her I was attracted to Carrie," he said. "When I saw her in the restaurant, I couldn't take my eyes off her. When she gave me that Coke, it was like a signal. So I waited for her. From that very first day, when we both discovered we loved black raspberry ice cream cones, we were kindred spirits. She was so much like me, and yet so unlike, like two sides of the same person. We liked the same things and shared the same sense of humor, but I was so cautious and controlled, and she was such a bold, free spirit."

The thick fog was turning into a steady rain. I turned my face up and let it run over me, welcoming the cool relief. My vision was slowly returning. Chris Davis was sitting beside me on a rock, a twisted version of my sister Carrie, seemingly oblivious to the rain, staring intently at his clenched hands. The cords in his neck stood out like wire cables as he spoke. His voice came out harsh and strained. "My mother and I are very close," he said. "Very close. I think you could say I'm devoted to my mother. She's a good woman; a Christian woman. An idea you probably can't understand. Carrie told me your family isn't religious. My mother is also a sad woman. I knew she wouldn't approve of my relationship with Carrie. My mother has always tried to protect me from the dangers of loose women. Always encouraged me to choose my friends from the people in our church. Now I understand why. Carrie was the devil in woman's form, sent to tempt me, like Eve in the garden."

An angry response came to my lips and it was a struggle to repress it. I wanted to shout, "Bullshit, you witless, immoral little cretin. Maybe you can't see it, but the evil one here is you!" I didn't say it because I didn't want him angry at me; I just wanted to keep him talking even though his monologue was particularly painful when I'd just heard the other side of the story from Carrie, in her diary.

"This all happened because I was willful. Because I wanted to defy them. Because I was tired of being controlled by them. I wanted a life of my own, a life they knew nothing about, so I let myself get involved with that harlot." His voice rose to an anguished cry. "And I was so weak! So weak I slept with my own sister." He tore at the skin on his arms with his fingernails, leaving long white streaks that began oozing blood. "I am cursed with this weak flesh." He lifted his face to the rain, maybe hoping for a little help from God.

"Don't kid yourself," I wanted to tell him, "God doesn't like you." I was lying on the sand near his feet, half propped up against another rock. The wet sand and rain had soaked through my jeans. My hair was plastered against my skull. Despite my leather jacket, my teeth were beginning to chatter and it felt like my bones were turning to ice — from the weather, but also from fear. I watched him warily as I considered my options. If he'd tied the rope over my jacket, I might be able to wriggle free, but I had to get him talking again. When he wasn't talking, he watched me closely, but when he talked he stared away into space. Then I could move safely. I tested it carefully and found some play in the rope. "How do you know she was your sister?" I asked.

"I should have known it all along," he said. "We were too much alike. Even our toes. I lied to her, you see, about my age so she wouldn't think I was too young for her. Got her to tell me how old she was first. I thought I was being pretty clever. You see where it got me. Wallowing in the mud, like swine. Now I've got to kill you, too, to protect my mother." His monologue had been delivered in sort of a wailing chant, except the last thing. He announced his intention to kill me in a normal, conversational voice which I found much scarier than when he acted crazy.

There was no doubt in my mind that he would kill me. It was only a matter of when. I began working my way out of the rope. Luck was with me. He'd wrapped it over the sleeves of my jacket, and not too tightly, either. By pressing my arms together, I could gradually wriggle one hand free. Gripping one sleeve with the other hand, I began the slow process of wiggling my arm up the sleeve. "I don't understand," I said. "How will killing me protect your mother? Protect her from what?"

"You know perfectly well how," he said. "You just talked with her yesterday. You know how important it is to her to protect her secret. No one must ever connect my mother with Carrie."

My hand was almost free. I wriggled my arm impatiently, trying to shake it free. He noticed the movement and bent down, grabbing my shoulder and shaking me roughly. "I told you to stay still," he said. "What are you doing?"

"Just trying to rest my shoulders," I said. "It puts a lot of strain on them, being pulled back like this. Let me get into a more comfortable position and I'll try not to move again."

"No, don't move," he commanded. "You sit still."

My response was a combination of anger at him for what he was doing to me and pop psychology gleaned from articles on how to avoid being raped or mugged. Talk to your attacker, the articles say. Try to make a personal connection. Try to humanize the encounter, make your attacker realize that you are a person, too. Phooey. What I wanted to do was pound the bastard into a bloody pulp, but first I had to get the rope off, so I talked to him instead. "I have to move. It hurts. What you do to people, Chris Davis, hurts them. You hurt my sister and now you're hurting me. Do you realize that, Chris? Do you know that my ribs hurt where you knocked me into a rock and my back hurts where you stomped on me and my arms and shoulders ache because you've got me tied up like this? I'm a real, live human being and you're hurting me. And I don't care what you want, I'm moving." I hunched forward, pulled my hand free, and leaned back against the rock. As soon as I got him talking again, I'd see if I could slip the loose rope off my other wrist.

"It doesn't matter... how you feel, I mean," he said, "you're going to die soon anyway. Now stay still. It makes me nervous when you move around." He got up, came a step closer, and kicked me. "Don't make me do that again." Not so different from Charlie after all, was he? Carrie sure could pick 'em. The blow was a surprise. I'd assumed he wouldn't be gratuitously violent, at least not until he made up his mind what he was going to do.

When you're scared like I was scared, you think it can't get any worse, but hearing him say I was going to die, so casually, so callously, was like being punched in the stomach by a giant fist. "You should give yourself up," I said, struggling to keep the fear out of my voice. "Killing me isn't going to protect your mother. The police already know about her connection to Carrie. If you go to them and confess, you might be able to make some sort of deal to keep your motive out of the papers. That would do your mother a lot more good than killing again. Besides, they know I'm meeting you. If anything happens to me, you'll be the prime suspect." I didn't expect him to listen to reason, he was too wrapped up in his own vision, but I had to give it a try.

"You're lying," he said. "The police don't know. You're just trying to confuse me. Like your sister. I thought she was just a sweet girl, and then she seduced me. She took my innocence. But I didn't see it, even then. I still thought I was in love with her. Until I heard her talking to my mother."

Now I understood. Now things made sense. His mother hadn't told him about Carrie. He'd overheard. I could imagine what a shock it must have been, finding his secret girlfriend talking to his mother. And his mother hadn't known that he was there. She still didn't know what he had overheard. But she must have told him. How else had he found me? How had he known I was Carrie's sister? Had he followed me yesterday? I'd been so oblivious, a whole army on camels could have followed and I wouldn't have noticed. I wanted to yell, "Nobody made you sleep with her, you stupid schmuck, you just followed your instincts. You aren't anything special. It wasn't fault or sin or the devil, it was just hormones."

Instead I said, "Tell me about that. What did you hear?" He took a deep breath and stared off toward the hidden sea. The waves were sucking softly at the rocks, subdued, as though they were trying not to interrupt. I pulled my other hand free and felt the rope drop off behind me. Now it was just a matter of time. This guy was not going to dispose of me without a struggle. The little bubbles of anger were gradually bringing me to a full boil as I listened to his self-serving justification for what he had done to my sister. It would have been nice to imagine that Andre was going to get my message and come galloping to my rescue, but

I'm a realist. I'd seen the connection because I'd read the diaries and talked to Lorna, but Andre hadn't. He had no reason to think Carrie's brother was a threat. I felt around on the sand behind me for a rock I could use as a weapon.

"My mother didn't know I was home," he said. "I'd been up late with Carrie, fornicating, and I was too tired to pay attention, so I skipped my second class, came home, and went to bed. When I woke up, I heard two voices. I recognized one of them as Carrie's. I opened my door a crack and stayed in my room, listening. Carrie was explaining to my mother about her search, about how she'd always wanted to find her real mother, and then she said that this was where her search had led. She asked my mother to accept her."

"I waited," he said, his voice shaking with emotion, "for my mother to deny it. To explain that it wasn't possible for Carrie to be her child, because Jeremiah and I are her only children. I waited, and she didn't deny it. Instead, she told Carrie the whole story. The whole, sickening, revolting story of what her uncle had done. And then she begged Carrie to go away and leave her alone to protect her secret. Carrie didn't want to. She wouldn't give up, she kept trying to make my mother acknowledge her, despite my mother's pleas and her pain. That's when I began to hate Carrie. When I first saw clearly that she was evil. Then Carrie left and my mother sat and cried. I shut my door and thought about what to do."

"When you talked to your mother about it, how did she react?"

"She doesn't know I overheard, or that I ever met Carrie," he said. "God, I wish I hadn't!"

"I'm sure she'd feel the same."

"Shut up," he shouted, "or the next time, I'll kick you in the face. You don't understand, that's all." Well, he'd finally gotten something right. I sure didn't understand.

He bent over, gripping his stomach as though he had cramps. He was crying now, his tears mingling with the rain, his breath coming in shuddering gasps. I didn't feel one bit sorry for him. I found a sharp rock which fit nicely into my hand. Gripping it tightly, I waited for a chance to use it.

"I was filled with revulsion, for myself and for Carrie," he said. "The night before, I had held her in my arms while she cried as she told me that she was afraid she might be pregnant. And if she was, the baby was mine. She said she didn't know yet what she'd do, but in a way she was very happy to be having my baby. And now I had discovered that I'd been having sex with my sister. That she'd seduced me into being no better than that wretched uncle who raped my mother. Oh, God. Jesus. Can you imagine? I was fucking my own sister?"

The lid flew off my self-control like a pressure cooker blowing a gasket. "You pious, self-centered Jesus-loving shit! You're not some misled saint, you know. You're nothing more than a horny guy who told a few lies and screwed a girl because she was available. She wasn't an inflatable doll, she was a person with people who loved her just like you love your mother." I was screaming at him, my rage at what he'd done to her, to me, to all of us pouring out in an unstoppable flow like lava from an erupting volcano. "No, not like you love your mother. The way you love your mother is sick. It's sick to kill someone because it might embarrass you or get you in trouble. Do you hear, sicko? It's not normal to smash someone's head and rape them with a stick because having sex turned out to be a mistake, like you did, you bastard. If your goddamned mother hadn't been so determined to suffer... if she'd told you about Carrie..." I was so mad I could hardly speak. "If you had to kill someone, why didn't you kill yourself, you despicable, low-life scum? You arrogant, self-righteous sinner. She was my sister!" Now I was crying, too. For poor Carrie and her dead hopes and dreams, for the rest of us who had to go on without her, and in frustration that the world could produce creatures like the twisted fool beside me. Arms tensed, I waited for the kick that I was sure was coming, but none did.

His arms were wrapped around his body to control his shivering. He went on as though he hadn't heard me, as if I'd never said a word. "My mother went for a walk on the beach. She always does that when she's upset. I went into the bathroom and puked until I was hollow. Then I decided Carrie had to die. It was the only way to protect my mother. The only way that my sin and her sin and the taint of incest could end. The only way I could see that goodness and order could be restored. I knew Carrie hadn't told anyone else about finding her mother. She was very private. Very secretive about things. A few days later I arranged to meet her. And I killed her."

"Why did you do that... that thing with the stick?" The question I didn't want to hear the answer to and had to ask.

"It just seemed like the right thing to do. I had to destroy the baby, too, you see." Not only remorseless and completely self-centered, the idiot didn't know anything about biology, either. Or maybe he'd read too much science fiction and imagined the baby would keep growing on its own and eventually come and get him, making a perfect tabloid headline — "Revenge of the Killer Baby."

Down at the water's edge, one rock slammed against another with a sharp crack. His head jerked around and he stared into the fog, startled. Clutching my rock, I launched myself at him, driving my head into his nose. The cartilage gave with a mushy crunch and his blood poured over both of us. He grabbed his face with both hands and I hit him with the rock. The first time I didn't hit him very hard. It's not easy to make yourself hurt someone even when you want to.

He lurched toward me, bloody and menacing, swinging a fist which grazed my nose. The stinging pain focused my anger nicely. "This is for what you did to Carrie," I yelled and hit him again. This time I put all my rage into the blow, hitting him as hard as I could. He dropped at my feet and lay still. I bent over him and felt in his neck for a pulse. It was the first time I'd ever checked anyone's pulse but my own. His heartbeat was strong and steady. I knelt beside him, listening to him breathe noisily through his battered nose. Blood poured from his nose and a gash on his head, almost black in the deepening gloom.

I was still holding the rock. An image of Carrie lying in the dirt, impaled on a stick, rose up before me. I saw Carrie in her white casket, saw the traumatized faces of Todd, Dad, and Uncle Henry. Remembered my promise. Thea will fix it. I'd found her killer just as I promised, but now a part of me wanted a more exact form of revenge than the law would allow. I wanted him just as dead as Carrie was. Just as battered, just as bloody. I wanted to hit him until his face was smashed. I wanted to destroy him just like he'd destroyed her. He stirred. Moaning softly, he fumbled a hand over his face. His blue eyes opened, stared at me. I saw the knowledge there of what was coming. He made a feeble effort to move away. I raised the rock again. "You've come to the end of the line," I said, "and don't expect to wake up in Heaven."

In the distance I could hear sirens and the shrill sound of tires skidding on wet pavement, followed by footsteps and voices shouting. The good guys coming to my rescue, now that I no longer needed rescuing. I looked down again at Chris Davis, huddled on the sand, a pathetic, self-righteous, God-fearing murderer. One killing was enough. I wasn't going to descend to his level. My self-control was returning, but I was so angry, so intent on killing him, I had to pry the rock out of my own hand. I dropped it onto the sand and rose to my feet. "Over here," I called, "we're over here."

Andre and two other men in yellow slickers emerged from the fog. I pointed down at the boy lying on the beach. "This is Carrie's brother, Chris Davis," I said. "He killed her."

"Are you OK?" Andre asked.

"Battered, but still standing," I said. "The heavy damage is all emotional."

I started toward the car. Andre put a hand on my arm, stopping me. I tried to shake him off. I was awash with adrenaline, trembling, shocked and sick at what I'd wanted to do and almost done, infected by Chris Davis's sickness. I wanted no company right now, not even his. "Your nose is bleeding," he said, holding out his handkerchief.

I touched my face, staring in surprise at the blood on my fingers, and took the handkerchief. "I was sure you wouldn't come. How did you know?"

"I'm a detective, remember? How would Carrie's brother know where to find you? You didn't tell him, his mother didn't know, and Carrie isn't in the phone book."

"Thanks for coming," I said. "You got here just in time." I didn't explain, but I thought he knew what I meant and that I needed to be alone for a while. Their questions could wait. I left them to deal with things and walked back through the cold gray rain to my car. When the shock wore off, I was going to ache in a dozen new places. If I had known how painful this would be, would I still have done it? It was a question I couldn't answer with certainty, but I thought the answer was yes. I'd done the job and I'd found Carrie's killer. I felt no flush of triumph, no sense of satisfaction. I only felt stunned, hollow, and possessed by a terrible sadness. Mechanically, I let myself into the car, started the engine, and turned on the heat. Then I leaned my head back, closed my eyes, and cried one more time for my sister.